SHINE

EYE

GIRL

ALCALY

LO

This novel is a work of fiction. Names, characters, places, and incidents are either the product of the author's imagination or are used fictitiously. Any resemblance to actual events, locales, or persons, living or dead, is entirely coincidental.

Copyright © 2009, 2022 by Alcaly Lo

Published by Isaiah Books

Alcalylo.com

Mail@alcalylo.com

@Alcalylo

For Ieasha,

Isaiah,

and Anthony.

One love

Shine Eye Girl

Guanguanco

Beaumont, Texas. It took us 3 days to get there, one week to find an apartment, another two weeks before we were able to go see Rodney. He knew we were in town, by then. Prison officials had contacted him about the required visitation paperwork and spoiled our surprise. Amad lounged by our apartment complex's pool, letting Eli and me go first.

I went through the mandatory checks and searches without paying any attention to the guards' meanness and nastiness. I've been inside enough jails in my life to know the drill. Eli was jumpy, feeling the vibe. I had been surprised to learn that we could have physical contact with Rodney. Inmates in his category received visitors in a room that was carpeted and sparsely furnished in red plastic. Snacks and drinks could be purchased from two vending machines. Bright lights hung overhead. The walls were bare. There were guards inside as well as out, behind a large window.

Rodney, too, was growing a beard. Must have been the Muslim thing. What else had changed? He had gotten much bigger. When he embraced me, barely leaving room for Eli, his body felt nothing like it used to. There was a hardness in his eyes that hadn't been there before, either. The hardness he had been looking for in the streets. The hardness of a real man.

"Hi."

"Hi."

He looked at me, noting the differences in my appearance as well. The last time we touched I was pregnant up to here. The last time we touched he kissed me goodbye and said, "I'll be right back."

Eli raised a hand and ran it on Rodney's face. Rodney took him in his arms. Eli started to cry but looked at me, looked at Rodney, and thought better of it. "Give your daddy a hug," I prodded. He complied, doing the thing with the arms and the head tuck. Rodney's smile was worth a thousand words.

I knew I should have waited. I knew it was too soon. I knew Rodney was nowhere near ready for what I had to say. But that's how I had pictured the moment in my mind, and I wanted to stick to scripts as much as possible from thereon. You couldn't go wrong when you sat down and thought about things and decided on something and turned that decision into a plan and that plan into a series of actions. I couldn't have waited twenty years for Rodney. No way in hell. Nobody is that strong. But he had told Brenda and me that the Miranda angle had brought the twenty down to an eight, thanks to his lawyer. I could do eight, no problem. To finish what Rodney and I had started. For Eli. To give our family a chance. So our son wouldn't grow up like we grew up—a total screwup. Out there with no father, no mother, no home, no future.

Rodney didn't see me go down on one knee. Other people in the room did, and they got real quiet. I took Rodney's free hand in mine. He looked surprised. "Rodney Andrews," I declaimed: "Will you marry me?"

Rodney pulled me on my feet and pressed me against his heart. Eli joined in. One for Daddy, one for Mommy. People clapped. Rodney started to say something and choked up. Tears streamed down his face. I took that as a yes.

"There's no Miranda," Rodney said through his tears, sending my head spinning. It wasn't joy I had read on his face seconds, eons ago. It was something akin to consternation.

"There's no what?" I asked, swept in a sea of freezing cold.

"No Miranda," he repeated, looking away. "My sentence wasn't reduced."

My hands started to shake. Everything in the room became red. The cold swells reached my head, burning the inside of my skull as they turned it to solid ice. I found it hard to breathe. Panic. It must be panic. I grabbed Eli and pressed him against me for warmth. "What do you mean?"

Rodney seemed defenseless, all of a sudden. A man lost. A man caught. "I ... I just wanted you to pay me some attention, Sally. I wanted to feel like you were still mine. To keep you from straying too far. To give me hope. I never thought you would actually come here ... make all these changes in your life."

He lowered his head. Crying. He was crying. Unable to look at me. Wishing the visit were over so he wouldn't have to face me, face up to his lies. I stumbled into a seat. No Miranda. The eight back to a twenty in one bold stroke. My plans up in smoke. My beautiful, beautiful plans. A lifetime's worth. No waving a magic stick. No getting out and going home early. No slipping through the cracks. They had meant it, when they gave him all that time. Twenty to life was just that.   What kind of deal had he struck? "But Brenda ... the lawyer...."

"I made my mother go along. I begged her. She did it for me. I was going crazy, you know. Crazy. I needed a reason to keep going. If you still thought about me, if you still cared, then I had something to hold on to. It was like a fantasy. I was feenin' for that feeling, that connection. And I would have told you the truth down the line. I swear I would have."

"No Miranda," I mumbled, stuck on the word.

A stronger woman would have dropped Eli on the carpet and jumped at Rodney's throat. She would have wrapped both hands around his windpipe and squeezed hard, squeezed with all her might. She would have strangled the conniving, weak, lying, orange-wearing, pathetic motherfucker to death. Nothing but the satisfaction of witnessing Rodney's last breath would have pulled her back. She would have squished him like a cockroach and never looked back. A stronger woman would have done the right thing. But my brain was as good as frozen. I couldn't think. I couldn't move. I couldn't speak. Inward. The explosion happened inward. No Miranda. What the fuck.

The guards started to push all us visitors out. I don't know where the time went after Rodney's confession. I remember sitting there, completely, utterly, numbly lost. Not thinking straight. Not thinking at all. Though Rodney sat only a few feet away, we were universes apart. He was dead to me. I was dead to myself. Dead. Back on that bus with Eli and Amad. Our first trip worth anything. Bye, bye, D.C. Leaving it all behind. New beginning. High stakes. My son's father. My family. Together we can make it. You, me, and the little one. Dragging my little brother into this. This ... this mess. Stupid me. Gullible, naive, square, out-of-my-mind me.

Out of my body, too. Riding the wind. Beautiful landscape of beautiful America. Flying through clouds in the infinite sky. Sun on my skin. Over mountains high and valleys low. Rivers, canyons, hardy cliffs, ringed geysers, lakes, buffaloes. Higher and higher above Earth. Anywhere but here. Deep into the sea. Majestic sea. Swimming. Tasting the salt. Holding my breath. Liquid dreams. Happiness. No lies. No games. No sadness. No hurt. No shame.

"I'm sorry," Rodney said before he walked away.

I couldn't find it in me to answer. I couldn't even look his way. I walked out of the penitentiary in a daze and remained in a daze for a long time. Eli was like a piece of wood in my arms. I felt nothing for him. Not a thing. He wasn't my son any more. He was his father's, the man who lied and conned, the man who played, the man I wanted never to be reminded of, the man I wished to forget. Had the ground opened to swallow us, I would have gone gladly. Come to think of it, I should have done it myself. Right then, on that cursed day, in front of that wretched jail. I should have thrown us under a bus and spared us the coming misery. Out-of-Town Girl

Kills Herself, Son. Saves Herself Years and Years of Heartache. Survived by mother, Rudy, brother, Amad, grandmother, Lizzie, and Mo, a friend.

  I should have. A bus, huge tires, screeching sounds, shouts of horror, two bumps on the asphalt, popping heads, splattering of blood, consternation. Better die than lose oneself the way I was preparing to do. Better a suicide than the disconnect. Better disappear than be in between, living but not really, living but not alive, going through the motions without meaning to, breathing against one's will, almost. Darkness.

"We're going back to D.C.," I told Amad the same day.

"I don't want to," he said.

"No choice."

"Because Rodney lied?"

"Exactly."

"You don't have to go see him ever again," he proposed. "We could stay and do everything we said we were going to do. Just live ... you know?"

"I don't want to be in the same town as Rodney. All that's gonna do is remind me of my stupidity. Besides, Beaumont is slow as shit."

"Feels fine to me."

"You just like the apartment. And the pool. And that Salvadorian girl next door."

"So what if I do? This better than D.C., no?"

"No."

Amad went to his room. I sat and looked around. It had been what, almost a month? Wouldn't take long to get rid of the little we had accumulated. I didn't care if we gave it all away. I didn't care if we moved back with only the clothes on our backs to show for the expedition. I didn't care one way or the other. Eli crawled close to me and started clamoring for attention. I pushed him away. It was the first time ever, and it made him cry. His face a jumble of tears and snot and loud noises and accusing stares, he kept raising his arms for me to pick him up. The wailing drilled into my temples. It took all I had in me no to kick my son in the head. "Wish you would shut up!" I yelled. Eli cried even louder, layer upon layer upon layer before Amad walked into the living room and scooped him up. "Take him outside before I hurt the little faggie," I told my brother. Amad gave me a worried look and rushed out. The screen bounced on the door frame.

I went to lie down. I was hot. I was cold. I was both in the moment and out of it. I was back in the visitation room. Was it true, really, what happened today? Was it? Couldn't be. Couldn't be. I must have dreamt it. Nobody would play with other human beings like that. Not with their own girlfriend. Not with their own son. Right? Nobody. I'm going to fall asleep in a minute. When I wake up it'll all be gone. All gone. Rodney will be loving and caring and honest.

But there was no sleeping it through. No sleeping it off. I opened my eyes and felt it in my stomach. It was still here, the spreading heaviness, the betrayal. It hadn't gone away while I had my eyes shut. Why hadn't it? I curled my body into a ball. It was night. My blinds were up, the AC was blowing. No light under the bedroom door. Amad and Eli must be in bed. Or maybe they never came back after I threw them out. Took a walk and kept on walking. I closed my eyes again. My head was pounding. When was the last time I ate something? This morning? Barely. I was excited to go see Rodney. Elated. Couldn't swallow a thing. In love. My heart was full. Stupid. Stupid. Stupid.

I woke up again. It was bright outside. For a moment I thought I was at the hospital after my C-section, such was the similarity of sensations. Groggy, parched, heavy bones, aching back, unable to line up two straight thoughts.

"It's 12 o'clock," Amad said. "You gettin' up?" Same concerned look as the day before. Barely sneaking his head into the room, as if I might jump and crush him against the wall.

"Don't feel too good," I moaned, hiding in my pillow. "Leave me alone."

"Want me to get you some medicine or something?"

I didn't bother answering.

"I got Eli," he assured me. "I know what to do, so don't you worry."

He closed the door. Before going back to sleep I heard him shush Eli when the latter laughed a little too loud. Gerber time.

I stayed in bed through the day, only finding it in me to get up deep into the night, when I was sure that my son and my little brother were asleep. Didn't want to see anybody. Didn't want to be seen. Didn't want to speak. Didn't want to be spoken to.

The kitchen was clean. Amad had cooked. Steaks, potatoes, a bed of greens. My plate awaited inside the fridge, filled to the rim and plastic-wrapped. Didn't know the little man could burn. I felt like congratulating him. Initiative, a desire to help, good with his hands, will step up and put unsuspected skills to use when the situation calls for it. A brokenhearted sister's dream. I took a few bites, rushed to the bathroom, put my head inside the toilet, and vomited. After drinking from the sink I took off my dress, the sky-blue sleeveless thing bought for Rodney that I had kept on for what, three days now? It reeked of sweat. I threw it in the trash with the rest of my clothes. My hair was matted. I saw how ugly it looked in the mirror and decided to cut it. Scissors. Where are the scissors. Rodney had liked it long, hadn't he, the asshole. Grow it, baby. Grow it for me. I like you best with a ponytail. It makes your eyes stand out. Your Bambi eyes. Zip. Off the ponytail went. You like it long, I like it short. Guess who wins.

I stood in the shower for a long, long time. When my legs got tired I lay in the tub, letting the scalding water whip my body. Then I got out and walked around the house naked. I had a taste for something strong, something to wipe the bile off my throat. Something like alcohol, though I didn't know how it felt to drink. Right then, I was certain it was what I needed. The one thing absolutely, definitely, sure to make me feel better. Not good. Better.

"We can stay for a couple of months," I told Amad in the morning. "I don't feel like facing all the questions and problems back home."

He looked at my hair and said nothing. I had chopped a good five years' worth without eliciting a single comment.

"Cool with me, Sal."

I could tell Amad was puzzled. He would wait and see. More changes were brewing. This wasn't good-old Sally. This wasn't his dedicated Big Sis. He couldn't take me at face value no more. "One day at a time," I told him. "That's how we're gonna play it."

"Cool," he said again.

Our phone got connected. No one to reach out to, but we had it. I knew Mo, Grandma, and Rene were all anxious for news. I knew Rudy and Mike were both waiting for a number to call collect. Every time I pictured myself talking to one of them, my stomach jumped. So the phone only ever rang for Amad. It was always Yanira, his girlfriend, the little Salvadorian next door. They spent a lot of time together. Parks, the pool, bus rides to the mall, movies. Hooked up quick. Her parents were never home. I didn't mind that Amad was seeing her. I didn't mind at all. "Take Eli with you," I would tell him whenever he readied himself to roll.

I got my hair evened out at a black salon, bought a TV in a pawn shop, a pair of sunglasses from a table vendor, and three open tickets to Washington at the Greyhound counter. Beaumont wasn't an ugly town. It just didn't interest me one way or the other. Paris or New York would have had the same effect, I suspect. Our people seemed relegated to a town section of their own, something the hairdresser said was common in the South. "Just be glad they don't fence y'all in and call it a zoo, like where I'm from," I told her. She laughed, unsure about the way to take my comment. Her name was Anna and she was in her forties. The butchered hair intrigued her to no end. "I was ready for a change," I explained. "It simply couldn't wait until the morning."
"Problems with your man?"
"You could say that."

Anna is the only person I remember talking to in Beaumont.

Mostly, I floated. Everyday gestures and tasks took too much effort. The grocery store. Cooking. Cleaning. Eli. Most mornings I didn't feel like getting up, bowing to the heat radiating from my heart as soon as I opened my eyes. Blood was leaking from it, of that I was sure. My poor little heart. And my head?

My head pounded and pounded. Pressure on top of pressure. Not enough room in there any more. Forehead in my jaw. Teeth ground to a shiny dust. Eyes shooting out. I felt ... oh, I felt as if I were about to die. Lie down, I thought. Stay in bed. Why bother? There's nothing waiting for you out there today. Nada. You'd only zombie through painstakingly, wishing the night would hurry up and come. Food? You know your stomach won't hold anything. You're getting skinny again. Nobody would even guess you have a child unless they saw Eli. Child? What child? Weird, what's happening with Eli. Can't stand him any more. Look at him and I see Rodney. Hating the son for the father's crime. Unfair? That's how life is. Momentary, though. Definitely. Mommy's gonna get up and feel better. Everything back to normal. Sally and son. Just not today, okay? Today, Mommy's tired. She wants to drift. Everybody out, everybody gone. Nobody to see her fall. Mommy wishes to lose it in peace. Walk alone for miles and miles. Through the desert. Hot sun, cactus trees, birds of prey circling in anticipation, no more water. Sweat and dust. Wind gushing through open plains. Tumbleweeds. Push on until the last stumble, the final step. Here lies Sally. Believed in Rodney, got a run for her money. Sally Too Tired. Sally Too Dumb. Sally Two Lives. Cop-out Sally. A heap of bones by the wayside. Crumbled hopes.

To laugh the laugh of she who can appreciate a cruel joke, even that which is played on her. Rodney, you dirty dog. You dirty, stinking dog. May you die a thousand deaths. May you rot in that cell. May loneliness shred your soul to pieces.

I wished only to sleep and look at the rain when it came drumming on my window. Something inviting about it. It's where I belonged, it seemed. With the dark clouds, thunder, and rainwater. With the drenched flowers, the overflowing gullies, the mud.

We packed up and left. Amad did all the work, little boy learning to become a man. He moved our furniture to Yanira's, who was taking all of it. He cleaned our place inside and out before we returned the keys. He prepared our bags. He took care of Eli. He flagged a cab. He bought us snacks at the bus station. He held the baby during the 3-day return trip, giving me room to breathe, letting me rest. Sally's tired. Sally's in a bad mood. Sally's a little out of it, you guys.

The closer we got to D.C., the worse I felt. Three months without a word. What had happened? What would I find? Who got sick? Who got locked up? Who got out? Who got a job? Who lost their job? Who got pregnant? Who expected to see me? Who put money on my return? Who foresaw the Texas debacle? Who would laugh at my misfortune? Who would cry? Who would be indifferent? Truth is, I didn't want to go. Another mistake waiting to blow up in my face, another wrong turn. Once you leave the home front you're not supposed to come back. You go and go and go and try to make it out there. West is the best. West and farther west. You push on. You pioneer. You Lewis and Clark. You trailblaze. You bushwhack. You kill natives. You break new ground. You dig roots. You hand-build. You tame nature. You innovate. You reach for the sky. You fulfill expectations, yours and those of the people left behind. You forever live in their memory as the gusty one, the one who took a gamble and hit the road and made it the hard way. Oh, I didn't want to go. But the money was finished and I wasn't about to find a job and settle in Beaumont, Texas. I wasn't about to do anything. It was coming, the Great Weakness. Just like winter is sure to drop in year after year after year. I felt it in my bones. A fatigue creeping through. A shutdown I wasn't about to offer the least resistance to. Not me. Not Sally. Why put up a fight? I'd been doing just that my whole life—a whole lot of good it did me. Enduring. Clenching my jaws. Balling my fists. Staring adversity in the face. Keeping my tears inside. Ignoring the pain. Thinking of others. Hoping against all hope. For years and years. But not this time. Oh no-no-no. Not. This. Time. This time I planned to surrender quickly and completely. I would let myself go under. I would let my arms drop. I would hang my head down. I wouldn't have a worry. I wouldn't have a care. No more responsibilities. Read my lips: No More Responsibilities. I just wished to land us somewhere where the living would be easy. Amad at Grandma's. Me with Rene down at Sursum Corda. Eli with me until I found something to do with him. Maybe Brenda would have him for a while. Another grandmother to the rescue. No, not Brenda. She was in on that con game with Rodney, remember? She lied. Mothers would do anything for their sons—what's a young girl's love? So no Brenda. Maybe I could put Eli up for adoption. Let him go nice and easy. Cut him loose. Other people would love and care for him better. Plenty of good folks out there who would be glad to have him. Black folks. White folks. Gay folks. Nothing wrong with the little boy. Healthy, cute, affectionate, a heart warmer. Good hugger, all his shots, potty trained. Only thing wrong with him is he reminds me too much of his daddy and I don't trust myself around him any more. Feel like punching him every time he looks my way. Sick to my stomach when he grabs me. Want to shut him up for good when he cries, which is unnervingly often. I know, I know, he's very attached. Firstborn, what can I say. But I'm weaning him off slowly but surely. Short with him nowadays. Barely spending any time. Noticing without much interest little changes like standing up, pointing at things, focusing at play, trying to form words. I'm weaning him off. No mommy-sonny embraces. No bathtub rubber duckies tender moments. No strolls on shady streets. No drawings in the sand. No laughter. No kisses. No patience. No love. I'm weaning him off. Believe me, by the time someone walks in his life he'll be happy to go.

Home still had that thing about it. The smell and taste of a D.C. Sunday. We saw more activity in five minutes than Beaumont registers in a whole week. I put Amad in yet another bus and sent him off to Grandma's.

"Come with me," he pleaded.

"I'll be at Rene's," I refused. "Be seeing you."

"Let's call Grandma first," he said. "What if she's not there? Who says she hasn't moved?"

"Don't be silly," I told him. "Just go. I'll check on you later on today."

He cried before kissing me on the cheek, as if we'd never see each other again. I didn't know my little brother to be so intuitive, for this was indeed the last time he'd see the Sally he used to know. Blood ain't no joke.

Rene was home. My banging woke her up at one in the afternoon, a feat the hallway noise hadn't been able to accomplish. Puffy-eyed, disheveled, fleshy, darker than in my memory. She didn't seem surprised or particularly happy to see Eli and me. Maybe it was the sleep clinging to her thoughts. Maybe Willie, the balding sugar daddy watching TV on her couch. "We're back," I said, looking straight into her eyes. "Thought I'd crash with you."

She nodded and hugged me. "Why did you cut your hair?" It was the first thing she noticed in people. That much would never change.

"Tired of it."

We walked in. Willie waved the fingers of his free hand and tried to look at my butt. "House is a mess," Rene apologized, not lying for a second. "You can have Tyree's room."

"Where is he?"

"With Tyrone and Rhonda. Finishing the summer."

The room, like the rest of the apartment, was upside down. I sat Eli down and pushed my bag under the bed. "Tired," I told Rene. "I'm gonna catch some z's if that's okay."

"Go ahead."

Eli stumbled out of the room. I let myself fall on the unmade bed after opening the window. Failure. Rene's apartment and behavior stank of failure. She hadn't accomplished a thing since we parted ways. It was in her eyes, Willie's posture, the smell of weed in the air, the nasty floor, the bathroom, the overflowing kitchen sink, the chipped and scribbled-on walls, the crumbs on Tyree's minute bed. Rene, too, had embarked on a descending curve. It satisfied me to no end. Call me evil-minded.

I woke up to an empty apartment and stayed in bed.

"Went to the grocery store," Rene said when she came back with Eli around 8. I sat up and rubbed my eyes. Hearing his name, my son tried to come close. I put a hand between us and he walked away.

A thud came from the other side of the wall. "Don't know what they be doing," Rene said of her neighbors. "But it's nonstop."

"Who's Willie?" I asked.

She looked at the ground. "My boyfriend. He lives in the building."

"Married?"

She nodded.

"You and your old dudes."

"I tried me a youngin' after you left. Didn't work out. Least Willie be gettin' paid."

"What does he do?"

"He sells Love Boat."

We went in the kitchen. Rene started fixing dinner. I went to take a shower after she refused my help. Eli ate and drifted off to sleep on the greasy couch. "You're not gonna give him a bath?" Rene asked.

"He can rot in what he's got on," I told her. "After what his father did to me, the little sucker better be glad I haven't murdered him yet."

Rene laughed. "What *did* happen?"

She shook her head after I told her. "That was dirty."

We ate and caught up on the rest of our lives. She wasn't working. Willie was constantly in and out. He conducted business at his own place two floors up, dipping Newports in a formaldehyde vial and handing them out for $20 apiece. His brand was so strong they called it "Deader." "I tried it once," Rene confessed. "It had me lunching the fuck out. Felt like taking my clothes off and flying to the moon just like Stephanie's man did. Rocket Girl."

Willie was an uncomplicated man. Satiate his physical appetites and he was happy. Half of his money went to his wife to shut her up. The other half was Rene's. He slept with both. Raw with Hon, condoms with Rene. "He's a freak. Ten times a day if you let him. You'll hear us bonin' a lot."

"As long as he's good to you..."

"He is."

"...and you keep him away from me."

"Trust me."

Willie did try it with me. The first time he touched me in my sleep I punched him in the face, bloodying his lip. The second time, I took hold of his genitals and squeezed hard. He didn't dare howl for fear of waking Rene. Or maybe because he actually liked that I was touching him. But he managed to stay out of my way afterward, like I out of his.

Rene wasn't seeing anybody from the old days. Chevon was still hanging uptown, driving an even bigger car and wearing her expensive threads. Stephanie was doing porn full-time. The Amoco was getting robbed regularly now that the taboo had been broken. Of Mo, not a chance encounter or sighting.

"He's still got his little booth as far as I know. You're gonna go see him?"

"What for?"

"Thought you might be missin' him."

"I don't. Too soft for me. How's Pepsi?"

"Still on top. More so now that Doug is dead."

"Doug got got?"

"Just like we knew he would."

Rene filled me in on everybody but Juliet, the Sursum Corda girl who had become her best friend in my absence. She must have felt she had let me down. She must have feared I'd be jealous. It's from seeing the two of them interact that I understood how close they were. Routines, automatisms, tics, jokes, trust, secrets I didn't share, common acquaintances I didn't know, points of reference I was oblivious of. Juliet was likable enough. A year younger than us, skin and bones, her chocolate as dark as Rene's, short hair, fine features, pleasant face. Everybody has a trait or asset that sets them apart. My eyes, though some people would point at my nose. Rene's cheeks. Stephanie's knockers. For Juliet it was the upper lip. It curled above her teeth, setting off a barrage of signals, not all of them justified, some downright contradictory. Humor, innocence, lust, sexiness, sassiness, exuberance, gourmandise, coquetry, sexual savoir-faire. She was easygoing and fun to be around. I quickly got used to her, though her moodiness threw me off at first. Crack was the center of her life. She was happy when high and sad when in need. Boys in Temple Courts knew her as the $50-a-pop whore. Though her family, Trinidadian in origin, lived in a townhouse inside the complex, she seemed to have no fixed address. Men rented her time for cash or drugs, sometimes for weeks on end. She was a wild one, Juliet. A girl who, by her own admittance, had never had a true boyfriend. "Nobody ever claimed me," she told me once, regret in her voice. "It's like I ain't good enough."

"Your rep must scare the shit out of them," I explained. "They know you for that one thing. You'll need to drop out when you're ready for something serious. Disappear for a while, let them forget. Change your persona before you come back, hit them with a whole new 'tude."

"One day," she said.

It was weird to see someone who looked as good live the way she did. In another life she would have been a knockout on the strength of her shape and that upper lip alone. In another life we'd all have been princesses. What had gone wrong with Juliet wasn't readily apparent. Her folks, one generation removed from their tropical island and now on America's welfare rolls; stuff she had suffered through or been exposed to in Sursum Corda, like poverty, abuse, parental neglect, depression; a predisposition for substance abuse; identity issues; restlessness.

Juliet's the one who gave me my first line of coke on a slow Sunday morning, the bells of a nearby church ringing, the sun filtering through. On the living room table, a mere two feet from Eli. "Want some?" she asked Rene and me. I bent over to snort the white powder, immediately feeling the rush. It illuminated my brain and flooded my heart with goodness, goodwill, happiness, clarity, a brand-new confidence, a deep understanding of life's inner workings. "How does it feel?" Juliet asked, smiling.

"Good," I laughed with delight. "Gooder than a motherfucker!"

Rene went next. Snort-snort. Thumb wiping the bottom of her nose. I could tell she had done it before. "Good shit," she agreed.

"This be just an appetizer for me," Juliet proclaimed before doing her own lines.

Eli came to lean on her thigh, his eyes on the TV screen. I pushed him with my foot. "Go in the room."

He retreated promptly, knowing by the tone of my voice that a beating wasn't far away.

"Let's go out," Juliet proposed.

"Where?" Rene asked.

"To the mall."

"No money," I said.

Rene pulled a wad out of her purse. "I got you."

Juliet pulled on her collar to flash the bills folded in her bra. "Got you, too."

The thought of Eli held me back. "This damn baby," I told them.

"Lock him up in the room," Rene suggested. "Make sure there's nothing in there he can hurt himself with."

"Good idea."

For good measure, I spanked Eli before we left. He could cry himself to sleep. By the time he woke up we would be back. What were the chances of a fire or building evacuation or anything bad? What did I care?

We caught the metro at Union Station and went to Pentagon City. The coke was making our minds race. We were young and beautiful and fast-tongued. Not a care in the world. Juliet's hot box of a beeper kept going off. Behind each number was an urge, tricks to be turned, hallways or bedrooms or motels or alleys or parked cars or offices or basements. Preferences, anecdotes, $50 or more, group discounts, money upfront. Juliet was in demand. "They've been asking about you in Temple

Courts," she revealed: "'Who's Sally?' 'Who's the redbone?' 'She down?' They're wide open. You could charge a whole lot more than I do.

I was feeling better than I had in a long time. More alive. In a different skin altogether. Yet another Sally. High for the very first time. A whole new world was opening up. Anything seemed possible. Nothing was off-limits. Life was this unexplored territory. Do it all. Try it all. Go all the way. Hold nothing back. I can. I might. I will. What the fuck. What had taken me so long?

"We'll see," I told Juliet.

It was night when we got back. Eli was sleeping peacefully. Two days later we did it again.

Rene borrowed Willie's Monte Carlo and drove us uptown just so we could stomp our old grounds. "Didn't know you had your license," Juliet remarked.

"I don't" Rene retorted.

C.T.U.'s renovations weren't yet underway. It looked empty and sad. We hadn't done much with it while we ran it, but at least it had been alive. Brother Haj came to my mind. And Jerry. And Bam Bam. And Flying Man Troy. And Robert.

High and hungry, we raided the Amoco for snacks. Nikki was running the register. She had to do a double take to recognize me. "My God, you've changed!" she exclaimed. We exchanged a few words. She had more questions than I had answers. No need to pretend: I reconnected with my attitude and shut her down. She pursed her lips and called for the next customer in line. Rene, Juliet, and I talked loudly and goofed around and play-fought while shopping. We counted our change and left without saying goodbye.

As luck would have it, Pepsi was gassing up as we stepped out. "You look familiar," he told me, opening his arms for an embrace. No timbre in his raspy voice; no more than mild amusement, as if he were beyond surprise. A man who'd seen it all and done it all; a man who lived through filters; a man who'd successfully stripped the last inklings of spontaneity and impulsiveness from his soul. I'd heard the face wound he suffered in his teens had damaged his nerves. I'd heard that was the reason Pepsi never smiled fully. I wasn't so sure.
"So do you," I said.

We stayed glued to each other. There was a message in that hug. It meant something. A new direction. A break from the past. A promise. A beginning. Like jumping together. Like reaching for we weren't quite sure what.

Pepsi smelled good. His hair was neatly cropped. His beard was trimmed. His body felt toned. His grip was firm.
"Welcome back, Sally."
"Who said I ever went anywhere?"
He held a finger across his lips.

Emboldened by the coke, I kissed his cheek. If there ever was anything to what had been said between us before, this might prove the only way to find out. I'd held out all these years. The things I pursued, the ones I thought I wanted, the ones that were supposed to be right for me—none of them had worked out. I just wanted to know: Was he supposed to be my next move? Was he to be my destiny?

Pepsi looked fly in his tracksuit. His sports car

was silver and low and ready. I felt a stirring between my legs. I think he sensed it, too. "What are you up to?"

"I want to ride with you," I said.
"Let's go."

I waved at Juliet and Rene. They laughed and waved back and gave me the nod. Maybe this had been the plan all along.

The drive excited me even more. We didn't speak. We didn't even make small talk. Pepsi drove perilously fast. No music to drown out the engine. Blue cluster lights, restless tachometer. The speed wasn't just another rush. I saw ourselves crash and disintegrate. I saw an awesome ball of fire and exploding glass and mangled steel. I wouldn't have minded should it all have ended right then and there. I wouldn't have minded. I wasn't scared. It would have been more of a relief, I think. It would have been OK. It would have spared me a whole lot of trouble. It would have saved me yet more heartbreak.

Pepsi took me to a house in Bethesda, right off Democracy Boulevard. It had a circular driveway, red-brick walls, a pillared porch, wide windows, a fireplace, a jacuzzi, a bean-shaped pool. Quiet, except for the hum of the AC. Smelled of home-cooked meals. Blackie came running, her nails clattering on the gleaming hardwood floor. I looked around while Pepsi petted her. This is where the drug money went. Designer interior, electronics, custom furniture, Pop Art, landscaping, a personal chef, a relative's name or LLC on the deed, everything high-end and ultramodern and immaculate.

Pepsi unlocked the French doors and let Blackie out. "Go handle your business in the garden," he told her with a last pat. "I have company."

I wasn't invited to sit. I was offered neither drink nor food. Pepsi simply walked back to where I stood and grabbed my wrist. He came close. I held his gaze. There was no space between our bodies. Not an inch. No room to slip aside. No place to go. I started to smile but stopped in my tracks. His eyes showed nothing, at least nothing that I expected, nothing that I could say I liked. I started getting uncomfortable. One way to find out, right?

He kissed me and pushed me against the wall. The same hand that had been caressing the dog traveled all over me, probing, searching for, and finding, skin. Possessive. He was being impatient and possessive. I held my breath. I came back down to earth. Again, this wasn't what I had anticipated. No sweet-talk. No kindness. No tenderness. No preliminary. No participation required. I wanted to hold him and be held. I wanted to touch him and look at his body. I wanted to hear his heartbeat. I wanted to know his smell, his taste, his ways. I wanted to take my time. I wanted to explain. I wanted to teach him. I wanted him to learn me. I wanted to ask about feelings. I wanted to know: Was there ever anything behind what had been said?

But Pepsi was in a hurry. He was rushing and I didn't do a thing to stop him. I didn't know how. I wasn't sure. It's like I was there and I wasn't. No desire in me. Not an ounce. How to walk this back? It was me who'd sent the signal. It was me who'd jumped in the fire. It was me who'd said without saying, "I want to find out."

    Off flew my top, my jeans, my panties, my thoughts, my wishes, my will, my voice. Neglecting to undress all the way, Pepsi freed himself, slipped on a condom, flipped me, and held my face against the brick. It actually hurt. It did. But I dared not utter a sound. I just bit my lip and felt my own breath, the taste of paint, the pang of pain, the nausea of humiliation, the wet of tears. Seek refuge inward. Wait for it to pass.

He fucked me again, on the floor, on all fours, with something close to fury. I call it "fuck" for lack of a better term. Nothing else was at play. Pepsi had wanted me for a long time and here I was. It had nothing to do with me. I existed only as the one piece missing from his trophy mantle, the rebel, the holdout, the thorn in his pride. No mention, that night, of our previous conversations. How he had pursued me way back when, up to a few months ago, popping along any path I cared to follow. How he'd known me my whole entire life. The providential intervention in the projects yard. The parka with a Pepsi can spirited inside. The limo ride. Hains Point. How he was leaving the game and wanted me for his wife. How I was to become the one trusted woman by his side, the *capo di tutti capi*. This, I now realized, is how you groom a girl: You start her young, you don a mask, you play it smooth, you make her feel seen, you make her feel heard, you show her respect, you're slow and consistent, you persist, you pay attention, and, when it finally comes, you seize the moment.

The cold I had felt inside Beaumont penitentiary started to creep back into my skull. The cold of shame. The cold of torment. The cold of unspeakable hurt.

Pepsi got up as soon as he was done. "Get dressed. I'm dropping you off."

"I'm tired," I pleaded, meaning, I'm lost. So, so lost. "Can't we talk? Can't I spend the night? I don't want to be alone. It's late. I …"

He shook his head, a vague smile on his lips. "We don't talk. And nobody gets to spend the night. I would call you a cab, but they take forever."

"I see."

Cold. During the last moments in the house, when it dawned on me that I didn't know this man I had just given myself to, that he could kill me and feed me to Blackie and that it would be the end of me. Cold again during the silent ride, not to Sursum Corda or, at the very least, uptown, where he'd found me, but to the nearest metro station, the end of the Red Line, a dark and deserted platform, endless tunnels, an empty train with stained carpeting and orange seats.

"For your fare," Pepsi said, throwing a few crumpled bills in my lap. The thought of leaving the money didn't even cross my mind. That's how far I was from the person I used to be. How removed from my old self, and reality, already. Idling by the curb, Pepsi fished a small object from his pocket. "I see you like coke," he said. "Try this, let me know what you think. Need more, come around Clifton. We got that. Only, next one won't be free."

I slammed the door. Pepsi took off, marking

the asphalt and making heads turn. Does a bear shit in the woods and wipe his ass with a rabbit?

Sleeping didn't push the chagrin away. It did succeed in blunting it a little. Same with the cocaine, crack, and heroin I started to smoke with the eagerness of a neophyte. Nobody sets out to become an addict, I think. It's a game of self-deceit, a dance of denial. You swear you got it under control all the way to the very end. It's always about needing something to lift up your head right now, at this very moment. You feel bad. You're tired. You're down and out. You don't want to deal with anything. A little smoke would help. Puff, she puffs. I need this today, right now, at this precise minute, but I can stop whenever I want, I can kick at the snap of fingers. Whenever I want. As soon as I'm ready. Long as I put my mind to it. I'm not a weak person. Not at all. Look at me, look at my accomplishments, look at everything I've been through. Somebody else would have been broken a long time ago. Broken in two. Addicted? Me? Never. I'm too strong. I'm too smart. This here is just to get me by, see me through.

But the moments become days. The days turn into months. The months morph into a life. The point is to not deal with anything. To do as little hard work as possible. To get by. To push all the broken stuff, the ugly stuff, the hopelessly tangled stuff, deeper and deeper inside, until it is safely buried, sealed tight. To go to that one place where you can bear being yourself, find a little peace, catch a little break. It's a trip all right. Doesn't matter that in a couple of hours you'll be right back where you started. Jittery, uneasy, raw, sad, scared, low, sick to your stomach, beating yourself up, sick of yourself.

Addiction has a logic of its own. One of its tricks is to have you hide in plain sight. And crack, man, let me tell you.... Crack is as bad as they say. It's as bad as it gets.

Skillet

So what if theirs isn't much of one: Beginnings are beginnings.

It's thanks to Rudy that Sally finally got to know Mo, that winter. It happened at the market's counter as he was ringing them up. Rudy looked straight at Mo and said, "My daughter likes you," making him take notice. Mo didn't seem to mind that Sally was pregnant. He slipped her his number and made her promise to call. Too shy to make good on her word, Sally had her friend Stephanie impersonate her on the phone while she sat across the couch munching on a macadamia cookie. "11 a.m., Takoma station, tomorrow," Stephanie reported, her fingers in a V. "He's got to be at work by 3."

Sally took it from there. She plaited her hair, borrowed the fare and white shoes and a suede sweat suit, and showed up on time, hiding in one of the bus shelters until Mo rode along in a trick bike that was way too tiny. "I'm not getting on that thing," she announced with a sleepy smile, as if Mo really expected her to jump and ride amazon-style.

They left the station and followed residential streets, passing apartment buildings and bungalows whose old-school porches were carpeted a dusty D.C. green. Mo's T-shirt, thermals, loose jeans, and counterculture sneakers made him look just as underdressed as Sally.

He got off the bike and walked alongside her. They stole glances at each other and made small talk. On her bedroom mirror Sally had appeared winter-yellow and very, very round. A natural kind of girl, she had decided not to put on any makeup and to just let her eyes and her lips do their thing. Mo was an improvement on the bookish type—not much of a body but a face worth looking at, glasses and all. It's what promised to clinch it for Sally, to tell the truth, for real for real, come what may: the face, the apparent unpretentiousness, the hair darting like so many rays.

They entered a yard behind Tuckerman Street. Mo parked the bike under washing lines and barked at Venus, the neighbors' female pit, a hard-to-find white with candy-red nails and a brown patch around the left eye. The basement's reinforced door opened into a narrow hallway that smelled like cement and contained a sink, a small refrigerator sitting on bricks, and a stove. The walls in the living area were paneled in the same varnish as the hall. Books and a stack of records stood at the bottom of the stairs leading to the sealed-off upper floor.

Mo sat in the middle of the bare carpet and invited Sally to do the same. Sally looked around, her attitude kicking in. She was hot. She was cold. She was tired and already bored.

"Don't you have a radio?"
"In the room. A small one."
"I feel like some music."
"Go ahead."

In the bedroom also the sun filtered through a single window. What did Mo do for light? A mattress was laid at the foot of the wall. More books were strewn about. Where were the TV, the CDs, the posters, the picture frames, the video games?

Sally found the radio and turned it to something old and soft. "Can I use your bathroom?"
"Yeah."

It was blue, tidy, cool, and insufficiently illuminated by a plug-on bulb.

"You live like a nomad," she told Mo after she came to sit next to him, a beaching whale, one knee before the next, a whale stuck smack in the middle of Mo's immensely empty carpet of a sea.

"Never did care for material things."

"Lucky you."

He got up to make tea, using loose leaves and a kettle the like of which she had never seen. It was very small, with a fat belly and a long and curved beak. "One of the few things that traveled with me. The tea, I was able to find in a Chinatown grocery store. Same brand we use back in Mogadishu."

"Do you miss home?"

He nodded. "My father, Yonis. I last saw him when he handed me a stash, put me in a Land Rover along with my sister Aster, and two armed guides, and instructed me not to stop until the Kenyan border. November '93, right after Black Hawk Down. We were all freaked out, and more than a little bit."

"So you were fleeing the war?"

Mo nodded again. "Somalia has more Kalashnikovs and rocket launchers than people. It stopped making sense a long time ago. Everybody who could get away did."

"Why didn't your father come along?"

"He's a big man in our clan. My stepmother and half-siblings also stayed. I don't think they could have survived what Aster and I went through. Dadaab camp, especially. Maybe Yonis knew."

"Couldn't you just fly?"

Mo laughed. "That's what Aster asked when we cut her hair and disguised her. Going through a refugee camp increases your chances of obtaining asylum in America. Not the same as landing at JFK or Dulles fresh as a rose. Definitely."

Sally tried to imagine it. "How was Dadaab?"

Mo lowered his head. "Twigs and sheeting, an ocean of blue plastic domes. Different tribes, different languages, different customs. Dust for days. Showers and toilets one big bloody joke. Malaria the biggest problem. The makeshift hospital enough to break your heart. And the children ... no food, no water, no school. Kenyan soldiers treat you like dogs and have eyes out for young girls, old girls, pretty girls, ugly girls, starved-and-traumatized girls—any damn girl. The U.N. people no better. Aster and I left after finding out that the asylum process could take as long as three years. Road and rail to Nairobi. Rented room in a slum. Math and English lessons for rich kids. The American embassy first thing every morning—the queue starts long before dawn, some people spend the night. Good move, overall: My papers arrived in half the time."

"What about Aster? Where is she now?"

"In Mombasa, with other Somali expats, safe and sound. I talk to her once a week and send her money every month. Her own documents should come through soon. Next fall, hopefully."

"Like it here?"

Mo shrugged. "I'm an immigrant. Never imagined I'd be stocking shelves and sweeping floors for a living. I had different ideas for my future before my future disappeared."

Sally smiled. I'll be your future from now on, she thought, but said, "Work is work," instead.

"True."

High-five. Sally then does her best not to lose Mo through her stop-and-go story the way she loses even herself sometimes. Mo makes it easy to open up. She looks his way and sees him considering her intently. Mo the listener.

"My mom and dad were together until I turned seven," Sally says. "We had an apartment on North Capitol and K. After my parents separated, Rudy and I went to stay with her mother on Eastern Avenue. That's where my brother, Amad, was born from a man named Ned. By then Rudy was using heavily. Bad thing upon bad thing, trouble on top of trouble. She caught a battery charge before Amad turned one. My uncles and aunts all lived at Grandma's with their own children. A wild bunch. Nobody had their stuff together."

"And your dad?"

"Running a crew in Southeast and making babies with his new girlfriend. Two brand-new little girls back-to-back. Took me out every once in a while and bought me things: an encyclopedia, a gold-plated watch, a glass doll that Amad broke. When Grandma's basement caught fire the menagerie dispersed."

"'Menagerie'?"

"That's us: the world-famous Harris Traveling Circus, higgledy-piggledy. Rudy, Amad, and I went to stay with my cousin Chi-Chi up Clifton Terrace. I spent an entire summer with my father and one of his girlfriends before he got locked up."

"Drugs?"

"And guns. He's still in."

"How old were you?"

"Thirteen. Rudy got approved for a two-bedroom in the building next to Chi-Chi's. We still call C.T.U. home except for Amad, who lives with my grandmother on Atlantic Avenue."

"Why isn't he with you?"

"Social Services. They damn near took me away, too."

"What does 'C.T.U.' stand for?"

"Clifton Terrace University."

"What's to learn in that godforsaken place?"
"Bad things. Bad things only."

They got quiet. Sally stretched her legs and scratched her nose. Her back was starting to complain. She ignored it. No couch, not a single chair. A nomad, this Mo. A nomad. Then Mo: "School?"

Sally frowned. She was hot. She was cold. She wasn't bored any more. "Stopped in the 8th. Too much trouble. Rudy had it hard trying to take care of all four of us. I made sure Amad never missed a day."

"'Four'?"

"Me, Amad, Rudy, and her habit. Couldn't make it. Not enough to go around."

"Rudy ever worked?"

"She hustled. Hooked up with thieves and peddlers and small-timers. A whole bunch of sorry dudes. My surrogate dads. Things got better when I met Rodney. Until I got pregnant, that is. Until he, too, got sent away."

"What for?"

"Murder Two."

"D.C. Jail?"

"Beaumont, Texas. They transferred him not too long ago."

"Your first boyfriend?"

Sally shook her head. "Robert. I was fourteen. Killed in a drive-by right in front of Clifton. Right in front of me."

Detached, Sally. Easy breezy. Not her talking. Not her at all.

"That's tough," Mo commented after taking it all in.

Ready in about twenty minutes, the brew was unusually bitter. Sally thought about the baby. "I shouldn't be drinking this."

"And I should have known better," Mo acknowledged, taking her glass away. "When are you due?"

"Ten days to go."
"Scared?"
"Ready. My back is killing me."
"Boy or girl?"
"Boy."
"Got a name?"
"Elijah. Eli."

He ordered a Paradiso pizza even though Sally insisted she wasn't hungry. It was enough to sit next to each other and talk. They clicked. She already knew they would. She knew the first time she saw him. Just knew. "How old are you?"

"Twenty-eight.... Too old?"
"No."

She paused for him to ask her age. He didn't. He must find her old enough. She was pregnant, wasn't she. There was nothing innocent about her.

Waiting for the food, she was thinking about the things left out of her story when Mo came close and kissed her. She closed her eyes and felt his fingers slip under her clothes. Mo the fast one, his touch and his scent both exciting and off-putting in their newness. Sally resisted the impulse to let herself fall back on the carpet. Behave, Sally. Behave.

"It's on, then?"
"Till it's gone."

They rode the bus to the Amoco and hugged before Mo went in. Rayshan watched them from her alley stoop. Nosy Rayshan, her eyes as big as see-it-all, record-it-all cameras, her tongue itching to run tell it.

Sally walked the long block home and took a nap.

"How's my baby?" Rudy called when she came back from her shift at 8 to find her knocked out in front of the grainy TV.

"Tired," Sally said before giving her mother a kiss. "How was your day?"

"Glad it's over."

They ate the burgers, fries, and boxed apple pies Rudy brought from McDonald's every evening.

"Gotta go," Rudy said a little after 9, rushing to make her 10 o'clock curfew.

"Be safe," Sally said, more out of habit than true worry.

"I will."

Sally's friends gave her a baby shower, blessing her with much needed stuff, used stuff, hot-stolen stuff, good stuff, useful stuff, stuff for now and stuff for later: diapers, formula, layettes, shoes, hats, OshKosh B'Goshs, a stroller, a carrier, a baby bag, a nose cleaner, pacifiers, bottles, towels, blankets, and a plastic tub--all layawayed, snatched, traded, gift-wrapped, and offered with a smile by the four of them: Chevon, Rene, Stephanie, Tamika. It was the nicest time Sally had had in a while. The girls brought tears to Rudy's eyes and took advantage of her much- publicized resolutions and newfound softness to make her promise she'd stay clean and see Sally through. "Don't y'all worry," Rudy said. "I'm gonna stay kickin' this shit."

Good thing it didn't happen at night. Rudy came through with last-minute cab money, a packed bag by the door, and the dried half of a Quarter Pounder with cheese. "Lord knows you can't survive on that nasty stuff they feed you down there—good hospital and decent people, don't get me wrong, but the food, sweet Jesus, the food!"

Though Sally didn't want her mother in the delivery room, she couldn't find the heart to tell her, and so she didn't. Rudy had been excited about this baby from day one. No matter how ugly or embarrassing things were about to get, there would be no keeping her out of it. It was a big day for her, too.

So Rudy held Sally's hand and got in the way, her voice covering the staff's and her orders countering theirs to the point where they threatened to throw her out, not knowing she had a knife tucked under her scrubs and a second hidden in the bag and they would have had to kill her first, the crackhead from Clifton Terrace could take all of them in a heartbeat and win—Foxy Brown out of this motherfucker. Sally wasn't dilating enough, the baby wasn't coming out, the people got tired of her crying and shitting herself and her mother's interfering. After half a day in labor, they decided to cut her up. The fuss resumed when the C-section went to hell, the botched anesthesia causing Sally to feel the blade as it began to slice her skin. She hollered, levitated, and kicked everything moving until she found herself strapped to the table.

"Can't you useless bitches see she's in pain?" Rudy shouted, jumping on her feet and throwing her hands up high.

Sally thought she was about to die. She begged the doctor to make her numb. Tough as she was she couldn't take it any more, they could put her out for days and she wouldn't complain.

Eli was born on January 5th, 1996. Sally was home the next day, fighting her way up the stairs among a big crowd because the elevators stayed broken and a boy named Dogg had just been shot on the 3rd floor. Police and medics were all over the place. Tenants wanted to see, talk, and argue. Dogg was Sally's play brother, the son of one of Rudy's sorry dudes. He had lived with Rudy, Amad, and her for a while. Hearing that someone had taken a sawed-off to his face made Sally cry. She didn't go take a look, no, she didn't dare, but people told her that Dogg's blood and tissue fragments were all over the walls and all over the floor, that the blast didn't kill him, and that he kept pleading with the officers to finish him off because he didn't want to live any more —not never, not now, no way, no how, not like this.

So Eli's homecoming was all fire and thunder. Sally was a seventeen-year-old mother with pretty brown eyes, bad hair, mismatched knees, crooked teeth, and a gut cut in half by a brand-new, rosy scar. People came and went, telling her how cute her son was when she could see for herself that he was all cheeks and way too yellow. "All the fuss for this little thing," she derisively told her mother. "And he ugly, too...." But she loved her little pumpkin with all her heart and felt proud she had made him. Like a mother cat, she sniffed him and licked him and tossed him around and laid him on top of her, never for one moment letting him out of her sight.

Amad caught the bus from Southeast to come give Sally and his nephew a kiss. He said hello and countered Rudy's mock enthusiasm with mock interest, turning serious when he first set eyes on little Eli, nodding silently when Sally said, "So you're an uncle now." Amad was lighter of complexion than everybody in the entire family. His green eyes also set him apart. He promised to grow very tall and they wondered how and why, people on his father's side being just as short as those on Rudy's. Sally thought he looked awful, that afternoon. "Awful" as in "unkempt" and "raggedy." Cheap clothes, cheap shoes, lint in his hair, dirt under his nails. Letting himself go since he had been removed from her watch. That's what Amad was doing: Letting himself go. "It's not about the stuff on your back," Sally scolded him from where she lay. "There's no excuse for not being clean."

Amad shrugged. He was twelve, he was broke, he was stressed out and uncomfortable in his mother and sister's company. Living apart was making him forget how to live with them. Grandma had caught him smoking a cigarette in the bathroom, a no-no since the fire of six years ago. She'd chased him down Atlantic and shouted extra-spicy insults and a sermon the whole world could hear. Grandma, the court-appointed guardian who never spent on the boy a dime of the check she got for him.

Faced with her brother's silent distress, half of Sally was experiencing a familiar pang of guilt. The other half clutched Eli closer. "We're losing him," she told Rudy after Amad left.

"The boy's gettin' grown," Rudy admitted, missing the point completely. "Or so he thinks."

"Can't you get Grandma to give him more money? It's his."

"Ain't too much I can do," Rudy said lamely. "I start mouthin' off, she gets mad, the judge gets a whiff of it?" Rudy snapped her fingers to show how fast Amad could end up in foster care. "Better let Ma ride this one out until the day I can get my son back. One more reason for me to straighten up."

"Talk to her," Sally insisted. "Press her out ... or I will."

Rudy answered nothing.

Sally drifted off feeling sad for her brother. She ended up dreaming of him.

That evening, Rodney's little brother, Ben, and his mother, Brenda, came to visit after the latter got off work. Ben displayed his newly adopted street-tough persona: detached, dangerous, laconic, unsmiling, probably packing. Brenda looked mean and unbecoming in her blue zoo uniform. (Brenda always looked mean and unbecoming. Uppity woman was her thing. Too good for the block. Too good for the girl her son was messing with. Sally's deepest wish was that Eli turn out nothing like her.)

"You talk to Rodney?"
"We don't have a phone, Brenda."
"I forgot. I got some stuff for the baby. Come get it when you're ready."
"I will."

A whole five minutes, the visit lasted. Ben and Brenda halfheartedly took a few Polaroids to mail to Rodney. On the one where Brenda held Eli she couldn't even bring herself to smile.

"Stiff as shit," Rudy mumbled behind their backs. "Why couldn't she or Ben just bring that stuff to you instead of having you climb the hill all the way to the Amsterdam? Ain't that what you're supposed to do with a gift—take it to the person it's meant for?"

Sally started feeling sleepy again. "Brenda will always be Brenda."

"All of us is family, now," her mother reasoned. "I don't think the wench realizes that."

Rodney, whose six hundred dollars' worth of collect calls had surpassed her father Mike's five-fifty to get the phone disconnected for good, wrote Sally a long letter to ask why the baby should carry her last name and not his, and to remind her of the promise she had made to stay true and see him through his bid, the Big Twenty. "Stay away from all the dudes out there. Hold me down, you know." He was that faraway presence in her life, the voice that, though muffled by time and thousand of miles, came out of the ether to threaten and straighten out every once in a while—Rodney the disciplinarian.

Hard as she tried, Sally couldn't remember pledging to sit for Rodney's twenty-to-life sentence. What she did tell him was that she'd never turn her back on him, which was different from cutting herself off from the rest of the world. During her last visit to D.C. Jail he had downplayed the whole thing and angered her with advice on masturbation and government help. "They'll come through for you," he said with a benign smile. "They'll give you a place and money to spend. If you can learn to budget you'll be fine. Just sit tight, baby." His hair, which he always used to keep short and neat, was growing past his ears. He looked like a stranger in jumpsuit and flip-flops behind the stained and cracked glass. His voice came strong through the phone connection. There was no fear in his eyes either, maybe because D.C. Jail was still home. A lot of the people in there he already knew. Boys from around town, an old Dunbar football coach, a cousin or two. "Ray-ray says wassup. Remember him? That nigga in here doin' hair, cleanin' floors, bummin' cigarettes.... Straight fag." Rodney kept scratching his chin, eyes all over her. The phone became heavy in Sally's palm. It weighed a ton, it crushed her, it pushed her deeper into her plastic seat. She started to pay more attention to the men sitting on each side of Rodney, the officer standing behind the prisoners' bench, the chatter of conversations, the dirty hallway leading to she didn't know what. "You gon' always be mine," Rodney declared. "I know it don't look like it but I ain't gonna be here but for a hot second. My lawyer's working the mess out of this case, comin' up with all kinds of good things. He'll make it happen." Rodney waited for Sally to say something, but she couldn't think of anything to match his high spirits—how could she? Turning jealous as their thirty minutes started to run out, Rodney hurriedly tossed warnings and recommendations across the partition. "Watch yourself, Sal. You belong to me. I got people dropping dime. You do me wrong, I'll find out. Better know where your ass is at. Never forget who put clothes on your back and planted that seed in your belly. You *best* not forget."

She left without saying goodbye, feeling nothing for him, nothing at all, storming, talking to him in her head, saying all the things she should have said: You should have worried about losing me before you jumped out there and tried to make a name for yourself. You knew, because I made sure to tell you constantly, that you couldn't allow anything to happen. A baby was on the way that would need the both of us. You knew, but chose to do what you did. Now I'm out here on my own. Now I'm supposed to parallel your ordeal, sit in a cell at the same time as you and for just as long, only my cage won't have any bars around it. It will only exist in my mind, freeze me in time, keep me safe from joy and new experiences, protected against self-realization and flourish. A scion of 605, the Welfare building on Florida Avenue. Untouched by new influences and new people.

She went to see Mo as soon as she felt strong enough, as soon as she felt ready, finding him stocking canned goods on a shelf, fatigues and a T-shirt despite the cold seeping under the Amoco's glass door. Underdressed Mo. Counterculture Mo. Mogadishu Mo. Nomad Mo. A-future-before-future-disappeared Mo.

"So how did it go?"
Sally opened the blanket so Mo could take a peek.
"Messy. Little boy didn't want to come out."
Mo shook his head, bewildered. "Can I hold him?"
"Sure."
He stood against the microwave stand and took Eli in the crook of his arm. "He's so peaceful."
"Good baby. Hardly ever cries. A true soldier."
"He's got your cheeks. And your eyes."
"Long as he doesn't get my nose...."
"What's wrong with your nose?"
"Everything. Don't act like you don't see it, big as it is."
Mo got close and kissed Sally's nose to prove

her wrong. She started to give him her lips but he didn't notice and pulled away, leaving her with closed eyes and a warming heart.

The store's co-owners came from out back, all three sisters who had run it for as long as Sally had been living down the street. Hiwot approached first. She was easygoing and good-natured, always dressed in eccentric fashion: berets, velvet pants, flowing robes, sweatsuits. Something of a flower child, a late bloomer. Nikki, the eldest and most outspoken, jokingly asked Mo if Eli was his, to which he answered, "I wish." Mariam, the youngest and prettiest, was still childless. She took Eli from Hiwot and ran a finger along his face.

Sally and Mo stood in front of the store, watching the activity around the gas pumps and the traffic on 14th. A bunch of girls from the other side of Clifton stared at them as they drove past in a red box-Caprice. A Korean War veteran named Shake 'n Bake was hunched on a broom at the far end of the lot, a vodka-induced rasp of a song flowing from his lips.

Mo reached for his pocket just before somebody called him back in.

With the $40 he gave her Sally went and bought diapers, baby food, and groceries at the Giant up the street. She was craving fruit more than anything else, lately: apples, peaches, apricots, grapes, strawberries.

She went to see Mo every day after that. They couldn't talk on the phone and he couldn't visit her just yet—Rodney's friends and his little brother, Ben, would have jumped him if they suspected anything was going on, or Mo could get plain robbed inside the complex since everybody knew where he worked and people thought Africans always carried money around. Mo gave Sally something every time he saw her. "For the baby," he would say as he hooked her up, always on her way out, while they hugged and nobody could see.

"You do it to him yet? How was it?"
"Ma!"
"Just checkin'. Don't you go having more babies on me, Sally. 'Cause I'm satisfied."

Breastfeeding as a whole was painful. The sight of the milk pump made Sally moan. Much as she hated everything having to do with Welfare and the nosy government, she signed up for WIC vouchers. Something temporary so she wouldn't feel like one of the Assistance children she had promised her father Mike never to become. People like Ms. Betty, Tamika's mother, were always telling her how good she would have it if she learned to work the system. Ms. Betty had gotten a big house from HUD and she also received a monthly check. "You could do just as good," she claimed; "It ain't no thing." Sally knew better, and so did her mother. "Don't listen to that fake bitch," Rudy told her more than once. "You might run with her daughter, but Betty don't mean you no good."

The few weeks that Rudy hung in there felt precious and extra. She cooked, cleaned, washed, and taught Sally things she hadn't applied to her own children's upbringing.

The night Mo invited Sally to the movies, Rudy volunteered to baby-sit. "You ain't even gotta pay me," she declared. Sally frowned. "You're not spending the night at the halfway house?" Rudy smiled and looked away. "I'm off the hook. All I gotta do is keep a job."

"Let me see your discharge papers," Sally insisted.

"I lost them," Rudy said.

Sally pushed her doubts away. When the time came to leave she gave Eli a kiss and asked her mother how she looked. Rudy said she liked her hair and everything she had on, and kicked her out.

Ben was standing in the front yard talking to another boy. He took a puff of his smoke and remained silent as Sally went through the Clifton Street gate. She could feel his eyes on her back before she cleared the turn leading to the store. She could feel his eyes on her back and it burned like hell.

Sally and Mo strolled Silver Spring's ghost town of a shopping center and ended up going to Ruby Tuesday instead of the movies. Their waitress had a pimply face, tired eyes, and brusque ways. They ordered steaks and nibbled at each other's side dishes. Mo thought a middle-aged patron two tables across was a compatriot. It made him lash out at his country's old guard. "Syad Barre seized power and didn't let go until the coup that sent him packing and started a civil war. Under him we were all Social Scientists. We spoke Italian, Somali, and English. We aligned ourselves with the Eastern bloc. Everything we used or bought was Russian- or Chinese-made. Czechs and Poles taught in our schools. We dressed alike, thought alike, mistrusted one another, and never voted for anything. The countryside? One big time warp five minutes out of Mog: herds, compounds, petrol lamps, well water, sprinklings of open-air classrooms, bush medicine, bandits." Mo shook his head at the waste, the mess nobody knew how to get out of. "No wonder the world looks at us like something's wrong."

They had ice cream for dessert. Sally spared Mo the Strong Black Woman fairy tale of self-improvement, college degrees, and hard-won triumphs when he asked about her plans. "My son is my priority. Didn't think I would have to do it all by myself, but here I am. It's gonna be tough. Rudy wouldn't be able to watch Eli even if she weren't in a program. It would drive her crazy to sit around all day with my baby as I went to work. She wasn't able to do that for her own son."

"Nobody else you can trust?"

Sally took a deep breath. "You could say I got myself in trouble. No choice but to take it one day at a time. Whatever I need to do for Eli, that's what I'll do."

They sat on a bench across from the mall's glass doors to wait for the bus. A few people were coming out, leaving the restaurant. All-Latino cleaning crews were going in. Sally felt cold despite the coat borrowed from Rene, and she leaned on Mo's shoulder. "I'll help you," she heard him say as he played in her hair. "Don't know how much and for how long—Aster's counting on me and I can't let her down. But I'll do for you, too. Whatever I can." He squeezed her tight. She squeezed him back.

Nobody was on the bus but them. They could see all the way across the empty rows of seats to where the driver sat on top of the big wheel. They were flying, the trees lining 16th making it dark between the big houses, most of them still bearing Christmas decorations. It felt to Sally like a vacation from real life. "What are we gonna do about Rodney?"

Sally sighed. "I should write to let him know before he learns it from someone else."

"How will he take it?"
"Bad."
"Do I have to watch my back?"
She nodded. "His brother, Ben, is around Clifton every day. If Rodney wants to get us it'll be through him."
Mo yawned. "Guess we'll find out."
She kissed his cheek. "Sleepy?"
"Not really. I ain't had enough yet." "Enough of what?"
"You."
She kissed him again. "I'll stay, but not for the whole night."
"Miss your baby?"
"Yeah. And Rudy is waiting for me to come back."
"How is she?"
"So far, so good."
"I'll put you in a cab."

The bus dropped them off in front of Coolidge High. They did their best not to make too much noise unlocking the gate and going in. Mo caressed the pit's nose through the fence. "Such a good girl."

The house's furnace painted the paneling blue before Mo flicked on the light. The couple he rented from knew the family who owned the Amoco. They were quiet, left him alone, and took it easy on the rent. "The husband sells insurance. Self-deprecating, never says much. The wife likes to ask me up. When I go through the front door it'll be just the two of us, blinds all the way down, she'll be wearing this see-through thing. She's got an itch I'm supposed to be scratching."

"Where does she work?"

"Filene's. I don't think they make much. Early fifties, two grown daughters who don't pay them any mind, a mortgage, two cars. Not quite the life they used to have back in Africa. He was a big shot, apparently."

"Why did they leave?"

"Same with Aster and me: war. They're Tigrai people, from Eritrea, a province of Ethiopia. Lived in Addis most of their lives. When Eritrea fought to gain its independence from Ethiopia, they found themselves behind enemy lines. All their possessions were seized. They were stripped of their nationality and deported. They made it here and started from scratch. Might never get rich again, but they got free." Mo handed Sally a smoothie. "I'm making myself some tea. This should work better for you."

"That's all you're living on, isn't it? That tea."

He dropped the kettle on the stove. Sally took Rene's coat off and balled it to prop her head. Mo joined her on the carpet. His lips and fingers were so cold they tickled. Sally touched him, too. He got up with a sigh when the kettle started whistling. "How long before you can have sex?"

"Six weeks."

"Who was your first? Rodney? Robert?"

A shadow crossed Sally's face. "Robert popped that cherry. You?"

"Aurora. High school sweetheart. She still calls."

They laughed.

"Ever considered waiting for Rodney?" Mo resumed, more seriously.

Sally looked at the ceiling. "What the hell for?"

He shrugged and came back near her. "Why did you pick me?"

Sally closed her eyes, her mouth stretching into a smile. "Girls in my building were talking about you. How nice you are. How you buy snacks to a lot of kids out of pocket. That store's been there forever. Workers come and go. Nobody made that kind of impression. I felt like seeing for myself."

Mo kissed her forehead. "Every time you walked through the door you had a book in your hand. That got my attention."

She opened an eye.

"And that big belly. People told me you were a

sweet girl down on her luck. It made me want to reach out."

"I looked that forlorn?"

Mo kissed her closed eye. "It's me. Something happened to me when I was little that makes me care about kids and mothers."

She waited for him to say more, but he got up again. "All the single-mothers-to-be out there and you chose me?"

Mo smiled across the hall. "I know a good girl when I see one. Bottom line."

She asked him to call a cab when she felt herself drifting away. "I'll ride with you," he proposed. They huddled in the back.

She turned to watch him before entering Clifton Terrace. He waved from the taxi's open window. She blew him a kiss and nodded at the guard sitting behind bulletproof glass. The littered courtyard was deserted. Picked up by the wind, fallen leaves danced around her face. They clung to her clothes like so many emblems. She hurried toward her building's flapping door, pulling her knife out before she entered the stairway. On her floor's landing she saw Miss Barbra help her son, Jerry, stick a needle to an already badly butchered vein in his neck. They smelled like rancid sweat and cold cigarettes. Both flashed gap-toothed smiles as Sally walked by. The old lady was holding her son's head with one hand and the syringe with the other. "Hi, sweetie."

"Hi, Miss Barbra. Hi, Jerry."
"Where's your mother?"
"Asleep."

Her apartment was dark and hot. Rudy was snoring on the couch, her skeletal shape barely filling the dingy frame. Eli was lying on a makeshift bed inside a dresser drawer, too close to the coffee table and its overflowing ashtrays. Sally cracked a window open and peeled her clothes off, cursing under her breath at the roach that came out of Rudy's carryout remains. She picked Eli up and took him to her bed. They both went under the covers. His quiet breathing, the peaceful look on his face made her heart swell. She thought about Mo, wondering what could have happened to him when he was a child.

Rudy wasn't there when she and Eli woke up in the middle of the next day. She found her mother's uniform rolled under the bathroom sink and inspected the pockets, discovering nothing but tobacco crumbs and a half-empty lighter. She fed Eli before deciding against going out after Rene came to pick up her coat. "I have a job interview," she explained rather apologetically. "It's cool," Sally assured her. "Thanks for letting me use it."

"Let me know when you need it again.
"I will."

Rene had borrowed enough of her wardrobe in the past not to mind. Rodney used to buy Sally clothes all the time. Like trading cars at one of the Florida Avenue lots every other month, keeping her in style was some sort of statement. Half of the outfits and pairs of shoes that he brought back from the mall she had no use for. Her friends dug at will and carted armfuls away. People started recognizing the five of them as a crew, calling them the "C.T.U. Honeys." Back Yard Band shouted them out at go-go dances. Though the girls shrugged off the fame, it was true that they were so similar that they might have been sisters, their lives totally interchangeable. It's like Clifton Terrace only produced a certain type of girls and they were it.

Out of the pack Rene was the one Sally felt closest to. They went back to Easy-Bake Ovens, double dutch, Just For Me perms, and roller skates, their mothers having been friends first—pipe friends. Sally envied Rene's complexion and her ease with all beautification matters. The girl knew how to enhance a face on a shoestring budget. Not only could she braid the coarsest dome into an intricate design, she was the champ of rolls and flips, the curling iron queen. Despite her skills and mature looks, Rene was as impulsive and naive as Sally was guarded. Not one mean bone in her body. Truly kindhearted. An unshakable loyalty that Sally readily reciprocated. They were protective of each other. The core of their clique, the part that would never break.

Amad barged in a few minutes after Rene left, using his key. He threw his backpack on the floor and ran to the fridge. "Where's Ma?"

"Out."

He reappeared in the living room to flick an imaginary lighter with his thumb, waiting for confirmation on Sally's part.

"Could be," she ventured. "You know it's coming. What are you up to?"

"Pepsi wants me to take some stuff to this dude down on Grandma's block." Amad kneeled close to the couch to kiss Eli. Thinking he had just seen the baby smile, he beamed. "That's my boy."

"What does Pepsi want with you?" Sally snapped.

"He pulled up at the bus stop after I left here the other day. Gave me a ride to Atlantic Avenue. We went in Shooters and he bought me this jersey I got on." Amad proudly popped the fabric between two fingers.

Sally felt her blood turn cold. "What does he want with you?" she asked again.

Her little brother shrugged. "Work. To put me

on. You know.... Pushing weight."

Sally grabbed Amad's collar, forcing him on his feet.

Amad stood up, towering a good head above her. "What the hell did you do that for?"

"You're gonna be running dope for Pepsi? Is that what you're trying to tell me?"

Amad tried to pull away. "You're ripping my collar!"

Sally held on tight. "I'll shred that jersey to pieces if you don't answer me!"

"I don't got nothing to say to you!" Amad declared.

As soon as Sally let him go he snatched his book bag and made for the door. "Amad!"

She followed him into the hallway. Amad looked over his shoulder and ran. All Sally could do was yell at the shape flying down the stairs until she found herself out of breath. The hangers-on lifted their heads and started to laugh. When she returned to the apartment, Eli was crying. Wincing in anticipation, she gave him the breast. Frustration made her bite her lip.

She sat by the window until nightfall. Rudy didn't reappear. None of her drug friends came looking for her, which meant they knew where she was.

Sally wrapped Eli in a blanket and left the apartment around 8. The stairwell was full of children bouncing around. She fanned Eli's face to chase the smell and reefer smoke away.

Two boys in their teens blocked the steps between the 6th and 7th floors. Pushing Eli in front of her Sally smiled, but not too much. "Wassup."
"Wassup, Sally."
They moved to let her pass. Same thing between the 7th and 8th. Two boys. A nod. Green light. The door to apartment 808 opened before she got a chance to knock. Haywood stuck his head out, blocking her view. "He ain't in here."
Sally retraced her steps. Back in the staircase she went up one more flight, to the rooftop.

The wind caught her off guard. The darkness, too. She pressed Eli against her and walked on the gravel toward the shape silhouetted against the sky. Blackie sensed her presence first. She turned Sally's way, bared her teeth, and started growling. Pepsi tapped her muzzle. "Quiet, girl."

Sally got close. Pepsi's face opened into a rare smile. He went for a hug, careful not to squeeze Eli between the two of them. "Congratulations."

"Thank you."

He took a step back. The scar on his cheek seemed to come alive under the moonlight. His yellow eyes searched Sally's. She felt relieved that he didn't ask to hold the baby.

"Got good news for me?" he began almost playfully. "You ready to do this?"

"I didn't come to talk about that."

The smile vanished. Pepsi folded his arms behind his back. "What can I do for you?"

Sally took a deep breath. "I want you to let Amad be."

"I don't want nothing with him," Pepsi said evenly.

"He told me you're putting him on."

"He told you wrong. Little boy hungry, but I got me all the manpower I need. Not hiring right now."

Sally looked straight at him. "No more jerseys, then. No more rides."

A gust shook a plank loose on the shed a few yards to their left. The couch sitting next to it looked massive and incongruous. Pepsi shrugged. "I just wanted to show him love…. On the strength of you."

Sally stopped him when he moved to drape his jacket on her shoulders.

Disappointment curled Pepsi's lips. "Wassup with you and me?" he tried again.

Sally shook her head. "I got somebody."
Blackie trotted toward the parapet. Changing her mind, she jumped on the couch.
"Who?"
"He's not from around here."
"Think about it some more," Pepsi suggested, taking the blow in stride.
"I wouldn't lead you on, P. Me and you cool, but that's all she wrote."
Pepsi looked at her, caught between anger and resignation. She held his gaze. "I'll see you around."

He called her as she was reaching for the door. "Your moms grabbed me in the yard last night. Asked me for an 8 ball."
Sally's hand let go of the rusted knob. She didn't turn around.
"Shutdown time," Pepsi continued. "Had that baby of yours out in the cold. Made me wonder where you was at."
"Did you give it to her?"
She heard him spit on the gravel. "You know me better than that, Sally."

The yard was buzzing with sales. Powerful lights that had been meant as a deterrent to drug peddling only left a few corners out. Jerry was talking to himself as he walked behind a tree with his eyes on the ground, the man who once found a dropped bag of coke and never forgot. Back from her job search, Rene was chatting up one of the security guards while Tamika waited patiently, the twins tugging at her hands. Tamika had been lucky with her daughters: they had good skin and good hair, a welcome departure from the crow-like appearance cursing every member of her household. To thank for that was Spyder, the girls' father, a Puerto Rican in his mid-thirties whose extensive jail sentence promised to help maintain his own complexion a perfect beige.

Ben was sitting on top of the usual bench, cap to the side and hands inside his pockets, a replica of his big brother down to the scowl, oversized jacket, and black boots. He held out his arms and delicately took Eli from Sally. "My heart," he said for the benefit of the boys gathered around his observation post. They nodded absentmindedly before returning their interest to the action on both sides of the gate.

"I'm on my way to your house," Sally told Ben. "You walking with me?"

"Still on the clock," he apologized.

Sally followed his eyes to where the stash sat behind her building, under an upturned milk crate guarded by Lee, Kevin, and Wayne, Chevon's boyfriend. Little Mark made a quick run in front of them, dropping cash into Ben's palm before picking up a bag that he sprinted back to deliver.

Sally walked toward her friends. Rene was still talking to the man inside the booth. The twins ran to cover Eli's face with pecks. "Take your girls home," Sally told Tamika. "Don't you see they're ready to go?"

"I'm about to," she protested. "Soon as Rene finishes booking this dude."

"Why can't she just get his number and roll?"

"Complications," Tamika announced succinctly: "He's married."

Sally shook her head. "Rene will never learn."

Clifton Street was hard to navigate. Prospective buyers double-parked or drove by slowly, covering the short stretch between 14th and 13th before circling the block. Hawkers walked up and down the road. The best of them were fiends who knew the regulars and could recognize need in someone's eyes and body language. Working the crowd tonight Sally saw light-skinned Riri and her mother, Beth, as well as the husband-and-wife team of Bean and Jackie. Tony, in the military parka he wore year round, was catching people as soon as they made the turn from 14th and started to ease off the gas. They were all focused and busy at work. Rudy wasn't one of them. "I seen her go down an alley on the other side," Jackie told Sally.

Mo had the day off. Sally walked the two blocks separating her from Fairmont without stopping at the Amoco. "Need a ride?" an old man in a Cadillac asked.

The Amsterdam's lobby boasted a sculpture, a framed mirror, and potted trees. Both elevators worked. Nobody pissed in the stairs or tagged or smeared the walls. The mailboxes were intact. Junkies didn't run around with loaded syringes. Weed smoke didn't permeate the air. The security officers meant business—they signed visitors in, patrolled the premises, and didn't shy away from the occasional arrest. After a warrant got put out on Rodney two weeks after Tilden's murder, they had accosted him as he was visiting Brenda, tackled him, handcuffed him, and kept him in their office until the police came to pick him up.

Brenda opened at the first knock.
"Hi," Sally said, taken aback by her smile.
"Hey, girl. You've got my grandson with you? I was just thinking about the two of you." She seemed in a better mood than Sally had ever known her to be. The red highlights in her braided hair made her younger and more attractive. Brenda could look pretty when she wanted to, contrarily to what Rudy was always saying. She had dimmed the lights and lit

a stick of incense. A glass of wine and a plate of meatloaf and macaroni and cheese sat on a TV tray.

"Sorry to interrupt your dinner. I should have called."

"I'm glad to see you."

Before they sat Brenda delicately relieved Sally of Eli. Pictures of Rodney beamed from all directions. Sally's favorite had been taken on a football field when he used to play for his high school. Rodney was kneeling, fierce and ready, one hand on the ground and the other holding the ball. "The baby looks so much like him," Brenda said.

Sally frowned at the claim. "He looks like me."

"He's got a little bit of both."

The clothes Brenda had bought were of good quality. She took them out of a Macy's bag and laid them out. Sally felt grateful and told Brenda so. They talked about how Sally was handling things. Brenda spoke to her like an equal, as if giving birth instantly put them on the same footing. She insisted that Sally try some of her food. What a change from just a few nights ago. It was as though Brenda had been looking forward to the intimacy and complicity of the moment. Sally only picked at her plate, finding the chumminess too sudden to be sincere. Rodney and his mother had buried the hatchet and become much closer since he got transferred to Texas. Sally assumed that he had asked Brenda to keep an eye on the baby.

Brenda hugged her when she got up to leave. "I mean it," she said: "Stop by whenever you feel like it."

Walking home, the cold made Sally shiver. Warm houses have that thing about them: They make you forget about the bad weather.

Ben was topping his tank off as they walked out of the market. He gave them a long look before getting inside his car and driving toward Clifton. Sally half-expected the car to appear behind their bus. Her guilt was normal, she reckoned. But the fear—the fear was new and she didn't like it a bit.

Mo mistook Sally's unease for sadness. "What's wrong?"

"My mother," Sally lied. "She hasn't come home in three days."

"You worried?"

"Just disappointed. She had promised. I thought this time might be it."

"Because of the baby?"

Sally nodded.

The bedroom was too cool for her taste. They turned on Mo's small rotating heater and left the door open after tucking Eli in.

"Don't you need to feed him or change him or something?

"He'"s good to go."

Mo shook his head. "What do I know? You hungry?"

"A little."

"Tea?" He laughed at her grimace. She kicked off her shoes and sat on the carpet.

Mo popped their food in the oven and filled the kettle with water. "What are you looking at?"

"You."

"You like?"

"Yeah."

"I like you, too."

He served the Amoco sandwiches on paper plates and poured her a glass of juice.

"Amad and I stayed eating these," Sally said after taking a bite. "We used to buy them by the box."

"Nobody cooked, ever?"

She shrugged. "Not Rudy. That's another thing I had to take care of. When we had groceries, that is."

"So you can burn."

"Of course."

"Nobody taught me," Mo said. "My mother wouldn't let anybody but Aster into the kitchen."

They laid a sheet in the middle of the carpet, grabbed a cover, and turned off the light. The moon glowed through. Resting on their sides, they faced each other. "Truth?" Sally began.

"Truth."

"What's your dream?"
"Who says I have one?"
"You're better than that store. It's plain to see."
Mo smiled and said, "Getting published."
Sally nodded. "I knew it. What do you write?"
Mo's eyes widened. "Novels."
"Will you let me see?"
"They're on disks. I'd have to print them out and bind them."
"How many?"
"Four. They're not good at all, but each is better than the one before. I'm learning."
"When do you find the time?"
"Early in the morning. They let me use an old computer at the Takoma library. I could do it all day every day, but a man's gotta eat.
"How did you start?"
"Mog. After I read the last book and medical publication in the house I plugged Yonis's ancient machine to a car battery and started firing away. Existentialism was the rage back then. In my mind, at least."
"What's that?"
"A school of thought that came out of Europe and took hold around World War II. Before, during, or after—I don't remember. It's about humanism, engagement, morality, and justice. The right, and obligation, for each man to determine his own destiny."
"Religious?"
"No God. Man is responsible for everything, good or bad, past or present. That's the whole point."
Sally yawned ostentatiously. "Sounds exciting."
They laughed.
"What do you call yourself these days?"

"A survivor. Both me and you."

"True." She kissed him to give weight to her next words. "Don't give up."

"I won't. I'm happiest when I'm doing that. The stuff makes me hard."

Sally raised an eyebrow. "'Hard' how?"

"When I'm writing and it's going good, I get a stiff. Honest. Doesn't even have to be a sex scene. That's how I know."

Sally had never heard of such a thing. "That's wild."

"It is," Mo echoed. "My turn?"

"Go."

"Any dreams of your own?"

"No."

"Why not?"

"I'm stuck on realness. Dreaming would only get me in trouble."

Mo found it hard to believe. "Everybody needs at least one."

"Test me," Sally said. "You won't find me wishing for what I can't have."

"If you say so.... How did it feel to give birth?"

Sally sighed, reminiscing. "I thought I was about to die."

"That bad?"

"Yes."

"Was Eli an accident?"

More bad memories, but Sally kept her attitude in check. This was Mo asking, after all. "A lot of people assumed it was, but no. I wanted this baby. So did Rodney."

"Will you ever want another?"

"I'd like a girl. But not now. Not like this."

"I'd love me a little girl, too." Mo squeezed her cheek.

"Who do you call when things go wrong?"

"My uncle Skunk. He's the only one with pull in the family. Our go-to guy."

Mo didn't like the sound of it. "Anything happens from now on, you call me. I'm the man."

She promised.

"What does it take to make you cry?" Mo went on.

"Stuff that people close to me go through. Late at night, by myself, when nobody can see. I'm not a punk."

"Ever lost somebody?"

"Robert. Thought I told you."

"Sorry."

"No problem."

"Ever been scared? Really really scared?"

"Yeah. You?"

"Mog. A house two doors from us got blasted by the Americans by mistake. *By mistake*. Three people died." Mo rubbed her left breast until the nipple hardened. "You shave your legs?"

"Ugh!"

They kissed.

"Are you a crack baby?"

She bit his lip for daring to ask. "No. And if I was, you wouldn't be able to tell."

"How come?"

"My brother Amad is one. He's normal."

"Just checking. Got a crew?"

"You've seen them: the C.T.U. Honeys. Tamika, bless her heart, she ain't too bright; Chevon is a knife freak, I think she owns about seventeen; Stephanie is a hot little thing; Rene is my true dawg. We family. All five of us."

"You the jealous type?"

"Yeah."

"What would you do if I cheated on you?"

"Walk away."
"That's all?"
"After cutting your thing off."
Mo looked into her eyes. "I won't cheat on you."
"Good."

She turned to lie on her back, took his hand, and moved it to her right breast.
Mo came closer. "They're getting bigger," he said.
"It's the milk. I wish my hips would come out, too. I'm still shaped like a boy."
"They will."

Without looking, Sally ventured a hand on the other side, finding his skin warm under his shirt. They thought about the same thing at the same time, but he was first to speak.
"How many more weeks?"
"Three. We should get checked."
"Let's go."
She tried to imagine how their first time would be. No lights and under the covers—she would insist because she didn't like herself very much right now with the scar and bloated stomach. But nothing would be off. Not a thing. "I want to be able to do it without second thoughts."
Mo's fingers inched lower and rubbed her belly. "Me, too. Everything. You know a place?"
She nodded. "The free clinic uptown."

They didn't take off their clothes, aware that what it would start they wouldn't be able to stop.

When Eli woke them up Mo helped Sally get a bottle ready. Seeing him hold her baby made her think of Rodney. The moment belonged to him. He should have been the one making the soothing noises and hushing the fuss. Though she knew she hadn't done a thing wrong, it made her sad all the same.

They ended up sleeping late even though noises from upstairs disturbed the peace and the sun made its way through the rectangular window. The phone rang around 10. When Mo started talking in his language, Sally fled into the blue bathroom after checking on Eli. The lack of pressure made it hard to wash the shampoo off her hair.

Mo was still on the phone when she came out, speaking as if to a sad or angry child. Exploring the cupboards and the refrigerator, Sally found enough to get started on breakfast.

"That was my sister," Mo told her after he hung up, brushed his teeth, and kissed her good morning.

"How much more does she have to wait?"

"Six months at the most. You're making toast?"

"Yeah. Coffee?"

"Tea."

She rolled her eyes playfully. "What was I thinking?"

Mo showed her Aster's picture. She was his complexion. Curly hair, straight nose, dreamy eyes. "Skinny little thing," Mo said.

"People like that be the strongest," Sally commented, thinking of her mother.

"It's true. Aster is tough. Way tougher than me."

More pictures?"

"No. I'm a nomad, remember? A backpack was all I had with me when I landed in New York two winters ago. Craziest town in the world. I looked so out of place that people laughed at me."

"How did you end up in D.C.?"

"Some cousins of mine I never really associated with back in Mog invited me to come down. I got off at Union Station and walked from 1st Street Northeast to Connecticut Avenue Northwest."

"You *walked*?"

They finished eating and cleaned up. Mo took a shower and came back into the room whistling, his hair glistening. He dropped his towel and got dressed in front of her. As the time to leave neared Sally realized she didn't want to face the winter weather, the dirty and empty Clifton Terrace apartment, the boring day. She would have been the happiest girl in the world if Mo had asked her to stay and wait for him. She would have made herself small, she would have been quiet and good, she would have cooked and cleaned and washed and played with her son until Mo's return, counting the minutes, five, four, three, two, one, not bored or anything, content with the thought that her dude wanted her home when he was ready to come back, that she would be there to open the door and welcome him with a juicy kiss and a "Hi, baby you hungry?" and a warm plate, something to fill him up and make him fat, not Amoco subs or Ramen noodles but a homemade meal prepared with care—certainly a good girl could do that, and much more, for a man to make him feel appreciated.

She thought of all those things and took a long time packing Eli's bag. Mo didn't see her reluctance. Or he saw, but didn't know what to make of it. Either way, he didn't invite her to stay.

"What's wrong?" he asked as they were waiting for the bus in front of Coolidge.
"Nothing," Sally answered, looking away.
He pressed his cheek on hers. Eli, who was cradled in his arms, opened his eyes.

The bus came and they got on. It was almost empty, coming straight from Takoma station. They took their spot in the back. Sally put her head on Mo's shoulder much like on the way up. The bus rides, the way Mo held her son, the streets they passed, the comforting torpor ... everything was becoming so very familiar.

Ben got off his bench and started walking toward Sally and Rene as soon as they came out of the building, later that day. Sally took a look at his face and knew he meant business. "Hold Eli," she asked Rene.

Ben was standing in front of her before she managed to pull her knife out of her jeans. Holding the handle, she prayed she'd be fast enough. "What are you doing with that store dude?"

"None of your concern."

"You're my brother's girl and I'm looking out for him. Everything you do is my concern."

"I do what I want."

Ben inched closer. "It's like that?"

Sally didn't flinch. "It's like that."

Ben's eyes narrowed to a slit. He knew the whole yard was watching. So did Sally. She freed the knife from her pocket, opened it, and prepared herself to strike.

An amused smile floated on Ben's lips. "I don't wanna fight you," he said. "It's Mo I'm gonna get.

Sally put the blade between their bodies. "Do what you gotta do," she told him. "But if and when you do get Mo, get me, too. Because you won't live long after something happens to him."

Ben's face hardened. Sally's grip tightened. They both took a step back to see who would make the first move.

A distant but powerful bark raged out at the same time as Ben's pager went off. Sally stayed put. Ben raised his head and immediately dropped his hands. He made eye contact with Sally and spoke softly, all anger seemingly out of him. "Your lucky day."

Sally still didn't budge. "It don't gotta be. We can do this right here, right now."

Ben shook his head and started to walk away. "Keep talking shit."

The watchers broke their circle. "Just drop it," Rene said nervously, pulling Sally by the sleeve.

Sally looked up as they stepped outside the complex. Pepsi was standing on the roof's edge, Blackie at his feet. She could tell he was looking at her.

They walked all the way to 9th and T. It was a little before 5 and the streets were getting animated. They saw Chevon come out of the drugstore with little Javon. Chevon had yet to master the art of walking in stilettos. She scraped the pavement with every other laborious and overeager hip roll. The too-tight jeans didn't help. "Girl better watch it before she starts a fire with her feet," Rene told Sally: "It only takes a couple of sparks." Sally said nothing. Chevon's fortunes had risen with her boyfriend Wayne's after Tilden's death and Rodney's fall. (Wayne had been the one making the most of the reshuffling in Pepsi's crew. The new breakdown went something like this: Pepsi on top, literally; Haywood on supply, packaging, and storage; Wayne as yard manager and re-up guy; Ben as yard supervisor and money man; a flurry of runners for hand-to-hand sales and muscle.) Chevon had all the clothes money could buy, a new hairdo every week, a furnished apartment in a high-rise, and a Caddy on the way.

Though she was officially the most dolled up, best dressed, and richest Honey, she remained a thug at heart and the girls loved her for it. Stashed somewhere in those expensive and impeccably matching threads was at least one very long and very sharp blade. Featherweight Chevon, she of the buttermilk skin, delicate features, and inexpressive, pitch-black irises.

The friends hugged. "That girl Nita's been talking about you," Chevon informed Sally. "She's telling everybody you stole Mo from her. Calling you 'dusty' and shit. You need to cut her ass."

"Black Nita from the other side of Clifton?" Sally asked, still hot from the incident of a few minutes ago. "Rayshan's sister?"

"That one."

"I know where she lives."

"I'll go with you," Chevon proposed.

"Tomorrow."

Chevon nodded. "I'll leave Javon with my mother and meet you at 12." She pulled Eli's blanket and kissed him on the nose. "Why don't you use the stroller I gave you? Ain't he getting heavy?"

Sally shrugged. "I don't feel like hauling that thing up and down the steps. Plus I like the contact."

They hugged again.

Nobody was manning her uncle Skunk's corners. The only person from his crew that Rene and Sally saw was Never Scared Fats. He was sitting in a red truck in front of Golden Gate Liquors and gave Sally a nod. "Wait for me," Sally told Rene before she stepped on her uncle's porch. It was the first property Skunk had ever bought, an eyesore of a townhouse that fit right into this strip of shabby Shaw. Skunk only kept it as a base of operations. Dark, cold, and neglected, it didn't pretend to be a home.

"Anybody in here?" Sally shouted.

"Who's asking?" her aunt Ella answered from the first-floor bathroom.

"Hi, Auntie."

"Hey, baby."

"What you doin'?"

Ella looked up from the sink. "Dying my hair."

The cigarette left on the soap holder made Sally cough. She opened the window. "Need help rinsing that stuff off?"

Her aunt's grateful smile stretched the jailyard scar on her forehead. "You don't mind?"

Sally plunged her hands straight into the tangled mass and watched the water from the faucet turn dark. Without looking, Ella reached for her cigarette, flicked the ash into the dye's empty box, and took a drag. "Can you believe I'm getting a full head of gray?"

"Getting old on us?"

"I guess."

"How's Keisha?"

"Pregnant."

"Again?"

"Them damn conjugals. Like I need another grandchild."

"She gon' keep it?"

"She don't know yet. Rico ain't coming home anytime soon. I told her she better think real deep about this one. I didn't mind helping with the first, but the rest is on her."

"She still works at that dentist's office, ain't she?"

"Getting paid good money, too. But it's hard as hell. Baby stuff costs."

Sally nodded. "Tell me about it."

Ella switched sides and took another puff. "Where's Eli?"

"Outside with Rene. I'm looking for Rudy."

"She probably across the street."

"Ebenezer?"

"You know it."

Ella sat on the tub's edge while Sally rubbed her head dry with an old T-shirt. Black and big with overdue fat since she had stopped using, her aunt filled the small space the same way her man voice bounced around the walls. "Where's everybody?" Sally asked. "Sidewalks all empty."

Her aunt sighed. "We dry, baby. We so dry. Skunk's connect ain't been coming through, lately. Don't know if the nigga dead or what. Skunk's running all over town trying to re-up."

"Is that why Rudy tried to score from Pepsi?"

"She did?"

Ella lit another cigarette and got up to look in the mirror.

"See you," Sally said.

With a satisfied smile, Ella flicked a strand of her bush between two fingers. "Thanks for the hand. I'll tell Keisha you asked about her."

Sally and Rene crossed the street and stood in front of a boarded-up storefront church. Sally had gone inside five months ago looking for Rudy. What she had seen had almost made her cry. She didn't care to go back in. Nope. Not with Eli.

They waited until a pipehead stumbled out. He was a short man with a shaved skull, missing teeth, and stinking clothes.

"Get Rudy for us," Sally asked him after he

smiled at them. "Tell her it's her daughter."
"Rudy who?"
"Small woman," Sally said. "Brown-skinned. Slanted eyes. Bandanna."

Sadness filled Sally's heart when her mother joined them on the sidewalk a few minutes later, nodding vaguely before coming to lean against the rusty gate. "Hi." The progresses of the last three months had been all but erased. Rudy looked as bad as she had ever looked. Her bones showed, her lips were white and dry, her eyes had the telltale faraway, glassy look. She, too, smelled.

It seemed like a long time since Sally had last seen her. Not days, but years. Demon years. Devil years. "Happy birthday, Ma."

Rudy looked lost. "Birthday?"
"You forgot?"
"I guess...."
"Sorry I couldn't get you anything."
Rudy still couldn't bring herself to look up. "It's enough that you thought about me." Her voice was low and tired.

Still holding Eli, Rene took a few steps toward S Street.
 A shiver shook Rudy. She held on to the gate, arching her back into a pointy dome. "How's my grandson?"
"Eli's fine. How are you?"
Rudy shrugged and closed her eyes. Sally worried that she might fall asleep right there. A group of teenage girls passed them on their way back from school. Their laughter stopped as they approached and resumed after they walked off. Sally wondered if it showed that Rudy and she were family. Same

height. Same slanted eyes. The trademark Harris nose. Same frame, except that while her mother was shrinking, she was putting on weight. Both of them needed shoes, a coat, and hair care.

"Pepsi told me," Sally ventured.

Rudy shrugged again. "And?"

"Nothing. You do what you want. Just don't forget that you're on papers: you stopped reporting to the halfway house; you quit your job; your urine will test dirty. It only gets worse from here."

"You don't have to spell it out."

"I know. I just wish you'd stop running, Ma. 'Cause I can't do this much longer."

Rudy finally looked into Sally's eyes. "Nobody's asking you to do anything, baby. Let me be. All of y'all can let me be. Fuck work-release. Fuck them people."

Sally's head started to swirl. Too many emotions. Some running loose, most bottled up. Images, words from the past, unhappy times. She felt tired and old. "That's not the way, Ma. Try and face the stuff. Turn yourself in, do the rest of that sentence—we're talking what, eight months? Everybody gets off your back and you're free to do what you want afterwards. A fresh start."

Rudy shook her head slowly. Tears were welling under her eyelids. Pity overwhelmed Sally. "We need you," she told Rudy for the thousandth time. "Me, Amad, and now Eli. Try to take care of yourself."

Rudy didn't respond to the plea. Sally took a step forward and put her arms around her mother. The gate leaned a little farther. Sally kissed Rudy's parched skin. "I love you."

"Love you, too," Rudy mumbled. "Can I get

ten dollars?"

Sally sighed, thinking about the folded bills in her pocket. "Don't have it," she said.

She walked toward Rene and Eli. When they turned to look back, Rudy had disappeared inside the church. Sally wiped her tears. She thought she recognized Murphy at the wheel of an unmarked cruiser on U.

"Hungry?" Rene asked as they walked past Ben's Chili Bowl.

"Not yet," Sally answered. "I have one more thing to do today."

"I'll stay with you."

The sun set as they were climbing 14th. They waited for Brenda in front of the Amsterdam after buzzing her apartment in vain. Kicking around in the cold with a runny nose, Sally wondered when she would get sick.

"Here she comes."

Brenda was crossing the street after getting off the 62. The heavy pea coat she was wearing on top of her uniform was Rodney's. Grocery bags strained her arms. She looked pensive under the lampposts' glow. Tonight her burden showed. Sally remembered the days when she carried her head so high.

"Brenda?"

Brenda passed the building's entrance and walked over to where the girls were standing. Surprise overtook the resignation in her eyes when she recognized Sally. "Y'all must be freezing."

Sally shrugged, not sure how to begin. Brenda dropped her bags and held her hands out for Eli. Rene took a step backward. Sally moved into the gap and found the wind to let it all out. "Ben tried to fight me in Clifton's yard today," she began. "I'm here to let you know that I want both of you to leave me alone."

Brenda looked perplexed. "I have nothing to do with whatever happened between you and Ben," she protested calmly. "But I'll talk to him."

"Stay out of my life," Sally continued, not listening. "I don't take to threats too well."

Brenda stiffened. "I'm sure Ben…"

"I'm through with him," Sally cut her off. "And I'm through with you."

Brenda lowered her head and chose her next words carefully. "You don't have to deal with either one of us. But what about Rodney?"

Sally didn't hesitate. "I'm done with him, too. You can tell him yourself and save me a stamp."

Brenda sighed and grabbed her bags. "You're taking the easy way out, little girl."

"I'm doing what's right for me and my son."

"Maybe. But don't just turn your back on everybody." "I'm not a hypocrite like you."

The word stung. Brenda's shoulders seemed to get heavier the longer she stood in front of Sally. "One more thing," Sally added. "You won't see Eli any more. As far as I'm concerned he only has one family: mine."

Brenda shook her head sadly, turned around, and resumed walking. The guard held the door for her. "You're all Rodney's got," she shouted before going in. "How hard is that to understand?"

Sally felt light as a feather. "I thought the lady had more fight in her than this," she told Rene as they walked away.

"You went off on her," Rene mused. "Hard."

"I'm not scared of them," Sally proclaimed, a little for herself. "It's whatever."

Kantouri's was packed but the wait reasonable. Stephanie was on her way out with a red box and two drinks. Her discount-mart glasses were catching all the light. Her body stretched the fabric of her jeans to its limit. She looked the way she always did: good to go. "Where's Troy?" Rene asked.

"Home with the baby. Probably bought himself a dipper and smoked it as soon as I left." She nodded toward the car parked out front. "I'm about to go get me off."

"Who with?"

"Lonnie."

"You whore."

"I like his sex better."

Sally didn't find it as funny as Rene, or maybe her mind was simply somewhere else. Rene paid after they ordered.

"Did a couple of heads last week," she explained as they strolled past Big Wash and Sally thought of her full laundry bin. "Two more customers lined up for tomorrow and the day after. I'm gonna keep doing hair until something bette pops up."

"You should teach me," Sally suggested, not for the first time. "That's one thing I can do that'll earn money while Eli sits right next to me."

Rene nodded. "Nothing to it. Nimble fingers, a good back, and patience."

Sally clutched her knife as soon as they made it to Clifton Street. The yard hummed with the usual comings and goings, but no Ben. Rene wanted to stop and talk to the man in the booth. "Leave this old dude alone," Sally said, pushing her on.

"What's wrong with him?"

"He's old."

Sally welcomed the apartment's warmth, if not much else. "I think Eli's due for a diaper change," Rene said.

"You've had him the whole time," Sally commented. "I know your arms tired."

Rene's chocolate face lit up. "I enjoyed every minute of it."

The two of them had fun bathing Eli. He was being extra-good, tonight. Little noises, smiles and things. New expressions every day. New moves. The girls felt happy and didn't think twice when someone knocked on the door, even though with everything that had happened during the day it could have spelled serious trouble. "Go see who it is," Sally, whose hands were busy, asked her friend.

Rene came back almost immediately with a bulging shopping bag. "It was Ben," she announced.

"Ben?"

"He gave me this."

The bag contained a black parka. The puffy, expensive kind. "Damn," Rene said.

Sally wasn't amused. "Why did you accept it?"

"He said it wasn't from him," Rene told her. "And he apologized for earlier."

They looked inside the bag but found no card. "Check the pockets," Sally intuited, and here it was: a glistening Pepsi can.

"Damn," Rene said again.

Sally bit her lower lip, reflection wrinkling her forehead. "Didn't expect this one."

They finished taking care of the baby and went into her bedroom, taking the chicken wings, biscuits, and fries with them. Rene was on hot coals. "Wassup with you and Pepsi?"

"Nothing. He's been trying to talk to me ever since Rodney got sent away."

"You don't like him?"

"I do. They don't come smarter or tougher."

"Why won't you go with him, then?"

"I'm scared."

Rene laughed in disbelief. "You're crazy."

Sally squeezed jelly on her biscuit. "I struck out twice already," she explained. "Robert and Rodney. Two hustlers, two C.T.U. boys. One dead and one locked up, maybe for life. Pepsi ain't gonna cut it for me."

"He's different," Rene countered. "Smart. You said it yourself."

Sally's voice hardened. "He's heavy in the game," she said with finality. "That's all I need to know. What good am I if I don't learn from my mistakes?"

They ate.

"Why didn't Pepsi bring the coat himself?" Rene wondered as they were cleaning up.

"To send a message. Two of them, actually: he sill cares; he's got Ben under control. It was him who stopped us before we got into it. Must have a phone on the roof along with that couch of his."

"You think he really sits up there and watches?"

Sally grunted. "Probably not. Nobody can say for sure. But there's the end of that couch sticking out every time the crew looks up, and Blackie running loose and barking up a storm. It keeps everybody in check."

"Of all the girls Pepsi could have, why you?"

Sally nudged Rene triumphantly: "Real recognizes real."

They went back in the room to lie down, Eli between them. Rene tickled him on the chest.

When her friend's mood seemed to swing suddenly, Sally knew what was wrong. "You miss Tyree, don't you?" Rene said nothing. "How long since you last saw him?"

Rene exhaled. "Three months."

"You should go visit."

Rene nodded.

"I'll come, if you want me to."

Rene nodded again.

Words of advice filled Sally's tongue. Fearing they would only add to Rene's distress, she didn't speak them.

They left the apartment a little before 11.

"You're not wearing the coat?" Rene asked.
"Are you crazy?"
"Why not?"
"Got my own message to send."

　　Rene walked Sally as far as the Amoco's parking lot, although Sally kept telling her she didn't have to. "See you tomorrow.

Sally was ready for a long kiss by the time Mo got done and the night shift took over. Mo felt it and made it thick and juicy and didn't stop to take a breath until he knew she had enough—yeah, he missed her, too. "How was your day?"

She smiled wearily. "You don't want to know."

Mo grinned as they were walking out. "No bus tonight. We get to drive Hiwot's van home."

"How come?"

"They want me to start buying stuff for the store. I'm going to the Florida Avenue wholesalers in the morning." He popped the key in and held the door for her. "You can come with me if you want."

Midway through 13th, they started talking about a car seat.

"I don't want to wait," Sally decided after Eli went to sleep.

"Me neither."

She looked at Mo hoping he did, thoughtful as he struck her to be: "Got protection?"

Sure enough, Mo nodded and grinned and pulled a box out of the bathroom cabinet. "We're still gonna go check ourselves," they agreed.

He started to undress her but she gently pushed him back. There was a plan to follow (no lights, slipping under the blue comforter, she did her own stripping) and everything must go according to it, which it did until what they were doing felt good and it started to show and all inhibitions went out the window. Sally did Mo first. She used her lips, her tongue, her fingers. She put it down and laid it thick. When Mo's turn came he fumbled and hesitated inexplicably. Sally realized that she knew more about sex than he did, and so she held back a little—no need to blow his mind, not yet, not smart. Not that it was boring or subpar, in the end. Though Mo wasn't a natural like "Lightning Rod" Rodney, he knew enough. Besides, the wait made making love for the first time that much more felt: Everything went straight to their hearts. It didn't hurt the way Sally had feared it might. Pretty good, all in all, for opening night.

Resting, they played the Truth Game with Mo calling most of the shots, not knowing Sally sometimes felt standoffish at such moments for no particular reason at all.

"How many, Sally?"
"Three, including you."
"I had two."
"Including me?"
"Including you."
She patted him on the head. "Good boy."
"Aurora lasted a good long while, bless her

heart."

"Then came me," Sally sang.

"Then came you," Mo sang, too. "Not much of a choice in Mog. If it's not guns and grenades blocking you, it's religion. Puts a brake on messing around, for all intents and purposes."

"Real existentialists don't get stopped," Sally quipped.

"Buy it or not, Islam is big," Mo retorted, the irony hurting a little.

"Not for you, certainly?"

"Not any more. Poor Yonis tried his best. Koranic school and all that stuff. I still remember fragments. You?"

Sally frowned. "Not a church girl by a long shot. But I do believe in God."

"You stopped," Mo remarked after a while.

"I stopped what?"

"Books. Ever since Eli. The only thing you carry around is his bag."

It pleased her that Mo noticed things. "I'm on his schedule," she said. "He sleeps, I sleep. He's up, I'm right there with him. And books scare me nowadays."

"Books scare you how?"

"I lose myself."

"That's what you're supposed to do."

She shook her head. "I go too far. That encyclopedia that Mike gave me when I was little? I would leaf through it for hours and hours. Rome, Ancient Egypt, Timbuktu.... It took me places."

"Better than TV," Mo argued. "That's the real brain killer."

"True."

"'Searcher,'" Mo informed her, drumming his fingers on the carpet as if he was letting her in on a scoop: "That's the title of my new and upcoming joint."

"What's it about?"

"This detective..."

"African American?"

"Of course. He's on a quest for the Soul. Gets paid good money by a council of luminaries, the Diaspora Fifteen. Visits all these high grounds of Blackness looking for our lost ways."

"What's his name?"

"I don't know. He doesn't have one yet."

"How about 'Black.' That's what dudes call one another in the 'hood these days. 'Hey, Black!' 'Wassup, Black!'"

"I might do that."

"Does he find it?"

"Ain't no finding the Soul, baby. It's gone. Whoever took it from us."

"If anybody stole it, it was us. We took it from ourselves."

Mo refused to hear it. "We had help in our undoing. Big time."

Sally wouldn't have it. "Don't believe the hype."

Mo got on one elbow the better to persuade her. "At the beginning was white people's sin. It spun us on our heads."

Sally conceded no ground. "We should look past that. There's such a thing as a statute of limitations."

It struck Mo to no end, the way she said that. He opened big, Tex Avery eyes as if he hadn't expected her to be able to stand on her own two feet intellectually. As if she shouldn't have opinions so definitive and articulate, what with her age and background. It shut him up quick, it shut him up good. She could almost see the computations and readjustments behind his forehead. Three little words and the C.T.U. chick had proven she knew English, she knew concepts, she knew politics, she knew race. It was too much.

"You're tough," was all Mo found to say: "Sally too tough." Not "smart," or "bright." Not even "precocious." "Tough."

Sally blew on her nails as she would on a just-fired pistol, and decided to let it pass. "I hear somebody out there is calling me 'Dusty' Sally."

"Who?"

"Your friend Nita. The one with the teeth and booty shorts.

"Wannabe friend. She followed me in the walk-in box last week and asked could she get some. I told her where to go."

Sally yawned. "I'm about to set her straight."

Mo flashed the peace sign, not taking her too seriously.

How about some more?"

"How about it."

He unpacked a fresh one, slipped it on, and started toward her. Fired up by the "too tough" thing, Sally pushed him flat on his back and climbed on top. "I got this."

They got up, ate, played with Eli, got ready, and took off in the burgundy van. "We'll shop for you first," Mo declared. "I don't want to ride around with a full load. People get jacked in the wholesale district." He looked at her. "Why you cheesin' so hard?"

"'We'll shop for you,'" Sally repeated. "I like the sound of that."

They put the coat out of the way first. A blue one, thick but not overwhelmingly so. A nice blue, too. Reflective material on the collar and logo, definitely a winner—Sally had yet to see anybody with it. Mo paid just under $100, got a real good thank-you kiss right in front of the counter (Sally caught herself before saying, "Now there's some Soul for you," so as not to hurt his feelings), and pushed his chest out. "Get some jeans, too. And a couple of hoodies."

They went in the shoe store next. Mo got himself a pair of running kicks with a neon bubble midsole, remaining a true Nike head despite all the bad press, the sweatshop scandals, the anti-globalization kids staring him down every time he ventured downtown. "Coolidge's track is calling me," he told Sally. "One of these days I'm going to answer and run me a lap or two. What are you getting?"

"These high-tops."

Her pick looked like moon boots, a clear sign that her tomboy days weren't yet a thing of the past. Sally always wanted what she wanted, taste or flavor of the times be damned—could nobody tell her different. Mo insisted she put her stuff on immediately, and while she was more than willing to oblige, it made her wonder how badly outfitted she must look to him and to the rest of the world. Maybe the girl Nita had a point calling her that name. Maybe that's what they were all saying about her: Sally's dusty. "You like?"

Mo joined her in front of the wall-to-wall mirror with Eli for a picture-perfect moment. They looked gorgeous, Mo in his wild-haired everyday workman getup, Eli bright-eyes-plump-cheeks cute, and Sally in her new gear, hands on her hips, something resembling happiness in her eyes, or what was it ... something long overdue ... victory, it looked like victory, yes, she would say, but over what?—life, probably, the whole shebang.

Every last wholesaler they went to was Korean. Okie Street between Florida and New York, fish market on the right. It was a part of her hometown Sally wasn't accustomed to seeing. Here were the crates of fruits and vegetables, the bundles of shirts, the pallets of sodas and chips, the barrettes and bows and incense sticks, the hats and gloves and knee-high stockings, the batteries, the drug baggies and crack pipes Hiwot and them kept in a special drawer and made a killing off. In each gigantic warehouse Sally stayed with Eli and the cart while Mo ran the aisles—he had a list and knew what to do.

She didn't have to ask: He thought of getting bulk baby formula and diapers without Sally even looking their way. They checked out her things separately and switched them to shopping bags once inside the van.

"Take it all home or leave some in the basement—your choice," Mo said. "You can also bring to Tuckerman anything you feel you might need."

Sally wasn't sure that he meant what she hoped he meant. She didn't see it fit to inquire further.

She knew just how blissful the morning and early afternoon had been when Mo eased into the Amoco's lot and she caught a glimpse of Nita and Rayshan sitting across Euclid on the sunny side of their stoop. "See you tonight?"
"I'll meet you here."
She kissed Mo, grabbed Eli and the bags, and hurried down 14th, feeling utterly and quite satisfactorily invincible when Ben stayed put on his perch as he saw her coming through the gate.

Chevon and Rene were in front of her building kicking up dust. "Nice coat," Rene said.
"Nice shoes," Chevon chimed in.
Sally nodded gracefully. "Let me put my stuff away and then we can bounce."

She dropped her clothes on the bed and hid her knife under the mattress so as not to be tempted. Chevon would be packing anyway.

Rene spotted New York Joe coming down the hill as they walked past S & L, the beer and deli facing the Amoco. "Here come the old pervert," Sally jeered. They stormed Joe for the fun of it, kicking and shaking his wheelchair until the look on his face turned to pure worry. Chevon slapped him for good measure, knocking the wool Cowboys hat off his whitening head. Then they crossed 14th into the west side of Clifton, rolling up on Nita and Rayshan as soon as they cleared the bend leading to their alley, C.T.U. Honeys on the prowl.

It was a textbook jump from beginning to end. No interference. Clear view all the way to the Amoco, where old Shake 'n Bake was doing his thing with the broom and vodka legs and bobbing head. Nita clenched her fists. Rayshan looked unsure about what to do. Rene stood far away with Eli. Chevon took position. Sally smiled her sweetest smile at Nita. "You wanted to see me?"

Nita started to answer but Sally stunned her with one to the face. A three-piece followed on the same spot. Rayshan let out a yelp but dared not move past Chevon. Nita ducked. When she straightened herself and tried to swing, another punch sent her reeling toward the building's door. She held on to Sally's coat, scratching the fabric with her nails. All hell broke loose, Sally going blow after blow without breaking stride, feeling deeply and decidedly calm all the while. Nita grabbed the door handle and took refuge in the lobby. Rayshan sealed the deal with her complaint: "Enough."

All anger went out of Sally. A little boy called Anthony came out of the building as she and her friends were leaving. He ran and took Sally's hand. It was Tina's son, a handsome three-year-old with sagging pants and a full head of braids. "Dag," he said. "You punished that bitch."

Mo, who wouldn't have known hadn't Shake said something, wasn't amused. He even raised a finger, lying down as he was. "Don't be fighting."
Sally felt anything but apologetic. She sounded like it, too. "I don't mean to. People test you out here. They don't let you be." She made the piece of bubble gum she had brought to bed pop.
"You can't beat up every girl that likes me."
"Only the ones talking trash."
"Promise you won't."
"I can't."
"Why?"
"Don't want to lie to you, Mo. Don't want my hands tied when it happens. Where do you think we're at? Does 'It's like a jungle sometimes' ring a bell?"
Mo knew the song. Who didn't? He understood. "This is not the first time, is it?"
"Of course not."
"Who taught you to fight?"
"My uncles. My mother. They made sure I knew how to defend myself."
"What if Nita presses charges?"
"It'd be a punk move. People know you be talking to the police, they spit on you. Nobody likes a snitch. Nita has no choice but to take her ass

whopping and sit on it."

"No get-back?"

"She's not cut out like that. And I won't let her off this easy next time around."

Mo mulled over Sally's answers for a minute or two. It didn't feel like they were under the same cover. They were lightyears from last night. He had barely talked to her inside the car. "Did Rodney ever beat you?" he began again, breaking new ground.

"Sometimes.... I let him."

"You *what*?"

"I let him. Didn't want to embarrass him in public. He knew where to stop."

"I don't get it."

"You fight your man back, you weaken him to the eyes of whoever's watching. I didn't care. It was a different story behind closed doors."

"What happened then?"

"I used everything I had. And believe it or not, I had the upper hand. If not physically, then with my head."

"Give me an example."

Sally let out a joyless laugh. "Once, I woke him up in the middle of the night with a loaded gun to his temple. His own gun. He had scratched my face with a brush the day before. That made him think."

Mo nodded emhatically. "I'll never beat you."

Crossing the bridge, Sally kissed his cheek and rested her head on his chest. "I know."

Mo was the first to get up when Eli woke up at 3. He tripped on the used car seat Hiwot had given them. They had brought it inside because even though Takoma was gunshot-and-drug-corners-free, it was still D.C. and people stole anything they could get their hands on. His bike had been snatched from the yard a few days ago, Venus and all.

Sally, who hadn't had a manicure in a while, went to the strip mall on 14th the next morning and got Mo's name painted on her nails. Mo thought it was the cutest thing. He liked it even better when she put them to use later on that night (no lights, under the comforter, the doggone things came alive).

She flew in a rage the following Sunday when Rene, Amad, Eli, and she came from a trip to the Laundromat to find her mother and Ella cutting crack in the kitchen. "Finally got us a package," Rudy explained to the group as they barged in with trash bags full of clothes.

Ella threw in her bit with a satisfied smile, just as unaware of the storm gathering in Sally's chest. "Skunk's connect came through. Think Mo can get us a discount on baggies? We need about two hundred."

Maybe it was the baby bottle cooling off inches from the baking soda and single-edge blades.

Maybe the can of malt liquor sticking out of a raggedy backpack. Or the whiff of whatever the two women had smoked first thing to calm their nerves when they entered the apartment and found they had it to themselves.... Sally lost it. "You can't do this stuff no more, Ma. There's a child living with us. My son. Your grandson. Have the consideration for him you never had for my brother and me. Is that too much to ask?"

Jolted by her tone, Rudy stood up. "This is *my* house!"

Sally didn't even think to back down. "Mine and Amad's, too."

The tips of Rudy's bandanna shook like atrophied wings. "You can't tell me what to do!"

Sally ignored her mother and took a step toward the table. "Nobody's cooking rocks in here. Not today, not ever again!"

Ella put her bearish hands around the cocaine nugget

"Murphy's on vacation, honey. It ain't safe out there on 9th. And hard as merchandise is to come by nowadays.... Skunk said..."

Sally got on her aunt's case. "It ain't safe in here, Ella. Not while I'm standing in front of the two of you. You can go tell my uncle I said so."

Ella and Rudy looked at each other, shock straining their faces. Eli started to cry. Sally's patience ran out. She dug her palms under the wooden table and started to lift it, flip it, throw it out the window. "Get out!" she shouted. "Out!"

Ella snatched the drugs and paraphernalia and jumped from her chair. "Okay," she said. "Okay. Calm the fuck down, will you?"

Sally took a deep breath and looked around. Rene had retreated to the bedroom with Eli. Amad looked scared out of his wits. Rudy's pursed lips were full of pent-up hate.

Ella stuffed the backpack and zipped it up. She and Rudy avoided to look Sally's way as they filed out. "What's wrong with her?" Sally heard her aunt say as she pushed the lock behind them, two of the once-formidable adults who ruled over so much of her life. "She's the first girl on Earth to have a baby," Rudy answered. "That's what's wrong with her."

Rene, too, looked shaken. "What's gotten into you, lately?"

Calm as an angel, Sally started putting Eli's fresh clothes away. "Can't nobody play with me no more, that's all. It's a new day."

"What do you mean?"

"Been thinking a whole lot since Rodney got sent down South. Everything that's wrong with my life I'm going to try and stay away from. I'll have Eli out of C.T.U. before he turns one. Gotta start working on them numbers."

"What numbers?"

"Statistics."

Rene looked lost.

"That's what we are to a lot of people," Sally explained. "Categories. Slices. Packets. Brackets. I'm trying to get out of the one I'm in."

"Which is?"

"Hopeless Helpless Minority Single Teenage High School Dropout Mom."

Rene stopped what she was doing. "What's that got to do with what just happened?"

Sally smiled sweetly. "I'm not sure. It just felt good to let my mother and my aunt have it."

They laughed. Amad went to sit in front of the TV.

"It's up to me to improve," Sally elaborated. "I know where I'm at and where I want to go. The things and people bogging me down, I'll leave behind. Everything and everybody that's helpful, I'll keep. Then I can really begin."

Rene found the word. "You have a strategy."

Sally nodded. "You should think of one, too."

"I've been doing just that. Starting with Tyree."

"You're ready to go see him?"

Rene's eyes brightened. "I'm ready to go get him. Sweet Thang said she would take me. You coming?"

"What do you think?"

They dragged Amad and Eli along. Sweet Thang put her dinner on hold, fired up her hooptie, and let her enthusiasm flow. "About time you showed youngin' some love," she told Rene. "I was starting to wonder what was wrong with you."

Sweet Thang's real name was Delores. She was a deep-voiced and good-natured mountain of a woman whose inclination to help everybody around made her well-liked. She had raised Rene because Bess, the girl's own mother, was no good. Sweet Thang put the F in "family," unlike Rene, who had given birth to Tyree two years ago but had yet to become a mother to the little boy. She had treated him with an indifference bordering on neglect until the child's father, a C.T.U. Fruit of Islam guard named Tyrone, stepped in and took him to his wife, Rhonda, a retirement home night nurse. Whatever explanation Tyrone gave Rhonda to justify Tyree's existence must have proven satisfactory, because Rhonda immediately took to the baby and started loving him as her own. Some women just have the maternal fiber, bless their hearts. Or Rhonda must have understood that, at 15 and a few months, Rene was nowhere near prepared to take care of another human being. Any bad blood that Tyree might have brought between the spouses stayed inside their Kenyon Street townhouse. Tyrone's fling with Rene had fizzled long before he stopped handling C.T.U. security detail (he stabbed an outside youth and the Nation lost the contract for the whole complex, ending an era of relative security for the residents). Rene didn't love him. She didn't even know why she had gone with him—it seemed to a lot of people that Rene didn't know much about much. Tyrone and she barely spoke whenever she happened to pop in on Kenyon on a guilt-trip visit. She ignored much about her son's life, as her more motherly or more courageous friends and her doting aunt often felt free to point out: Does Tyree eat? Does he cry all day? Does he have clothes? What's his favorite cartoon? Is he getting his shots? Is his teeth growing right? Who babysits for him? Do other kids beat him up?

    Tyrone opened the door in his slippers and wifebeater. He thought better of running his mouth once Sweet Thang stepped into the living room, the woman having never had anything good to say to or about him. Still, when Rene stated the object of their visit, his resentment showed. "You never did jack for the boy and now I'm supposed to hand him to you?"
    "We could share," Rene suggested.
    "You can visit and that's it," Tyrone countered.
    Emboldened by Sweet Thang's presence, Rene shook her head. "Not enough."
    "Don't push it," Tyrone said.
    "Work with me," Rene pleaded.

    Back and forth they went, until Sweet Thang jumped in. "Why don't y'all let the boy decide? Tyree! Tyree! Come here!"

Tyree came down the stairs in boxers, roller blades, and a helmet, hiding a cap gun behind his back. His smile at the sight of Rene did it.

"What about Rhonda?" Tyrone protested.
The truth came out of Amad's mouth: "Easy come, easy go."

"Rhonda can come see the boy whenever she wants," Sweet Thang assured Tyrone. "My house is always open."

They got in the hooptie and started singing a different tune two blocks from Clifton when Tyree threw a tantrum that promised to last well into the night. "No wonder his father gave him up so easy," Sweet Thang lamented. "Little boy is *bad*!"

Later that night Sally and Mo dropped Amad off at her grandmother's. Sally had brought Amad to the store to meet her new boyfriend a while ago, but the chemistry just never took hold. Mo didn't listen to hip-hop. He didn't play video games, he didn't watch sports, he didn't care about clothes. The only thing he ever asked Amad about was school, which wasn't such a hot topic for a twelve-year-old with a grudge. (Culture clash or mere spiritual foray, Mo spoke of asceticism as a desirable alternative to America's over-the-top consumerism. "Do you know who Siddhartha is?" he once asked Sally.) Still, Amad looked sad to be leaving their company. It had been an okay weekend, outburst and all. "Be good," Sally told him before he went in. "I'll be checking on you."

"Nice kid," Mo commented as they were pulling away.

"Nice enough," she agreed. "He's hurting for a father figure."

"We'll take him with us every time we do

something fun," Mo proposed. "Or just to hang out. That way I can get to know him."

"That'll be good," Sally agreed, thinking, *If only.*

She made Mo drive past 9th so she could check on Rudy. "Do you want to stop?" he asked two streets before they reached the corner where she stood talking to another woman, Rudy unmistakably Rudy, bones and more bones, her ragtop, her ghost of a body.
     "Looks like she's got a customer," Sally said. "Let's go." Rudy didn't look their way. They didn't so much as wave. "I kicked her out of the house today," Sally revealed with a pang of guilt.
     "What made you mad?"
     "Her damn drugs. That's all she thinks about. I can't take it, sometimes."
     "What is she on?"
     "Heroin and coke, any way they come. Smoked, if she can manage. She chases, too."
     "How old is she?"
     "Thirty-five."
     "She looks double that."
     "It's the life she lives."
     "Where will she spend the night?"
     "My uncle owns a house one block down. And there's an old church right across the street where

she can crash. Rudy doesn't sleep much, if at all. She sells and binges, sells and binges."

"She comes to the store every once in a while to ask me for money. I never told you."

Sally wasn't surprised. "Do you give it to her?"

"When I have it. No more than a few bills here and there."

"I used to do that, too. Every day when Rodney was home. Up to $70 a pop."

"That's called 'enabling.'"

"Ever seen your mother lie in a corner with a twisted face and twisted insides? At least I knew she didn't have to go out and do something dirty in order to get high."

Mo's eyes left the road for a second. "Ever used anything?"

"Me? The stuff scares me to death. I've seen what it does to them.... Never so much as tasted weed. Further I ever got was Newports."

"Serious?"

"Serious. I'm the only totally clean girl in the group. You?"

He shook his head. "The big thing back home is chewing *khat*. Makes you lazy and chatty. Yonis would have killed me. Only did cigarettes here and there, like you."

"We're two very lucky people."

"So it seems."

Eli was feverish and it took a lot to calm him down. Once again, nursing him made the both of them think of Rodney. "They say he killed one of his boys for small change," Mo ventured as he held the baby in his arms.

It wasn't the worst rumor Sally had heard. "Those who talk don't always know."

"Tell me what happened."

She hesitated, but felt it was better to speak. "Tilden owed Rodney dice money and kept bragging that he'd never pay up. The dis' was more about competition than anything: Tilden wanted Rodney's spot in the crew. One of them had to go." Sally was talking evenly, looking at Mo. "Rodney did what he had to do."

Mo didn't like the sound of it, she could tell by his face. Maybe he saw a remnant of her love for Rodney beneath the words.

"I thought you said you were mad?"

"I am. At the way Rodney did it."

"But not at the act itself?"

"Rodney could have contracted it. Or neutralized Tilden by taking his pride."

Mo's confusion seemed to increase. Sally poured herself a glass of juice. "Want some?"

He refused

"There are ways to render a man useless," she continued. "All I'm saying is, Rodney could have thought it out more thoroughly."

"So killing is okay?"

Sally took a deep breath. "Killing is ... necessary. This is a jungle, remember? The 'jungle sometimes.' You've lived in a war zone yourself. Certainly you must know what I'm talking about."

"I'm not so sure."

She took Eli from him. "Rodney's no murderer. The problem is, he found out too late."

"What do you mean?"

"It did something to him ... dropping Tilden. He wasn't the same afterwards. Too much guilt. I do believe that he would have turned himself in hadn't they arrested him first.... And no, I didn't have anything to do with any of it, if that's what you're wondering," she added to assuage Mo's fears.

Mo didn't buy it so easily. "Did you know beforehand?"

Sally nodded. "Yes. And you start to sound like the police."

"Did they interrogate you?"

"No need. Rodney confessed. There was no trial."

She wished Mo would drop the matter, but there were a few more things on his mind.

"What about you? Do you think you have it in you to kill?"

Sally didn't flinch. "Of course. And I wouldn't be sloppy or remorseful like Rodney."

"'Sloppy'?"

"Witnesses."

They tucked Eli in. "Did you ever write that letter?" Mo asked after they turned the light off and went under.

"No," Sally answered. "Didn't have to, after all."

"How did Rodney take the news?"

"He sent me a very short note."

"Saying what?"

"'*Die together*.'"

"Meaning me and you?"

"Me and you," Sally confirmed.

"Some dudes come in the Amoco mean-mugging every once in a while. Always at night. All stares and bad vibes. Like they have a beef I don't know about."

Sally laid her head on his chest. "Ben and his boys. Don't pay them any mind."

"I don't. Will you get me a strap?"

She yawned. Her eyes were closing despite herself.

"Guns are trouble, Mo. Get your own. Better yet: Don't get one."

"Why not?"

"Ben is a punk. That's one dude you won't need to shoot."

Sally knew Mo must resent the way she spoke without saying everything. One of those conversations that leave a bad taste all around. It was late and she had had a long day. Will you get me a strap.... The projects were working their magic. She had chosen Mo because he was so different from everybody around, and now here he was, Get me a strap. Mo: good family, happy home, surgeon father, all the way from Mogadishu. A strap. What was he thinking?

They skipped breakfast and went to Clinica del Pueblo the next morning in order to get their tests over with. Mo was surprised to hear Sally report chronic stomach pains to one of the doctors, a young white woman who addressed the Black and Latino patients as if they were little children. Probably volunteered her time and thought that made her a saint. After administering a full physical, she was leaning toward a cyst. "It'll have to get removed eventually," she told Sally. "You can do that at your own convenience."

Mo felt his poverty, and Sally's. Workers' Comp was all he got from the Amoco. To be out in this crazy world without insurance or any kind of coverage, now there was real cause for worry and a long-term goal for you. The news didn't appear to affect Sally on the same level, though. There was to be no stressing out or scheduling, the way she saw it. The day the pain got unbearable would be it: She would hop on an ambulance and dock at the ER. "All the women in my family have had that surgery," she declared. "I know it's coming. Hospitals can't refuse to treat me if I handle it that way."

Two young girls were in the clinic's waiting room when they returned to get their results a week or so later. Even though Sally and they didn't speak, Mo could tell they knew one another. "Those were Tilden's sisters," she informed him when they walked out. "We must have talked them up. They live in C.T.U. with their mother and Tilden's children. Every time we meet they give me this look like I'm somewhat responsible for their loss. I went to the funeral and gave his mother my regrets, but that's where it stops. This weight ain't mine to carry around."

All Mo could do was agree.

Mo only stayed at Grandma's birthday party up Chi-Chi's long enough to meet everybody. Chi-Chi herself, her husband, J.J., her father, John, Grandma, Uncle Paul, Uncle James, Uncle Will, Aunt Marie, Aunt Ella and her daughter, Keisha, Aunt Alice, Chi-Chi's five kids, and the man himself, Uncle Skunk. Mo kissed Grandma and handed her the card Sally and he had stuffed with $60—he'd asked Sally what would make the old lady happy and she said, Money, nothing but money will do. Sally's relatives all seemed to like Mo despite the age difference. Nobody made jungle, accent, or deodorant jokes. They all behaved and expressed relief that she had caught a good one, as if she had given them reason to worry in the past, as if their concern for her had ever translated into anything more than lip service.

It was a tranquil affair—Skunk's bodyguard, Never Scared, stayed out on the porch to make sure of it. The food was good and abundant. Chi-Chi's chicken and baked beans were on point, as always.

All the children went upstairs after dinner to play video games and gape at J.J.'s snakes. Grandma looked a sharp fifty-two in her mink coat, stockings, and purple heels. The men lit cigars and started to trash-talk. They saw one another every day and didn't have anything new to share. Short as he was, Skunk seemed to pull everybody and everything to him. He had the kind of aura that made his own relatives defer to him. Grandma had struck gold with her youngest son. He was the smoothest, the smartest, the hippest. The one with the houses, the women, the connections, the daughter in college, the Cadillac with Night Vision. His siblings could only dream about his lifestyle.

Chi-Chi, Keisha, and Sally got to play catching up as they washed the dishes.

"Got rid of that baby," Keisha announced as if it were no thing. "Couldn't see myself dealing with another one so soon."

"I don't blame you," Chi-Chi said. "Mine are killing me."

"You're doing a good job," Sally assured her. "All your kids are well-behaved."

"J.J. be on their backs. They know the man don't play."

"Y'all gotta help me take pictures," Keisha said. "For Rico."

"What kind of pictures?" Sally asked, as if she didn't know.

"Flicks," Keisha said. "Nasty flicks."

Chi-Chi shook her head. "Don't nobody want to look at your butt."

Keisha kissed her cheek. "Pretty please?"

"How will you get them out to him?" Sally wondered. "Don't they confiscate all that stuff?"

"One of the guards his cousin," Keisha

revealed. "You know D.C. a small town. I get Rico anything he asks for."

"What's been up with you?" Chi-Chi asked Sally after Keisha went back to the living room. Sally told her. They were each other's favorite cousin. Sally had always felt that, deep down inside, Keisha wished her no good. Keisha seemed sad when Sally shone, and she was happy when she saw Sally fall. By contrast, Sally liked everything about Chi-Chi, the one genuinely good soul within the family. Helping was her thing, and her word was bond. A laid-back kind of girl who was always joyful. The Harris family's Sweet Thang.

Rudy barged in to pick up the cake. "Skunk is about to leave. We'll do the song-singing and candle-blowing now."
Sally held the door for her. "Don't drop it."

Chi-Chi shook her head after Rudy rushed out.
"I see she's back to her old ways."
"With a vengeance."
"Thought she was in a program?"
"Thought so, too. Now she's on the run."
Chi-Chi sighed. Sally's disappointments and setbacks were hers. "Is she full-blown yet?"
"Nobody knows. She won't go to the doctor's. Probably scared of the truth. Last time I saw her come out of the shower I was able to close my fingers around her thigh. She keeps shrinking, but it could be because of the drugs."
"I hear they have stuff that keeps you going for many years even though you never get cured."
"Rudy's got a death wish. I don't think she'd

see the point."

"Is she being careful around you and Eli?"

Sally crossed her arms and leaned against the refrigerator. "Not always."

"Then you be careful around her."

Sally nodded. She was beginning to feel sad. "I already know. Sometimes I wish she'd just go ahead and do herself in. Less for me to worry about.... A fucked-up thing to say about your mom, right?"

Chi-Chi smoothed Sally's hair. She was tall, but not mannish in any way. Sally had always admired her shape. She, too, had the Harris nose.

"Y'all coming?" Ella called from the living room.

"Amad asked if he could come live with me," Chi-Chi said before they left the kitchen. "Grandma burned his last check at her church's Bingo Night."

"I'll talk to her," Sally declared.

Chi-Chi nodded. "I told Amad he could spend the night on weekends. My house is y'all's, too."

"Thank you."

"He misses you," Chi-Chi added, thinking Sally hadn't noticed. "He misses the way things were."

"I know," Sally said. "He used to be my baby before Eli."

"He's not jealous, is he?"

"No. It just seems Amad is the one losing everything, every time. He truly has nobody."

"He'll always have you."

Sally felt her eyes sting. "I'm not there for him like I used to."

Chi-Chi kissed her forehead. "You can't be everywhere. Just do your best."

After Skunk and Never Scared left Sally managed to coerce Grandma and Rudy into a discussion on the porch. Sally drew on her new take on things and people and she managed to speak to the old lady without much ceremony, mink coat and all. "You have to start giving Amad more money," she told her. "Or I'll make life very difficult for you."

Grandma's blood pressure seemed to shoot up instantly. Her glasses shook. Her nostrils flared. Those were sure signs, back in the day, that hands were about to fly. Lizzie Harris didn't take no mess. "Get your daughter," she warned Rudy. "Get her before I slap her good."

"This ain't my daughter," Rudy said. "I don't know where my Sally went."

"You have to stop being selfish," Sally went on. "All of y'all. Or face the consequences."

"I'd watch my mouth and stay in my place if I was you," Grandma growled.

"Just do what's right," Sally countered. "I'm not asking for the impossible. Skunk is at your beck and call. You already have everything you can possibly wish for. What's $30 or $40 here and there so Amad won't feel left out? What's a pair of shoes and decent clothes?"

Grandma's raised finger, too, was just like old times. "It's for me to decide what Amad gets. Your mother and you did a bad enough job raising the boy that I had to come to the rescue. Amad would be somewhere in the system if..."

Sally raised a finger, too. "You just smelled the money, Grandma. It was never about the boy."

Shock slapped the old lady still. Rudy's mouth hung open and her eyes ate half of her shriveled face.

"That's it," Grandma said. "I'm out. You can take your brother with you when you leave tonight. And don't you dare say another word to me. As far as I know you're dead, dead!"

She left the porch to go crocodile-cry in Ella's arms.

"Congratulations," Rudy told Sally. "You did it again."

Take Amad with her that same night Sally did. Mo drove them home in the van. Amad, who must have felt like he was finally getting his sister back, seemed happy with the turn of events. He fell asleep next to Eli on the back seat.

Mo tried to consider all the angles. "Sure you don't want to apologize?"

Sally was adamant. "Grandma's the one who owes me one. I didn't do anything but spit the truth. Too bad she can't handle it."

"What about the government people?"

"I'm not worried about CPS. They never visit. Grandma is talking just to talk. She'll keep cashing the checks as they drop into her mailbox and she'll stay put. Anybody asks questions, she'll know what to say. Where do you think my uncles and them got their crooked ways from?"

"She seems like a pretty harmless old lady."

"All this mess we're in started somewhere, didn't it? All this dealin' and hustlin' and usin'. None of her kids holds a degree. Eight dropouts out of eight. All went to jail at some point. Nobody's married, nobody's living right, no straight and narrow. And she's got the nerve to call herself a Christian."

"What happened to your grandfather?"

"Never knew him. Good-looking man, from the pictures. Very dark. Strong. He died shortly after they moved from Georgia. She was left with all those mouths to feed. Maybe that's where the bullshit started."

Mo nodded. "There you go."

He gave her a little extra before she got out of the car, sticking the bills in her bra. He had been writing all afternoon and felt ready for a good nut. They had talked about trying honey and the shower. It didn't seem fair to waste a stiff, but, hey, stuff happened. Sally gave Mo a long kiss and a good palm rub. Mo accepted the rain check gracefully. She felt like telling him she loved him, but something got in the way. Pride? Fear? Fear. You had to be careful with sharing your feelings.

"'Seeker,'" she suggested before he hit the gas. "That sounds better than 'Searcher,' doesn't it? Since your detective is on a quest and all."

"You've got a point," Mo admitted.

They kissed again and then waved.

He pushed the pedal, drove a few yards, slammed on the brakes, backed up, and called Sally.

"I'm gonna stick to my guns.... You know why? My detective is looking for the Soul.... He's Soul-searching."

Sally got it.

Amad carried Eli. They landed on their floor and there were Jerry and his mother doing the needle dance and looking just like the vampires Amad thought them to be when he was five. "Hi, Miss Barbra. Hi, Jerry."

"Hi, y'all."

They all slept in the same bed. Sally woke Amad up in the morning, got him an Amoco glazed donut and orange juice breakfast special, and put him on the bus. "Get your book bag and go straight to school. Mo and I will be at Grandma's around 7 with the van to get your things."

Amad clutched the $5 Sally gave him and kissed her on the lips. On her way back inside the building she saw Troy run around in the cold with Stephan, Stephanie's one-year-old. The baby didn't have anything on, not even a T-shirt or dirty diaper. Sally tried to stop Troy but there was no getting through to him when he was high on Love Boat and looked that ashy: He didn't see, he didn't hear, he didn't feel, he had no fear.

Sally regretted not trying harder after Troy jumped from a window and met his death later that day. "Who would have thought?" she told Rene.

"I knew something was about to happen," Rene commented. "Things have been way too quiet around here lately."

"Damn dippers."

Rene agreed. "Niggas be losing their minds."

"Suicide?"

"He probably heard that song, lunched out, and thought he, too, could fly. They say the radio was on."

"And baby Stephan?"

"Sitting by himself on the balcony, stark naked. It's a miracle he didn't catch pneumonia. It's a god watching over fools and little babies. I'm starting to believe it."

"Where was Stephanie?"

"At work."

Poor Troy had never made much of an impression on anybody, beginning with Stephanie. It was a baby's loss that young parents realized they didn't like each other all that much after the fact. Stephanie: round face, round glasses, round knockers. Still sucking her thumb despite becoming a mother and devoting so much of her late afternoons to Lonnie's hot sex. It looked ugly as she sat close to the casket, ugly and not quite right. They would have slapped her hand away from her face hadn't the occasion been so solemn. Well, semi-solemn. Families packed so many things into funerals these days. Between the food, the music, the T-shirt selling, the testimonies, the casket-hugging, and the high-leaping and low-diving theatrics, good luck concentrating on the pain and loss. But perhaps that was the point.

Tamika and Popeye drove Sally, Chevon, and Rene back home in the station wagon they had bought in common at Brentwood's weekly auction once their boosting business got going. Popeye was an honorary Honey. They all liked him because he didn't overdo the gay thing. No ass switching. No makeup. No nails. No heels. No Dupont Circle Pride Day Parade. No 17th Street Drag Queen Race. No leather angel, Carmen Jones, or Lolita costumes come Halloween. No drama. One of the girls, to tell it like it was. You couldn't be more down. Cool under pressure, a heart of gold, knew his way around a fistfight, a soulful chorister, a sure eye for style.

Quick as the ride to Clifton was, they all sweated through it and kept an eye out for the cops. Tamika and Popeye had been out all morning and the wagon was full of screaming-hot shopping bags.

"Do y'all ever come across computers?" Sally asked.

Tamika turned to look at her. "Who needs one?

Amad?"

"Mo. He be writing."

Tamika smiled. "How much you got?"

How much you want?"

"I'll do something with you. What you think, Peye?"

Popeye, all eyes and teeth and cheeks, turned to look at Sally. He was nearing 250 pounds and relished his size. More flesh, more skin, more brown sugar to offer. "We'll do some with her."

"Where should we go?" Tamika asked.

"Circuit City," Popeye proposed. "We're talking laptop or desktop?"

"Whatever's easy," Sally said. "I don't think Mo cares either way."

"You in a rush?"

"Not really."

Tamika looked around. "Anybody else placing orders?"

"I'm broke," Rene declared.

"I'm good," Chevon asserted. "Wayne got me."

They got it wrong at first: It wasn't Troy's four-story plunge that augured darker times, starting with a rash of shootings between C.T.U. and the 14th 'n Clifton Crew. Of course not. It was the eviction notices slipped under every apartment door at the beginning of spring. The eviction notices that caused an impromptu meeting in the yard on the day they were received. The eviction notices that said HUD was pulling the plug on Clifton Terrace. The eviction notices that gave tenants three months to vacate, no ifs or buts. Lease holders were to pick up new vouchers at the Section 8 building on North Capitol Street and use them as they wished and where they wished. People who felt so inclined were invited to reapply for their old units after the conversion into condominiums was completed two years from now.

"Bullshit!" summarizes the tenor of most people's response to the letter. A lot of things were vowed during that yard meeting. Things like fighting, refusing, coming together, overcoming, uniting, and so forth. By the next day the majority of families were counting their blessings and looking at *The Post*'s classified and free apartment guides. Nobody enjoyed being pushed around and told what to do—an eviction is an eviction—but a change was a change. It was time to go and start anew. "We runs," poet and C.T.U. activist-in-residence Brother Haj told anybody who listened to his pro-black ramblings. "We runs from a fight. We runs from ourselves. We runs from the truth. That's all we niggas do. We runs. We ruuuuns."

Three months, Sally thought. She had three months to figure out what to do. It seemed like enough time to come up with something. "What's Sweet Thang up to?" she asked Rene a couple of weeks after they got the news.

"Trying to get us a house already. She says the voucher won't be nearly enough to cover rent in Northwest. Not everybody takes them, and then there's the security deposit."

"Where has she been looking?"

"Petworth, near Princeton Place. There's a Safeway nearby. She's been checking on secondhand washers and dryers, too."

"Princeton? Ain't that where they keep finding all them prostitutes strangled and raped?"

"That's what I told her. You know what she said? 'Show me a damn street in this city ain't seen a killing.'"

Sally's mind wandered. Rene invited her to pay attention to the braid she was putting in a little girl's hair. "This is how you do a zigzag."

"Let me try and do the next one."

After Rene handed her the comb, Sally went to work. The little girl winced. "You okay?"
"My back hurts."
"Almost done."

Sally was getting the hang of it. Rene had been bringing customers to her place along with Terrible-Twos Tyree, whom she was slowly learning to rein in. They were usually finished by the time Amad came home from school, unless it was one of those two-day jobs like Senegalese or Nubian. Amad looked happier. He was on a schedule, he had his sister's attention, his pockets were never empty. Sally ran a tight ship: there was home-cooked food on the table at dinnertime, Amad couldn't stay out in the yard, she supervised his homework, the place was cleaner than it had been in months. They had reclaimed it from Rudy, her family, her fiendish friends, her crazy ways.

During a short visit Rudy did her best to duck the voucher issue, as was her habit with pretty much everything. "I'm not going down Section 8 so they can lock my ass up," she told Sally.
"They wouldn't," Sally said. "Different agencies."
"Government is government," Rudy insisted. "They all Feds to me."
"I don't think you understand, Ma: We're getting kicked out. People are already packing."
Rudy shook her head. "I don't know about this one, Sally."
"I do," Sally said: "Get the damn piece of paper, turn yourself in, start on what's left of your sentence, kick crack, nurse yourself back to health. There's some kind of new medicine cocktail that you

can be on. It'll have you in good shape. We'll keep the house going for you and you'll have something to come home to. How does that sound?"

Rudy sneered. "A house?"

"Why not?"

"Houses cost, baby. I'm not in no position to be paying any bills."

"I will be."

"You're gonna get you a job?"

"I'm learning to do hair."

Rudy exhaled. Too much information coming in at once. Decisions, decisions. Sally gave her the "please, Mommy, please" look to no avail. All Rudy did was rub her nose, fix her bandanna, and stare into the distance. Dark splotches were appearing on her neck and under her jaw, Sally saw. They weren't big, but they looked scary enough that she didn't ask and didn't touch. "I'll see you," Rudy said.

"Keep talking to her until she wakes up and does what needs to be done," was Mo's advice when Sally told him about it. Not, "I got your roof for you, sweetie," "Everything will be all right," or, "Let's live together": Keep talking to her.

Sally hid her disappointment, or she tried to anyway. "Rudy waking up? Amad and I will be out cold before that happens."

Mo grunted (this was a discussion he was going to have to think about before he got himself in too deep) and took the easy way out: He pulled some cash from his pocket and handed it to Sally. "What do you want to do for your birthday?"

Sally smiled despite herself. Money still had that kind of power over her back then. "Chill with you," she cooed.

"It's been a long time," Mo approved.

"I'll have Amad stay with Grandma so we can be free."

"Isn't she mad?"

"Not no more."

"Who won?"

"Amad."

When her birthday came Sally couldn't go out to meet Mo at the Amoco because everything west of 14th had become off-limits for C.T.U. residents. After a few misses, two dropped bodies had been confirmed that day, one on each side: Geech on his mother's Euclid Street porch at 3 in the afternoon; Bam Bam in front of Sally's building at 4:30. Drive-by, both times. People who weren't in the trade knew what to do: Dig themselves in and let the drug boys sort out their differences. Sally was glad she had sent Amad off to Southeast the evening before. She thought about Mo waiting and waiting and she hoped that he'd understand. It's true that she could have called from Stephanie's phone. Eli kept her busy, and then she dozed off without meaning to.

Knocks on the door woke her up around 11:30. It was Mo. "I was worried," he said, "and so I came."

Sally packed Eli's bag. She thought she could read on Mo's face how bad he felt about the way she lived. The broken couch. The messed-up TV. The scratched floors. The dripping faucet. The peeling walls. The dopey neighbors. The screaming kids. The menacing youngsters. The weed smoke. The empty drug baggies. The shitty stairs. The hallway craps games. The flapping building door.

The yard was completely empty. In his booth, the guard daren't fall asleep lest the bulletproof glass prove less than bulletproof, though enough points of impact dotted its surface to attest of its quality.

It's only when they got on Georgia that Sally started to breathe. "What's going on out there?" Mo asked.

"Pepsi stirring stuff up," she said.

They passed a Hunan and Mo caught her looking. "Beef and broccoli?"

She nodded. "Extra-spicy. And a Rock Creek fruit punch."

She dug into her food after they resumed driving. "Want some?"

"A little bit."

She fed him a couple of forkfuls at the next light.

"So what's the deal?" Mo asked again.

Sally snapped the flaps shut on her carryout carton and proceeded to break it down: "C.T.U. will be gone in a couple of months. Pepsi has all this good product but soon nowhere to dump it and nobody to buy. Across 14th it's the opposite: So-so supply, in-house clientele, all the space you want, car accessibility for on-the-go sales to suburbanites. Clifton and Euclid connect through University Place to form a drug seller's dream: an almost-perfect horseshoe."

"Why is that a dream?"

"Easy to guard—one entry point and one exit. So there you have it: a takeover."

Mo thought about it. "Who runs the other side?"

"Boy named Doug."

Mo knew Doug. Cool kid. Tattooed all over. Never said much. Had a pretty girlfriend and a little boy. "Any chance he's coming out on top?"

"Not in a million years."

"How are you so categorical?"

"I grew up with Pepsi."

They got home and decided not to eat yet. Mo put Eli in bed while Sally undressed and got in the shower. She sang, scrubbed her body good, rinsed the soap off, let the water run, and stepped back into the bedroom stark naked, birthday girl in her birthday suit on her birthday night. Eli was sound asleep. Mo looked up from his book, smiled from ear to ear at what he saw, and licked his lips. Sally curled a finger, turned around, and put her hands on her hips. Water droplets shone like crystals on her spring-orange back. Glorious. She was glorious. "Come and get it," she whispered.

Mo gave her her present before they drifted off to sleep. She had hoped it wouldn't be perfume, having forgotten to tell him how allergic to strong fragrances she was. It wasn't.

He kissed her good morning and goodbye around 8. "I want you and Eli to stay here with me," Mo told her. "At least until things are safer uptown. Be back a little after 3. You need anything, call." She let her eyes do the smiling, moved her head up and down, and went back to sleep.

She thought it was Mo calling when the phone rang around 10. Yonis thought he had dialed the wrong number, hung up before she could say anything, and called again.

"Mo's at work," Sally told him.
"Who are you?" Yonis asked.
"I'm Sally," she said.
"Sally who?" he asked.
"Sally Harris," she said.
"What are you?" he asked.
"Mo's girlfriend," she answered.
"Girlfriend?" he said.
"Girlfriend," she repeated.
"Thank you," he said.

The phone rang again around 12. This time it really was Mo. "Everything okay?"
"Everything kosher. Your father called."
"Was he rude to you?"
"Just curious. You should have told him."
"My bad."

She cleaned a little to keep busy. Not touching too much, not looking too hard, not presuming anything. If Mo was anything like her he wouldn't appreciate somebody going through his things. There were but a few. He could pack and move tomorrow should the fancy take him. No clothes. One extra pair of sneakers. Printouts and a thick notebook. Books. The useless records at the bottom of the stairs. Mo was Siddhartha. The only thing missing was the river.

She called Grandma at home and Amad at school to let them know where she was. "Can I come?" Amad asked. "It's too small," was what Sally told him. "Stay on schedule. Do your homework. Eat. One hour of TV or games. Sleep. Set your alarm."

"Love you," he said before hanging up.

"Love you, too."

She cooked spaghetti on the little stove. No ground beef and no way to go get some, so she fried some chicken. The hallway was no kitchen, half-eaten by the house's furnace as it was. She looked hard but couldn't find a smoke detector. It hadn't occurred to her to check before, though the fire that gutted Grandma's Eastern Avenue house was never far from her memory. She opened the entrance door, willingly trading warmth for light. The yard was sunny behind the screen, and temperatures seemed mild. Venus rattled her chain. Had she had a key, Sally would have gone walking with Eli.

Transferring the chicken into a plate, she thought of the day she and Amad had found Rudy passed out on the kitchen floor with a needle in her arm. Sally must have been eight or nine. It was between Grandma's house and C.T.U. They were living with Kim, Skunk's longtime girlfriend. The thud of Rudy's fall got Sally and Amad off the couch. Hard as they tried, they couldn't rouse their mother. Kim was at work, nobody else was home. Sally turned the oven off and called 911, her hands shaking. Amad sat in a corner, crying. It took the paramedics twenty minutes to get there. Shame, fear, guilt, or hatred: When Rudy came to, the first thing she did was slap the children. "Get out of my face," she told them. "Get the fuck out of my face!"

Mo came to pick Sally up right after work. They strapped Eli and drove to the grocery store.

Presume too much she did well not to, though the routine into which she and Mo quickly settled inside the basement could have fooled somebody more experienced, so easy it was. Mo would get up early, tackle Coolidge's track, write a little, and go to work. Sally would sleep late, get up, mind her son, cook, talk with Rene on the phone, read, talk to Amad. Mo would get home hungry and tired. They would eat, play, go for a ride, come back home. If Mo felt like writing, Sally would make herself and Eli small. If he didn't, they'd find something—cards, most evenings. She missed TV, but Mo was right: brain killer.

Mo broke down in the middle of her second Takoma week and bought a stereo. They played his records, '70s roots-reggae stuff she had never been exposed to but took to liking immediately. Harmonies. Bass. Drums. Pulse. Sufferers. Sufferation. Botheration. Reasoning. Overstanding. Kaya. Countryman. "Man in the hills." Country living. Social living. Duppy. Ska. Versions. Sessions. Rocksteady. Dancehalls. Sound systems. Deejays. Studio One. Treasure Isle. Channel One. Randy's.

Harry J.'s. Black Ark. Susupon. Backbite. Shit-stem. Government yard. Tenement yard. Trenchtown. Concrete Jungle. Ghost Town. Tivoli Gardens. Halfway. Hypocrites. Isms. Schisms. Babylon System. Get up! Stand up! Zion Train. Marcus Garvey. Rice and peas. Repatriate. One God, One Aim, One Destiny. Rally round the flag. Yellow for the gold that they stole. Natty Bongo. I & I. Brethren. Sist-thren. I-thren. I-threes. Grounation. Cassava Piece. Uptown Rockers. Rootsman. Herbsman. Mellow mood. Skank. One drop. Dub. Small axe. Big trees. Screwface. Spliff. Sycamore tree. Guava jelly. Nice time. Weeping, wailing, gnashing of teeth. Rude boys. Crazy baldheads. Rivers to cross. Slavery days. Soul Rebel. Tuff Gong. Rat Race. War. Botha the Mosquito. Conquering lion. Twelve tribes of Israel. One love. Pass the kutchie. Three Little Birds. Two Sevens Clash. Kingston Fourteen. Nine Miles. St. Ann. Bull Bay. Montego Bay. Negril. Chalice in the Palace. Redemption Song. Dread! Dread! Dread! Oh, dread! Jah, Ras Tafari. Rastaman vibration. Roots. Rock. Reggae.

Sally's favorite was called "Shine Eye Girl". It went a little something like this: *Shine eye girl / Is a trouble to a man / She want uptown / She want downtown / She want fancy car / She want superstar.* Not that Sally thought it described her. She just happened to like it.

Yonis did not call again after that first day. Sally assumed he must phone at work, like Aster. Mo never mentioned her much, but Sally saw receipts for the money he was sending. Little Sister was alive and well.

Sally went to check on her apartment and found a letter from Rodney. It was much longer than the last and a little kinder, too. He was letting her go. No hard feelings, no bullshit. He didn't want to tie her up and stress her out. He understood: She was young, she had a life to live, why should she wait, wait for what, wait for how long.... He understood. Life was short. Nothing that had happened was Sally's fault. He took the blame for everything. Everything. He wanted her to be happy. All he asked for was a little news here and there. Pictures of their son. As for life on the inside, well, it was what it was. (The routine, the food, the aloneness, TV, porn, the handjobs, the drain, the tattoos, the showers, the shanks, the cellblocks, the bunks, the roaches, the slime, the pushups, the boredom, the thoughts, Right, Wrong, Koran, Bible, Lord, why, what if, the regrets, the promise, time, the plans, the doors, the walls, the bars, the hours, the sun, the yard, the rifles, the gangs, the crazies, the punks, the race lines, the allies, the enemies, the taunts, the fights, honor, respect, blood, the guards, punishment, the Hole, the beatings, the Mace, the Tasers, the clubs, the searches, Strip, Hands up, Face against the wall, Bend over, Spread your cheeks, Squat you dumb nigger you, the sirens, the dogs, the alarms, the buzzes, lockdown, the peepholes, the nightmares, the mindsets, the rappin', the dissin', the ups, the downs, the moods, the drugs, the visits, holidays, money, I wish, the yearning, If only, dreamin', outside, reality, the programs, the books, a degree, power, will, I will, I can.) He would do his best to stay out of trouble, stay away from the Hole, stay strong. There were reasons to hope. The lawyer was still working the one crack in the prosecution's case, the procedural error, the Miranda joint. Ben was sending canteen money. Brenda was being wonderful,

wonderful. And she was sorry, by the way. Lonely, too. Lots of regrets about her attitude and past ways. Getting old. She cares about Eli, of course. A lot. And you. One love. Sincerely, Rodney.

Clutching the letter, Sally felt abandoned. Ask her why and she couldn't have said.

She made the trip to Southeast to see her brother, whose new thing was to get into fights at school: two in as many days. "Talk to him," Grandma pleaded. "You're the only person he listens to."

Sally reassured her the best she could: "I know what's wrong with him."

Atlantic Avenue made her cagey, starting with the bus ride from Anacostia Station. The disrespectful riders, the drunks, the trash, the defaced seats, the cigarette butts, the pools of piss. This was how Amad traveled every day. And the streets, they belonged to another city altogether. Broken pavement, missing lights, fenced lots, boarded-up homes, abandoned cars, overflowing project porches and stoops, busy sidewalks, fortified stores, screaming liquor posters, loud children, ghosts of adults, threatening youngsters. The ghetto, one step closer to Hell than even dreadful C.T.U. Hopeless, forgotten by the powers that be. The city might as well surround the whole quadrant with a wall and make the segregation literal.

Was life with Mo making her soft already? Only inside Grandma's building did Sally start relaxing. The apartment was cool and dark, the way the old lady liked it. Good furniture. Nice plants. Decent electronics. Full closets. Full fridge. Sparkling kitchen. Every nook and cranny its table or lamp or display. To Sally, the accumulation of objects and belongings yelled insecurity, an empty sunset, a desperate attempt to find in things an elusive solace. Grandma sat in her favorite chair, put her feet up, looked around, and thought, This is me; This is what I've accomplished. Never mind that she didn't own the walls. Never mind that Skunk's drug money had bought everything she possessed and cherished. Never mind that she lived in a neighborhood where somebody died from gun violence every day and even churches got robbed.

Amad was in his room. He knew why Sally had come before she opened her mouth to say hello. "Ain't nothing wrong," he affirmed. "I'm cool as a mug."

Sally took the controller from his hands. "I'm not here to talk about the fights," she said.

Amad sulked. "I *was* beating the game, you know."

"You can do so again after I leave. Look at me."

Amad turned his head.

Sally took a deep breath. "I love you," she began. "And I don't mean it like Rudy means it—we both know it ain't but a word to her.... All these years it's been me and you. Just me and you. Things are a little different now. But I want you to know something." She pointed at her heart. "You're here."

She pointed at her head. "And here."

Amad's eyes moistened.

"I'll never leave you behind," Sally went on. "Wherever I go, you'll go. Understand?"

Amad nodded. Tears started streaming down his face.

"Mo's the one taking care of me," Sally continued. "I'm trying to make it work. Things go my way, you'll be with us soon. That's a promise."

She hugged him, wiped his tears, picked up the second controller, and gave him a run for his money.

With only one month to go on the C.T.U. deadline, Sally realized that she wasn't good for Mo's keys. It happened the day Wayne and Ben got shot. Mo was dropping her and Eli off. They were almost at Sweet Thang's when Sally found out she had forgotten Eli's bag. Rather than give her his set as she suggested, Mo turned the van around and drove all the way back to Takoma. "You lose everything," was his halfhearted excuse.

"You shouldn't be with somebody you don't trust," Sally told him, not one to hold her tongue any more.

Mo said nothing. She, too, kept quiet until they got to Princeton Place. They didn't kiss or say goodbye. She slammed her door.

Sally went in and found Rene near tears. "Chevon just called. They were shooting uptown again. Ben and Wayne got got. Both of them dead."

Sally put Eli down and grabbed the phone. No answer at the Amsterdam. She tried Brenda at the zoo. "Not here," somebody informed her.

"Cancel Tootie's appointment," Sally told Rene. "Tell her we'll cornrow her hair tomorrow."

Sweet Thang took them straight to Howard University Hospital. Nothing. They drove up and down 14th without seeing anybody they knew. "Try Hospital Center," Sally suggested.

They found a distraught Chevon in the ER lobby. "He's gone," she said. All they could do was hug her and her son. "Ben's alive," Chevon went on. "He was hit in the arm, leg, and stomach. They brought him back."
Sally thanked God silently. "What happened?"
Chevon shrugged, folding her arms on her chest. "Not sure. They were sitting in Wayne's car on Fairmont. Somebody pulled up and started spraying."

Sally had no way to get in touch with Brenda. It took a whole day before she was able to see Ben. She went into the room with Eli and here he was, bandaged-up and groggy but nowhere near death. Brenda got up and took Sally in her arms. They both started to cry. From the bed, Ben smiled. Nobody knew what to say, really. It just felt good to be there together. It felt right.

Ben appeared moody. It wasn't hard to imagine what he was thinking about. Sally didn't want to stay too long. "I'll be back," she promised.
Ben held up his free hand. "Thanks for coming."

Sally lowered Eli to allow Ben to kiss his cheek. "Boy ready for some plaits, seems like."
Brenda walked them out.

"What's this Miranda thing?" Sally asked.

"They never read Rodney his rights. After the Amsterdam guards handed him over to the police, he was thrown in a cruiser and that was it: holding cell, arraignment, confession. His lawyer's working the technicality angle to get a sentence reduction. It's gonna take some time before we know, of course. And a whole lot of money."

"Is there really reason to hope?"

Brenda's face lit up. "One would like to think so. Rodney's doing as good as you can behind bars. It's a private jail and they cut corners but he's trying to take advantage of whatever's being offered, starting with a diploma." Brenda pointed her chin at the ceiling. "Now it's the other knucklehead I've got to worry about."

"You should move from uptown," Sally said. "Get Ben out of there before it's too late."

"That's what I've been telling myself all these years. The kind of money I make will never be enough. Besides, there're guns and drugs everywhere you go."

"Stay away from the projects," Sally recommended again. "Go as far as you can and take Ben with you. This is as close a call as it gets."

Brenda nodded. They got out of the elevator and crossed the lobby. "I'm ready for some fresh air. How are you getting home?"

"Cab."

The automatic doors closed behind them. They stood by the curb. The near-summer sun felt nice after a long winter and a cool spring.

"What's Eli up to?"

"Crawling around, already. He keeps me busy." Sally gave the baby a big, fat kiss. He laughed and grabbed her hair.

"I miss seeing the two of you," Brenda confessed.

Sally touched her hand. "You'll see us more often."

Wayne's funeral was a muted affair. Dancing, singing, jumping, and shouting were kept to a minimum. Pepsi had his boys posted up and down the parlor's street just in case. He only made a brief appearance and didn't address anybody who wasn't family. Haywood and a bodyguard shadowed him. Both Wayne's mother and Chevon got an envelope stuffed with cash. The latter seemed strangely detached from everything. Little Javon looked striking in his suit and shiny shoes. Tamika once again provided the return ride uptown. "We haven't forgotten about you," she told Sally. "The computer's coming."

"Don't sweat it," Sally replied.

She thought about death the whole day through. Rudy's death. She was, after all, the most likely candidate. No cheating the Reaper with the kind of life she lived. She had it coming as good as if she were on a list. They'd wake up one day and somebody would bring them the news: Rudy bought it last night, y'all. She was up on 9th talking to somebody when she dropped just like that, here one second and gone the next. Or an infection would take care of it. Complications stemming from an AIDS-related disease—isn't that how doctors said it? So Rudy would go. Skunk would pay for the funeral. Grandma would look cool in an expensive dress and a shawl and a veiled hat and one of her furs if the weather called for it, and maybe even if it didn't. Cousins, aunts, sisters, brothers, nephews, nieces ... everybody would be there, including Rudy's beloved junkie friends. That's what they should put in Rudy's casket to accompany her in the afterlife: a pipe, a syringe, a Newport, a lighter. How did you spend your time on Earth? I got high. What of your potential, your God-given human abilities? Hum ... I got high. Your kids, your two beautiful kids? I got high. I got high. I got high. The ceremony would be quite tasteful. Years later, people would ask Sally does she miss her mother and Sally would get smart. Mother who? What mother? I never had one. That lady, that Rudy, my mother? Gotta be kiddin' me. The woman was a joke. A joke. Not one damn good fiber in her body. Useless. The most selfish motherfucker on earth. I was the damn mother.

Mo took Sally to Kramerbooks to boost her spirits. "My favorite spot," is how he described the store, and it was easy to see why: They didn't have an African-African section. Rather incredibly, black authors were organized alphabetically within Mainstream Literature among their white counterparts. It meant that black books, good or bad, were freely offered to the masses' taste and good judgment. Kramerbooks let the marketplace decide, a revolutionary concept for retailers and the entire publishing industry at the time. Mo was in heaven. Gorgeous books filled the shelves, reggae piped from loudspeakers, the staff knew him by name. It was like a second home. He tried to stir Sally toward the Himes, Mosleys, and Pelecanos ("A D.C. native, you'll love him"), but she knew exactly what she wanted. "'Housekeeping For Dummies'? Are you serious?"

Sally nodded proudly. "They cover everything: sewing, embroidering, gardening, cooking, knitting, and painting. At $12.99, it's a total dream."

Mo laughed. " I respect that," he said. "I really do."

He had a set of keys cut at the True Value on 21st and P while she looked at potted cacti and bonsai next door. "Yours," he said. "Sorry I didn't do it sooner."

Sally smiled. "Apology accepted."

He helped her design a menu that evening, though he protested that anything she'd put together would be fine. "I'm really not such a big eater," he declared, as if she hadn't noticed.

"I don't mind," she insisted. "There'll be food on the table when you come from work, hungry or not. I can even learn to make dishes from your country, if somebody 'll teach me. You should let me speak to Aster one of these days."

Mo trashed the idea. Maybe because Aster was his and his alone. Maybe because he truly didn't care. "I appreciate the thought, but no, don't bother. Seriously. I miss only my people. Not the food, not the music, not Mog itself."

Come to think of it, Sally didn't see Mo do or say anything that an American wouldn't. You couldn't guess that he was a foreigner from looking at him. And you had to listen closely to hear it in his speech. "You're the most un-African African I know," she teased him.

"It's not like I'm in a rush to embrace everything," he said. "I'm not a chameleon. But alienation is overrated. Why look back when I already know that the path forward is here in this country? I'm aware of what I left behind. No need to turn myself into a walking shrine. There's work to do."

They looked up the word "alienation." Mo said it had been big, back in the day. Real big. Anybody who had been colonized or forced by circumstances to live in a white man's land could claim it. "Alienation." You didn't so much as hear it mentioned nowadays.

After that night, Sally took up the habit of consulting Mo's dictionary whenever she encountered a difficult word. It astonished her that she had never owned one, or even thought of owning one. (Dear Mike, a Webster's would have been nice to go with the blue and gray encyclopedia that screamed daddy love, thank you very much.) Maybe because she had always been able to deduct the meaning of strange words from their contexts. It didn't hurt to check, she found out. It didn't hurt at all. "Angst" was the second noun she and Mo talked about at length. It described a feeling she'd experienced through the years, and even now, as they spoke, without being able to properly define it. Not anxiety. Not fear. Not guilt. Not holding back or second-guessing. Angst.

And so she took the initiative to do more things around the apartment, like replacing the shower curtain and bathroom mats, and buying more utensils. It still wasn't presuming, she thought. It was trying to improve Mo's everyday as well as hers. It didn't matter how long she was there, she would strive to make the place better while she was. It helped that she started bringing money home for the first time in years after a day-long session in Sweet Thang's living room at the end of which Rene gave her half her earnings for half a head of twists. They had the next three days booked, which augured for a small but much anticipated manna. Sweet Thang was trying to get both of them hired in her U Street salon. Rene would go and apply after she finished training Sally; Sally would handle Rene's customers by herself; they'd get Sally in first chance and bring their clientele with them. "At least that's the plan," Sally told Mo.

"Sounds pretty good," he admitted.

She had forgotten how it felt to make your own money. Honest money, that is. She didn't have to wait. She didn't have to ask. She didn't have to depend on somebody for every little thing. Mo, too, seemed relieved that Sally might be of some help. He thought he'd make small talk. "So what was your last job?"

"Slinging dope for Skunk."

Mo's eyes opened wide. "Before I met you?"

"Way before. I was fifteen."

"That's not 'way before'! That's like barely three years   ago."

"Seems like ages to me."

"How did it go?"

She shrugged. "Easy. They only had to show me once."

"Who's 'they'?"

"Skunk and them. It was just for that summer. My father, Mike, was in jail; Rudy was in jail; I hadn't met Rodney, nothing was kicking in. Amad and I needed food, clothes, and a whole lot of stuff. And so I had to go get mine, handle mine."

"Weren't you scared?"

"I was hungry. So was Amad. We had dined on a cup of Kool-Aid the night before I started. My mind was made up."

"Anything bad ever happened?"

She took the time to remember. "Nothing that I care to talk about."

Mo played it off as something light. "That wasn't a real job, though. More like a hustle."

"It was a job," Sally insisted. "That's how Skunk told me to approach it, and I took that to heart. He didn't want no young girl goofing off and messing his operation up. I had very strict rules, and I stuck to them. They disguised me the same way you did Aster. I was the Dyke Bitch on 9th and T. I knew my stretch of sidewalk like the back of my hand, and I used everything: roots, cracks, empty cans, cigarette packs, parked cars. I took the money and told people where to pick up their stuff. I didn't make a single mistake. Not one."

"Were you on commission?"

"Salary. I began each shift with forty bags, brought back $400, took home $50."

"Forty chances of something going wrong."

"It barely ever did, I'm tellin' you. And I can see how some people want nothing else but being on the grind 24/7. It's a rush. You're on edge. You feel alive."

"What about right and wrong?"

"You ever wonder where your next meal is coming from?"

Mo took offense. "Mog in wartime? Every day."

"You had Yonis and your stepmother. You had your clan. This was on me and me alone. Nobody stepped in to help when Rudy went under. My family doesn't believe in handouts. My family barely believes in family. I considered myself lucky when Skunk agreed to let me work."

"Was it worth it?"

Sally heard the pride and calm confidence in

her own voice. "I did everything that I set out to do for me and my brother."

"Why did you stop?"

"Rudy got released, I met Rodney, 9th got too hot, Skunk got scared and pulled me out."

"Five-O?"

Sally nodded.

"What was Rudy's reaction when she learned?"

"She thought I might make it permanent since I was that good. That way she wouldn't have to worry about my brother and m-—the little she worried about."

"Did Amad know?"

"He never found out. I made sure to hide it from him. I never carried any drugs on me. I never showed him the money. All he knew is that things got better for a while."

"I should write a book about you," Mo said. "Compared to yours, my life is a walk in the park."

"You don't know half of it. And I'll write my own damn book, thank you."

He took her to her word, grabbed a fresh notebook, and pushed it across the carpet. "Carry this with you. Scribble whatever crosses your mind. Soon enough you'll have plenty material."

He had said something to the same effect before. She had thought he was playing, up to this moment. "You're for real, ain't you?"

"Of course. Give it a try and see what happens."

She felt giddy with excitement. "You're the writer. Not me."

"Anybody can do it, Sal. It's just a matter of starting and keeping at it."

It made her happy, the way he seemed to think of her as a smart girl. It had always been the way she thought about herself. There were two of them at least now. Three, if she wanted to be completely honest. Mike had been the first person to understand that she didn't mind learning: It's school she couldn't stand.

As the deadline grew close and closer still, Sally hounded Rudy about getting her voucher. "The building's emptying, Ma. The T-shirts and hats that used to say 'C.T.U. Sports,' 'C.T.U. Forever,' and 'C.T.U. Mafia'? They now read 'C.T.U. Rest in Peace.' It's time to go."

"I ain't made up my mind," Rudy groused.

"Don't think: Just do it."

"I'm scared."

"No point."

Rudy turned teary. "You don't care if they send me away, do you? It'd make you happy."

"Ma!"

"You're forgetting about Amad and me. Ever since you had your baby and met that boy. I shouldn't have said anything to him that day at the store. He's probably gonna take you with him to Africa."

Sally made her stop. "I wouldn't be here if I didn't care. You need to go get that paper so we can start looking. Do it for Amad, if not for you or for me. He needs a place of his own.

"He and my mother cool again."

"For now. But don't you want to have him

back? He's your son, not hers."

Rudy sighed and took a drag from her cigarette. They were in Skunk's sorry excuse of a house. "We need to move our stuff," Sally continued. "Think we can bring the furniture here until we're ready?"

Rudy looked around. "That's a lot of work."

"It's either that or coming up with storage money."

"I'll ask Skunk," Rudy promised. "Got something for me?"

Sally fished $20 out of her pocket.

Sally was on Butternut with Eli when her heart went wild. The house was small and pink and sat on a grassy lot. A tree, tall and knotty, grew out front. Toys dotted the fenced back: a slide, a swing, a bouncy castle, a plastic bike, huge colorful balls. Sally wished she knew how to describe it. All brick, no porch, red-roofed, one-storied, green shutters, three bedrooms at the most. It wasn't one of those wartime bungalows Takoma is famous for. She had never seen a pink house before. She hadn't even known she liked the color. It was an all-around revelation. Here on this tranquil corner of Butternut was everything she had ever dreamed of: comfort, peace of mind, security, simplicity, values. For her, Eli, Mo, and Amad. The roots from which their lives could spring forth. A foundation. She wanted it, oh, she wanted it as soon as she saw it. She wanted it bad.

She must have stood there daydreaming for a good ten minutes when the door opened, startling her. The middle-aged white man in a suit who came out called her as she started to push Eli's stroller away. "Is everything all right?"

She wouldn't have stopped if it weren't for the kindness in his voice. "I was just admiring your house."

The man smiled and shook his head. "It can be yours for a little below a 100k. The people who owned it moved out last week. It's on the market. I'm a realtor having a first look."

"Why did they leave all the toys?"

"You're looking to buy?"

Sally laughed. "I just like the way it looks. Something about it...."

"It'd be perfect for a young family. What we in the business call a starter home."

"We're nowhere near ready."

The man approached and shook Sally's hand. He was perfectly groomed, from his beard to his pointy shoes. Smooth, too. "Toby. May I ask your age?"

"Sally. Eighteen."

"Buy as soon as you can afford it," Toby told Sally.

"It's the best thing you can possibly do for you and your son."

"I know."

He gave her his card. "Thinking about a profession?"

"Beautician."

"Give real estate a try someday. I'm sure you'll enjoy it. You get to see houses all the time, perhaps not as pretty as this rambler, but all worth something to someone. The money's good and it's about to get better. D.C. is coming back in a major way. People just don't know it yet."

With only two weeks left Sally decided to take matters into her own hands. She had Popeye make her a picture ID in Rudy's name, and she took it to Section 8 along with the Clifton Terrace lease agreement and their stack of birth certificates and Social Security cards. She took care to transform herself into Rudy down to the bandanna, blotches, bitten-up nails, ringed eyes, stubbed-out cigarette smell, and attitude. So convinced was she that everything would go well that she brought Eli along, passing him off as her grandchild. The person who took her was either blind, dimwitted, or careless. (It helped that her phone kept ringing and that the case worker at the desk next to hers kept asking for guidelines.) She chewed gum noisily and didn't bother looking up. "Same people on the new lease?"

"Plus my daughter's son."

"Documents?"

Sally handed her the folder. The woman's nails were long and curvy. She stamped the paperwork and sent Sally and Eli on their way. "Notify us by phone when you find something, but only if your mind is truly made up. We'll set up an inspection. Sign here, here, and here."

Sally's hand and her heart were steady as she forged Rudy's scrawl.

"I got it," she told her mother with no small measure of pride.

"What you just did was totally illegal," Rudy pointed out. "You got some guts on you, you know that?"

Sally was too elated to care. "Let's go get it, Ma."

"Why do you even bother? Ain't Mo treatin' you right?"

"He is. And I like living together. But it's too soon to tell which way it's gonna go."

"That's why you wanted this voucher so bad? To have something to fall back on? Like a base or something?"

"I wanted this voucher so we can have us a house. Everybody needs one."

"You're still thinking about that?"

"Of course. No more apartment buildings. No nosy neighbors. No craziness. No living with aunts and cousins and friends."

Rudy cursed loudly. "$800 ain't gonna take you that far away from D.C., baby!"

It wasn't a good experience. Sally should have done it all by herself. But whatever she settled on was to be Rudy's as well, and she insisted on taking her along. Landlords took one good look at her mother and knew what time it was. Out went the unctuous smiles and pitches, in came the condescension, sighs, and foot-tapping. And Rudy was right: $800 didn't go a long way. Not in Northwest it didn't, unless you wanted another open-air drug market or drive-through drug street. Off Georgia, near Chi-Chi, could have worked. They didn't get the Harvard Street rowhouse they looked at because of a jacked-up last minute security deposit. It broke Sally's heart every one of the four times they applied and failed to secure a deal. It wasn't easy to balance her hair braiding lessons, Eli, Rudy's antics, the walk-through appointments, the trips to property managers' or owners' offices, and her household duties, however self-imposed. "Something's got to give," she declared at the beginning of the final week.

Mo saw an ad in the paper and drove her to Second and V, Northeast. The three-level townhouse needed work, but the landlord, a Mr. Drake, seemed eager to rent. Maybe he liked the idea of Sally, Mo, and Eli living at his place. Maybe the prospect of having the D.C. government guarantee his money month after month talked to his retiree's heart. Maybe he knew exactly how much work the townhouse was in need of and thought he could get off easy.

"It's not what I had in mind," Sally told Mo. The stained carpets, dirty kitchen, overgrown backyard, and unfinished basement dampening her enthusiasm. And there was the neighborhood itself. The houses on the block were well tended to, but a bodega up the street had all the requisites of a trouble spot: spacious front, idlers, single beers, cheap cigars, rolling paper. Sally also knew that the Rhode Island Avenue projects were only minutes away.

Mo saw possibilities. "Put that housekeeping book of yours to use," he suggested.

Sally turned the sentence around without coming to a satisfying conclusion about its meaning. Was Mo trying to tell her it was time she move out of the basement and back with Rudy and Amad? The guess she could have taken wasn't the kind she hoped for, and so she pushed her doubts aside.

Chi-Chi, whom she spoke to regularly now that a phone was close at hand, thought she saw some cracks in the relationship, what a host on a radio show she listened to every Friday called "red flags." The cousins discussed Mo's penchant for solitude, his devotion to Aster, his aloofness with Eli (he didn't interact with the baby past helping to feed and change him). More disturbing to Chi-Chi was the fact that Sally and Mo hadn't yet told each other they loved each other, something Sally attributed both to her own pride and to cultural differences: She still wasn't about to jump out there and say it first; they weren't big on feelings and affective displays in Mo's country

"Do you think he cares about you?" Chi-Chi asked.
"I do," Sally replied.
"Would he walk through fire?"
"That, I don't know about," Sally admitted.
"That's what bothers me," Chi-Chi concluded. Still, Sally thought she had it good.

DCRA inspected the place and ordered Mr. Drake to change the carpets, fix the kitchen sink, repair a leak in the upstairs bathroom, and paint the whole first floor. He asked Sally for an extra week she didn't have. "Only if we can bring our furniture in now. Our old apartment complex is shutting down the day after tomorrow."
"Bring it," the old man said. "My guys will work around it."

Sally had been sorting through her family's things here and there. Pictures, books, and all documents of value were already at Mo's place. Rudy owned next to nothing. The same went for Amad and herself. She didn't want the couch or either of the two tables. The clothes worth taking barely filled two trash bags. Her bed and dresser were relatively new. "It can all fit in one trip," she told Mo.

He helped her load the van and drop the stuff off at the new place.

The building in its death throes was even more heart-wrenching than it had been alive. People hadn't cared about it while they resided there, and they cared even less as they readied themselves to leave. Fixtures were removed. Doors were taken off hinges. Broken stuff cluttered the halls. Windows were smashed. Pipes were ripped off some of the walls.

Sally went to C.T.U. for the last time on closing day. She removed Rodney's gun from its hiding place under a kitchen tile and put it in a shoe box before taking a final look around. The years spent in this place, where did they go? What did she, her mother, and Amad have to show for them?

Though she had thought she might be the last to turn her keys in, it didn't surprise her that Pepsi beat her to the punch. He owned the damn place, didn't he? "Need a ride?" he asked as they met at the security booth, Blackie waiting in the shade.
"I'm okay."
Pepsi looked at her legs. Summer had come in heavy and bright, as Washington summers always do. Minis were all Sally wore. Denim, not too short, with white "slouch" socks, white high-tops or wheat-colored Tims. Her complexion had turned a muted copper. She was gaining weight, just like everybody had told her she would. The top was heavy and full. Her hips were pushing out. She was finally getting that shape, the womanly shape. It

pleased her a lot that boys were looking, though she kept her game face on and never gave them the time of day. "Phat to death," was little Anthony's comment to his equally little pals when he saw her cross 14th Street earlier. "I'd crush that any day," one of the boys had concurred.

"Still the prettiest," Pepsi said. "You're just now rolling out?"

"Thought you knew everything about me?"

"Been busy. But I'll catch up. You know I always do."

They walked toward the gate. Sally was carrying Eli with one arm and the box with the gun with the other. "Heard you and Doug workin' it out," she said, just to say something.

"For now."

"I see Blackie. What did you do with the couch?"

"Took it across the street."

Sally turned right, toward Cardozo and the 13th Street hill. "See you around."

Pepsi turned left, toward his new turf and new digs. "Bet."

The house was ready when Mr. Drake said it would. For the last Section 8 appointment Sally dressed Rudy in her own clothes and shoes and made her up inside Skunk's house. Blotches and needle marks went under. Rudy's pretty eyes were made prettier. The iron tamed her short curls. The bandanna got the day off. "Keep the ghetto act to a minimum, Ma. Smile. Don't say too much. Don't ask for cigarettes."

"I can be a lady when I want to," Rudy shot back. "Think that old man Drake single?"

They hugged when Rudy came out holding the new lease and the new keys. "I'm gonna need help with those bills, Sally. Don't let me down."

It seemed to give everybody a jolt, this fresh beginning. Rudy liked to live in the dark—maybe because she knew it was better if some of the things she did never saw the light of day—and so she took for herself the basement whose naked floor Mr. Drake had covered with rubber mats. She saved the biggest room for Sally. It was on the top floor and faced the street. "It'll be here," Rudy told her, "in case you need it. Mo's welcome, too."

Amad got the bedroom across the hall. Sally took her meager earnings and got all the utilities turned on by the end of the first week. Mo pitched in. "No cable?" Amad complained.
"No cable," Sally confirmed. "TV kills. Bring your console when you come around, take it with you when you go back to Grandma's. I don't have to entertain you. Better be glad we got us light, water, electricity, and a phone." "I'm glad," Amad said. "I'm very, very glad."

The first meal that the three of them shared in the townhouse, takeout fried chicken and orange soda, felt like a victory of sorts. They ate and talked and laughed on the carpet while Eli zoomed around in his diaper. Had they been the kind of people to toast, they would have.

The novelty waned quickly. They all resumed their pre-V Street routines. 168, as they began to call the house, didn't see any profound changes in their respective agendas. Rudy, whose heart belonged to 9th Street, wasn't about to become a homebody even though Sally offered her a copy of "Housekeeping...," forgetting that the woman couldn't read too good and that she wasn't the type to sit still, plot, ponder, organize, improve, and embellish. Amad was still at Grandma's, attending summer school. As for Sally, she did her best to keep the busiest schedule she'd ever had: up early with Mo, hair session with Rene at Sweet Thang's if they had someone booked, bus ride to 168 to check on things, Takoma to get dinner going, Eli while Mo wrote, bed early, weekends with Amad. It's a routine she could have gotten accustomed to. Things weren't exactly where they needed to be, but she felt like they were moving in the right direction. She was learning a trade. She had accomplished something by moving her family into a house, empty as it was.

Her father, Mike, tracked her down to 168 and called. It was all him to pop up out of the blue. "I phoned Chi-Chi to check on you," he announced, "and she gave me your number."

"Easy on the collect calls," Sally warned. "I need to keep this phone on."

"You don't sound too happy to hear from me," Mike ventured.

"I am," Sally lied. "I'm just trying to keep it short."

"How's my grandson?"

"Getting big."

"He talkin' yet?"

"In a few more months. You don't know much about babies, do you?"

"Why don't you ever write?"

"No time."

"How's that African dude treating you?"

"All right."

"Think you might come see me one day?"

"In Youngstown?" She said it as if she thought the idea as ludicrous as contemplating a trip to the moon.

Mike sighed. "Talk to you soon, then...."

Sally wasted no time hanging up.

It always felt like she was talking to a stranger. The connection Mike tried to maintain just didn't exist on her end. Resentment was keeping her from opening up. Years and years of it. The return on the points Mike had earned for the encyclopedia had maxed out long ago.

Though she was sure Brenda had given Rodney the new number and address, he never wrote or tried to call. Sally felt both relieved and sad. Mostly sad.

Look around and everybody's gone.

Summer brought its share of heartache and drama, as Washington summers almost always do. It was rough on the Honeys, who seemed to suffer hit after hit without knowing where and if it would ever stop. They tried to do what's best in those cases: Roll with the punches.

"Tamika got knocked last night," Rene told Sally as she walked into Sweet Thang's early one August morning.
"Where?" Sally asked.
"Circuit City," Rene said.
"For what?"
"Take a guess."
Sally knew. "The computer."
Rene nodded.
"What about Popeye?"
"He hauled ass with the twins and ditched the car."
"They had the twins with them?"
"It's not on you," Rene assured her. "They must have gotten careless or something. Stores be

getting hip to this credit card thing."

Sally wasn't about to let herself off the hook that easy. "Of course it's on me. I'm the reason Tamika was there in the first place."

Popeye got out of Dodge with the quickness, moving with distant relatives in North Carolina. The twins were at Ms. Betty's, Tamika's mother. The woman had profited handsomely from Tamika's activities and now she was inconsolable. It wasn't about her daughter getting locked up or the girls having to do without a mom for who knows how long. All Ms. Betty complained to Rene and Sally about were her charges, her charges, her charges, as if they could somehow take the relay, keep the money coming, keep her flush. "I feel real bad about what happened," Sally confided to her friend, "but I'll be damned if Ms. Betty thinks she can start pimpin' me, too."

They went to visit Tamika in prison. It reminded Sally of the last time she'd been there. Rodney, who was never very far from her thoughts, stayed with her the whole day.

Two was Chevon going crazy on them and turning into a stickup kid. "Chevon? Our Chevon?"
Rene nodded. "Chevon. She told me herself."
"Why?"
"She's hurting for cash."
Sally was incredulous. "How hungry can the girl be that she needs to start robbing people?"
"Hungry enough to roll up on drug boys in alleys with a big pistol."
"But Chevon's a knife girl!"

"Not no more. She traded those blades in for a piece, I'm tellin' you."

Sally still couldn't believe it, and so she called her friend. "What are you up to?" she asked innocently.

"Making that cake," Chevon answered, sure enough.

"In alleyways?"

"Wherever I gots to."

"You ain't scared?"

"I have a son. And bills."

"Me, too. And so do Rene. It ain't that bad that we're jumping out there, though. That stuff's trouble."

"It's been good to me," Chevon gloated.

"You be careful," Sally begged.

Chevon shrugged her off.

"It's like she's actually enjoying this," Sally told Rene after hanging up.

"It's the life she had gotten used to while Wayne was alive," Rene explained. "That fast money went to her head."

"I still don't know about this one," Sally mused.

"Chevon a grown woman. She'll do what she wants to do. Might as well stop worrying about her."

Stephanie was next. They had been slowly losing touch with her after Troy's funeral. A lot of things had been going on—Sally and Rene realized that much after seeing her get out of a white man's car on U Street. It was the first time they had seen Stephanie wear a dress and heels. She had shed a few pounds, grown some hair and lost the glasses, but the forehead, mustache, and knockers were unmistakably hers. "Who was that?" Sally asked.

Stephanie took the time to light a cigarette. "A trick."

Rene laughed hard and loud.

Sally raised her head to the heavens. "I don't believe this!"

Stephanie flashed a few bills. "Y'all can go ahead and judge me," she said. "It don't make me no difference."

"The girl was high," Rene told Sally after they resumed walking.

"I thought so, too. Her eyes."

"Lonnie probably put her up to selling ass."

"They're together, ain't they?"

"If that's what you want to call it."

Four was Sally getting harassed by a neighborhood thug as she came out of the V Street bodega. It didn't seam to matter the least that she had her son with her. Those damn miniskirts. "I'll give you $100 to sit on my face," the boy, tall and muscular and wearing black, announced, to the other loiterers' benefit.

Sally didn't bother looking his way. "Call your mother," she said. "She got you."

The boy followed her on the sidewalk. "Bitch."

Four houses to go, Sally told herself even as she made a point not to walk too fast. "Asshole."

"Hood rat."

"Pervert."

She made it to 168, sat Eli on the porch, and turned to face the punk.

"Don't ever talk to me like that," he said, getting in her face.

Sally stood her ground. "You're the one started it, nigga. You want the motherfucker, come get the motherfucker."

He slapped her. She balled her fists and punched his eye. They tussled. Sally saw the boy's friends running their way to get a closer look. Rudy jumped out of the basement with a golf club and tried to hit the aggressor with it. He snatched it from her and raised it high above their heads. Rudy held her elbow up. Sally jumped in the middle. The club whacked her arm twice as she tried to protect her face. Rudy pulled a knife and punctured the boy's side, drawing blood. He let go of the club, screaming. "Crackhead cut me! Fuck!"

One of his friends pulled him away. "Come on, man."

Rudy got Eli and Sally inside. "Take me to the hospital," Sally told her mother. "I can't feel my arm.

It was the right one, too. Broken in two spots. The cast they put in at Howard took forever and started itching right away. The discomfort didn't trouble Sally as much as the prospect of losing her livelihood. No more hair braiding for a month and a half, going on two. And let's not even talk about crawling around on all fours with Eli, getting in the bath with him, or carrying him everywhere the way she had gotten him used to. "Just 'cause dude thought he might get him some pussy," Rene commented bitterly. "Now that's some bullshit."

"Dude" was Frank, who lived one street behind 168. Smalltime hustler, two kids from two different girls, lived with his mom. Pressing charges was out of the question (the code). Amad was boiling with rage but Sally forbid him to say or do anything, trying instead to work on Mo in order to get some retaliation action going. It was already one week after the assault. Mo had been real nice to Sally, buying her clothes and catering to her every need. She couldn't have cared less. It hurt her pride that Frank still walked the streets untouched. Rodney would have handled it the same day and everything would have been forgotten. "I know where to find Frank," she told Mo.

"I'm not fighting him," Mo declared point-blank.

Sally couldn't believe her ears. "They don't avenge their women where you're from?"

Mo stared her down. "Of course they do. But this ain't home. There's a line I cannot cross. If I so much as get convicted of a misdemeanor they can revoke my asylum and send me back to Africa."

"What about my honor? Anybody can beat me up and get away with it? What do I have you for?"

"This is not just about you. One single mistake and I'm gone."

"It's not the way we do things," Sally said. "We're soldiers. Anybody who touches you or Amad or Rudy would have to reckon with me, and there would be hell to pay. Hell! I expect the same from you. You're my man, are you not?"

Mo looked at her sideways. "Want to contract it?"

She couldn't tell if he was joking or not, and so Sally just shook her head and let it pass.

Rudy took it to Skunk. He loaned her the truck and Never Scared Fats for an hour or so. They showed up at Frank's house and had his mother wake him up while they sat on the couch, Never Scared grinding the cushions. Frank walked into the living room with downcast eyes. Never Scared looked him up hungrily. Only Rudy spoke. "We C.T.U.," she told Frank. "Deep as they come and thicker than blood. It's two ways out of this: either apologize to my daughter or get brand new holes in that scrawny chest of yours."

Frank walked to 168 with two of his buddies two hours later. Sally came out on the porch. It was their first time laying eye on each other since that afternoon. "I'm here to ask for forgiveness," Frank told her. "It was a bitch-ass thing, what I did. I'm totally disgusted with myself."
"Squashed," Sally said.
They shook hands.

Of course there was no way Mo would get off that easy. A big chunk of the respect Sally and her family had granted him from the get-go was gone. "From now on make him pay for that booty," Rudy intimated. "Don't give it up. Don't even let him smell it. He can't fight for you, he can't bust a nut for free. Simple as that."
"I called the radio lady about your case," Chi-Chi informed Sally. "Dr. Pamela Brewer."
Sally was tickled. "You went live?"
"I did. You know what she and other listeners had to say about your relationship? Red flags! Red flags! Red flags!"

Sally didn't join into the Mo bashing, though she stayed upset for quite a while. If she told him no every time he wanted to make love after the incident, cast and all, it's more because she didn't feel romantic in the least. Hard questions were popping up in her head, and the Truth Game held more appeal than sex. Something had been lost. Maybe talking could help recoup, regain, and rebuild.

"What happened to you as a child?"
"Yonis was on his way to Italy for a PhD. My

mother, Lafia, and he decided to leave me behind until they got settled. They were young and broke. I was six months. Lafia's godmother had helped rear her. They thought she could be trusted. They thought she was safe." Mo looked at the wall. "A year and a half into their stay abroad my mother got an anonymous letter telling her she'd better hurry and come get me if she wanted to see me alive again. The old lady apparently had a grudge that she was taking out on me. Or perhaps she was just plain crazy. When Lafia flew back for me she found me scared of everything and everybody, including her. It all went downhill from there."

"Is that why you are the way you are with children?"

Mo nodded. "I love them fiercely and unconditionally, but from a distance. Don't even have to know them. Poor kids, mistreated kids, suffering kids.... Taking care of them, protecting them is okay. As soon as I get close I feel inadequate."

They looked up the word.

"With most people there's a big wall," Mo continued. "Like I'm a prisoner in my own mind. Defenses I unconsciously put up that keep me in, keep me safe. I never confided in Yonis or Lafia. I never warmed to my stepmother and half-brothers."

Sally understood. "Aster's the only one."

Mo acquiesced. "I'm more connected to her than to any other human being. No self-consciousness, no second-guessing, no conflict. She sees right through me."

"What about your first girlfriend? Aurora."

"She. too, was mistreated. Kind of like me, but by her own mother. So we understood each other."

"How is it with me?"

"Better."

Sally thought up a tough one. "Will you want

children of your own one day?"

Mo didn't hesitate: "Yes."

"If we're still together, what of Eli?"

"I don't know. You can never love other's children the way you love your own, can you?"

"I think I could," Sally told him after taking the time to think. "Of course I could. A child is a child."

Mo shook his head. "I'm not so sure."

Sally started feeling sad. "What else is going on with you?"

"Depression," Mo confessed. "Here and there. And sex. I get hang-ups, so I'm not very good. I'm sure you've noticed."

"You just need more practice."

"Don't joke."

If she didn't have to lie on her back because of the cast covering her arm, Sally would have held Mo tight. She thought he must have drifted off, but he said, "My turn," after a few minutes.

"Go," she invited him.

"That thing with Frank: Was that the worst to ever happen to you?"

She shook her head. "The cop Murphy was the worst. But New York Joe is a close second."

Mo inched toward her. Now it was she who couldn't bear to look at him. "Joe happened right after we moved to Clifton. I had fallen asleep watching TV. He came in the apartment with Skunk. I felt somebody touching me and so I woke up. Joe was sitting on the other side of the couch, the only other person in the room. I told my uncle when he came out of the kitchen. He got his brothers on the phone. They made me watch as they beat Joe and broke both his legs. How's that for vindication?"

Mo let out a long, soft, and heartfelt whistle.

"Murphy was during that summer I spent hustling on 9th," Sally resumed. "White boy, rookie, thickheaded. He jumped out of his cruiser one afternoon, pushed me into an alley, took my money, called me 'nigger whore,' and felt me up. My uncles didn't break his legs: They used me as bait, filmed Murphy as he went for it a second time in the same alley a few days later; rushed him, taped his confession, and made him work for them in exchange for their silence. He's still out there protecting Skunk's corners." Sally stopped talking.

"Wow," was all Mo could say. "Wow."

Sally shrugged. "You asked."

"Do you fight it," Sally asked Mo the next day, a Sunday, "that feeling?"

He nodded. "I try to recognize it when it kicks in. I try to beat the inhibitions. I try to get out."

She sipped tea with him and thought about his life. No friends. No fun. Double shifts. She had no doubt he was going to make it, but what about the other side of things: his head, his emotions, his happiness? "Can doctors help?"

"Yonis may be a doctor but he never liked the idea of therapy—not sure why. And tough luck, in Mog."

"You're not in Mog any more. Yonis ain't around."

"No insurance, Sally. Remember?"

"There are always ways."

"I won't go."

He picked up his notes and went into the bedroom. She followed him with Eli. "What about me: Is there anything I can do?"

"No. It's gonna be me helping me."
How?"
"Writing. Spitting it out."
"The stiffs?"
"The stiffs."

They laughed. It was good to see Mo relax. The last thing she wanted to do was to push him in a corner.

"How's 'Searcher' going?"

"So-so. I'm switching focus midway through. The new version isn't about the detective looking for the Soul but about the man who wrote the book about the detective looking for the Soul."

"What good will it do?"

"I can examine myself a little better and try to make progress."

"What's the roadmap?"

"No roadmap. I go wherever the narrative takes me. I tackle things as I go."

They looked up "narcissistic" in the dictionary.

Sally finally got to read a few pages of the manuscript. Mo paced the floor nervously, awaiting the verdict. "Give it to me," was his request. "Give it to me as straight as you can." Sally struggled through the first two chapters. She didn't think she saw a hit. "It's stuffy," she announced.

Mo stopped walking in circles. "'Stuffy'?"

"Too much thinking. No dialogues, no action, no storyline. You want to make it interesting. You want to draw people in. You want to compel. And keep an eye on your proportions."

It gave her a measure of his self-confidence that he didn't even think to put her expertise into question, reacting, instead, the same way he did every time she struck and unexpected chord: "Too tough, man. Sally too tough."

It bugged Mo all day long, what she had just said. It made him see just how far he was from the rest of the pack, the household names, the heavy-hitters, the trailblazers, the Himes, the Mosleys, the Pelecanos. "Years and years of sweat, four manuscripts, still no voice. I might as well give up."
Sally tried to soften the blow. "You're not writing in your native tongue and you only have so much time to dedicate to it each day. Give yourself a little credit."

She didn't tell him she felt that she, too, had the gift. She'd been meddling with the notebook he'd given her, scribbling in it every chance she got. The stuff was taking shape. It came easy, stirring and then bubbling inside her until she couldn't hold it any longer. Nobody knew about it. It was hers and hers alone. The notebook was in the shoe box with Rodney's loaded gun and the C.T.U. pictures she didn't want Mo to see. It would take time before it amounted to anything. But it'd be funny if she turned out a better writer than Mo, wouldn't it?

Maybe one of the advantages she had was time. She stayed home with Eli at 168 or in the Tuckerman basement, trying to make the best of her temporary infirmity at the same time as she was cursing it for holding her back. She started watching Tyree here and there once Rene got the green light and joined the staff at Upper Cuts, Sweet Thang's salon. She visited Tamika in jail. She visited the twins. She visited Brenda at the zoo at lunchtime and found out that Ben was still in recovery and had long ago lost his headman spot on Pepsi's team. "That's the best thing that could happen," Brenda mused. "Hallelujah."

"Still thinking about moving?" Sally asked.

"It won't happen," Brenda said regretfully. "No money."

"Can't Ben go live with his dad?"

Brenda laughed. "Both he and Rodney hate their father's guts. He's dead to them, remember? Besides, the man lives in Philly with a white woman and two half-white kids. And his project is way worse than mine."

"So what's the plan?"

I don't know. Ben's walking with a limp and he has to carry a shit bag for a few more weeks. He's hurting. Never leaves the room, doesn't even want to see his girl. The people he thought were his friends stopped calling a month ago. I'm scared he might try to get back at the boys who shot him."

"He should learn from Rodney."

"He should. But that's not how it works.

It was a sunny early September day. You could already feel fall in the air. Eli had a cover in the stroller. He was having a ball looking at all the animals. It was the first thing Sally and Brenda had ever done together. "I never hated you," Brenda confessed. "When you came into our lives I had too much on my hands. Nothing was going right with my job, my relationships, my sons, my neighborhood. I felt like, Why should I be nice to anybody? I wasn't what you call a 'positive' person."

"I really thought you didn't like me. But I saw a change when Eli was born."

"It got different after Rodney got incarcerated. My worst fears had just been realized, so why bother being scared any more? Rodney needed me. I had to do my best to be there. It gave me a new purpose."

"I feel like I failed him," Sally said, acknowledging the thought for the first time. "Even though when it was all going down he didn't seem to have that many options. It was kill or lose everything."

Brenda squeezed her arm. "If anybody failed Rodney—or Ben, for that matter—it's me. I should have tried harder. I should have gotten them out of uptown before they bought into this whole Thug Life shit. I should have put my foot down when I realized what they were up to. Cutting school, smelling like cigarettes and weed, staying out late, clothes I hadn't bought, money I hadn't given them.... Oh, I didn't exactly look the other way. I screamed and I yelled. I searched their room. I raided their pockets. I made a fuss every single night." Brenda sucked her teeth. "It seemed they were bent on doing wrong. I found out I didn't know how to handle them. The power, the authority I once held over them was gone. My worry turned into meanness. More distance, more problems. I stopped short of kicking them out—they were all I had. So no, whatever happened reflects on me and my shortcomings."

Eli screamed at the sight of a baby chimp hanging from his mother's neck. Sally and Brenda both looked at him and laughed. "Might be too late for Rodney and Ben," Brenda resumed. "But we'd better do a good job with this here baby. One more chance to prove ourselves. One more chance to beat this thing that's killing our sons. If anybody's ever going to save black men, it's us."

Sally agreed.

They decided to meet the following week and do it again, or do something different. "I'm proud of you," Brenda whispered for no reason at all as they were saying goodbye. Sally almost cried.

It made her work harder on herself and on Amad, that zoo conversation. It stayed on her mind a long, long while. Looking back, Sally even wondered if it wasn't what people call a "defining moment." One thing is for sure: She took it to heart. The bigger picture. Her place, her role in the struggle. Black people. Poverty. Projects. Mothers. Families. Work. Choices. the future. Sacrifices. Raising sons. Raising brothers.

She stayed on Amad's back. She talked and talked and talked. She called. She hung out. She showed love. She tried to stir him toward a better, if harder, path.

They school-supplies shopped together. Mo provided the ride. Grandma entrusted Sally with Amad's whole check, and Sally budgeted wisely. It was to be Amad's best start ever—every item on the list was crossed out. Clothes and shoes, too. Instead of the video game Amad wanted, Sally bought two books. "'Black Boy'? 'Malcolm X Talks to Young

People'? I'm not reading that!"

"I'm not giving you a choice. You're gonna read them and write a report on each. Either that or I confiscate the console."

Amad looked at Mo, who hammered it in. "You gots to read, little brother. That's where it all begins."

"What?"

Mo tried to keep a straight face. "Freedom, little brother. Freedom."

Amad laughed despite himself. "Y'all bringing out the drums, Kente cloth, and medallions, too? Taking us back?"

Sally didn't join in the fun. "You have one month," she said. "So I suggest you start tonight. How about five pages each day?"

"Whatever," Amad said.

They all gave a hand for the Amoco's Back to School Party, that weekend. "Unabomber," Backyard Band's ubiquitous hit, played over the taped-off parking lot. Smoke from the barbecue pit filled the air. Amad and Mo did the hot dogs. Hiwot and Sally judged the dance, beads, hula hoop, and yo-yo contests. Nikki and Mariam gave away notebooks and pencils and book bags. "It's just not the same with C.T.U. gone," Nikki told Brother Haj.

"It's not just C.T.U.," Brother Haj corrected. "14th 'n Clifton, Fairmont, Girard.... Everybody's gonna be gone as soon as the Columbia Heights metro stop is completed. In three years you won't see nothing around here but yuppies. Just remember I told you so."

"We runs," Amad quipped. "We ruuuuns."

It felt good to be out and to do good. It always did. Mo and Sally agreed: It's something they'd be happy to be doing every day for the rest of their lives.

They had trouble agreeing on anything else, that night. A bad feeling washed over Sally as soon as Mo said, "There's something I need to tell you," and so she braced herself as they sat on the carpet after dropping Amad off and tucking Eli in. Sitting next to her, Mo was grim-faced and slow to get it out.

"What is it?" Sally asked.

"Aster," he announced. "She's coming."

Sally held her breath. "When?"

Mo lowered his head. "Tuesday."

"Do you need me to leave?" Sally heard herself ask.

Mo paused before he answered, as if he wasn't sure. "You can stay. It's small and all, but we'll give it a try."

Sally's stomach started to hurt. She lay down and looked at the ceiling. "How long have you known?"

Mo's voice got even smaller. "A few weeks."

"And you're just telling me now?"

"I was afraid it would change things."

"I should go to my mother's house," Sally proposed again. "Give the two of you some space."

Mo ran his fingers through her hair. "Stay. I want you to."

Sally tried to imagine how it'd be in the basement with an extra person. "Do the upstairs people know?"

Mo nodded.

You tell the landlords before you tell me?"

"They're easy. They're not the ones living with me."

"Is Aster even aware of my existence?"

"Of course."

Sally pulled Mo's hand from her hair.

They had only one day to clean and tidy up. Sally felt like moving out altogether after Mo decided he wanted Aster to have the room, but Mo insisted again and convinced her that she should stay. He went and bought a crib for Eli, something they'd been talking about for months. Fresh groceries stuffed the fridge and cabinets. "The girl doesn't really eat," Mo said. "She snacks all day."

"I'm still not feeling it," Sally told him later that night.

"Everything will be fine," Mo assured her. "Aster's not a bad person. She's more outgoing than me. No hang-ups, no inhibitions, no inadequacies. You'll love her."

"The question is, Will she love me?"

"It'll be all right."

Mo talked about his sister until they fell asleep. He hadn't been able to say anything at all in the past. Now that Aster was on her way, he bared it all. Aster is fun-loving. Aster fell on a pot and scarred her forehead when she was three. You should see when Aster dresses up. Aster was so brave in Dadaab ... so brave. Aster can cook a mean barris *iyo digaag suquar*, man. I love me some Aster. Oh, how I love me some Aster.

Aster's plane landed at 4 p.m. Mo went straight to Dulles Airport from work. Sally chose not to go. She spent the day at 168 to give them time to reunite and she only got acquainted with Aster late that evening. The basement smelled different as she walked in with Eli. All the lights were on. Aster was bug-eyed and couldn't have weighed much more than ninety pounds. Her English was bad, her voice was grating, her social skills sucked. But Mo looked as if he had come alive for the first time in months. Sally didn't think that anything they had talked about or done together had made him this happy.

Brother and sister lay on the bedroom's mattress, spoke Somali, and kept Sally out of their catching up. Sally put Eli in the crib, turned the light off, and tried to go to sleep on the living room carpet.

Hearing the shouts and laughter coming from the room, she gave herself one week at the most.

Sally woke up feeling differently. It didn't make sense to get mad at a brother and a sister who hadn't seen each other for over two years for expressing their joy. Mo had been waiting for this moment. It was the culmination of his efforts, the end of the journey begun that day in Mog with a little bit of money, a Land Rover, and two guides. It meant everything. Of course. She knew she was looking at it from the right angle when Mo talked to her before leaving for the store. "I'm putting Aster in your hands," he told her, using his father's words. "She doesn't know the first thing about this country. You could be her first American friend. Nothing would make me happier."

So Sally played the host. She showed Aster around and took her where she needed to go. They went with Eli on the green and orange trolley that stops at every Washington landmark. They went shopping using the subway and buses just so Aster would learn the system. They went to a Connecticut Avenue ESL school to get her registered. They went to a few museums. Aster remained quiet, looking at everything with the same sullen expression. Perhaps it was too much too fast. "You like it?" Sally asked.

"I like the city," Aster said. "It's green. Not too big, not too small. And you?"

"I guess it's all right."

It dawned on Sally that she didn't know much about her hometown. Take her out of the blocks she grew up in and she felt a complete stranger. It was a black thing, she thought. People like her didn't feel accepted, they didn't think they belonged, and so they never ventured too far. As if they expected somebody to challenge their right to stomp the nation's capital's grounds. Or maybe it was a class thing: Limited money makes for limited movement and limited leisure. Sally resolved to break the barriers in her mind and make D.C. hers. She had to step out of her comfort zone. Washington was bigger than uptown. It was bigger than the projects and a couple of shopping malls. There was a whole world out there she had to make sure she wasn't excluding herself from.

Mo found two words for her: "insulated"; "marginalized."

The friendship so hoped for by Mo never took hold. Sally didn't think it was the language thing (Aster knew enough to understand when spoken to and to make herself understood). It wasn't a bad disposition or lack of effort on Sally's part, either (she was nice to the girl and she tried to show her a good time). "We don't click," Sally told Mo. "Ain't no getting around that."

"You can't force chemistry," Mo agreed. "It's either there or it's not."

"It's not like we're enemies," Sally went on. "There's just no spark at all. Nada."

"It's okay," Mo said.

"And I don't think she cares for Eli."

"What makes you say that?"

"She never touches him. She looks at him like he's this thing from outer space. She sighs every time he cries. Doesn't she like babies?"

"She does. It's just that..."

"What?"

Mo looked embarrassed. "Well.... It's not my baby."

Sally's face started to burn. "I see."

Mo tried to explain. "You don't. Back home, out-of-wedlock kids and their mothers are still ostracized."

Sally didn't have to look up the word to know what it meant. "Welcome to America," she told Mo. "And tell your sister I said that."

The problem was, they had to live together. Aster's privacy and comfort were hard to respect since you had to cross the bedroom in order to access the bathroom. When she wasn't lying down listening to the radio, she was cooking for hours and hours in the kitchenette/ hallway, infringing on Sally's turf and duties. The dishes Aster prepared, the ones Mo had dismissed when Sally wanted to make them, were too spicy and foreign for Sally's taste. And then there were the looks. Sally knew what they meant, having lived long enough in other people's homes to know when she wasn't wanted around any more. It wasn't enough that Aster had relegated Eli and her to a corner of the living room. Dadaab's Finest wanted them gone.

So Sally made up her mind. "I'll be at 168," she told Mo, bag in hand. "You want me, come find me."

Mo grabbed her elbow. "Why are you doing this?"

Sally snatched it back—the angry woman, the wife wronged, the rebel. "I'm not the one."

Mo opened his palms. "Stay."

Sally all but shuttered her face. "I can't."

We hang on to good things and hope they last. Sally could never say she'd had her share. A few sprinkles here and there, magic sparkles to illuminate the gray: Robert; Rudy during two drug-free stretches; Amad as a bubbly and endearing little brother; the Rodney of early days; Mo.

Mo and she had been the big, big one. She wasn't ready for it to end. We never are, are we? But it seems we sometimes say or do things that go too far. Things we don't necessarily mean. Things we can't take back. "I dig attitude," Sally's father, Mike, had recently told her on the phone. "But you, baby girl, you take pride to a whole 'nother level."

Maybe it's what did her in: pride. Sally couldn't tell for sure. She had thought she should avoid the showdown with Aster before it came. She had tried to keep the impression of becoming unwelcome from gnawing at her. All she knew now was that she last saw Mo on the "You want me, come find me" night. He dropped her off and that was it. No talking. No kissing. No helping with Eli and the bag.

She gave it a month. One whole month. Mo didn't come and he didn't call. Sally felt betrayed. She felt miserable. She felt lonely. She felt lost. "Gone," she told Rene. "All gone. As if nothing ever happened. For a few wretched words."

"You should try," Rene suggested. "Go see him. Maybe all he needs is a gesture from you. Men got pride, too."

Sally couldn't. It would have taken too big a chunk out of her. "He doesn't love me," she said. "He never did."

Rene thought otherwise. "Don't believe what Chi-Chi's telling you. All that 'red flag' shit. Mo do love you."

"Then why ain't he here?"

"Problems," Rene suggested, very helpfully; "Problems."

Rene took it upon herself to go to the Amoco and buy a Hot Mama pickled sausage just to see what Mo was up to. "He got skinnier than a mug already," she reported. "Hair needs a good slab of grease, too."

"That spicy stuff Aster is feeding him," Sally lamented. "That *barris lyo digaag suquar* stuff. What does the heifer know?"

"He didn't ask about you," Rene added, crushing Sally's hopes. "Just said hi and disappeared in the back."

Sally did a good job concealing her disappointment. "That's all right. Mo wanted a way out and I provided him with one. Nothing else to it."

"He could have been man enough to do it

himself, no?"

"Mo's a fluke."

And so Sally decided to let it be.

Opinions and feelings around her ranged from A (asshole = Mo) to Z (zip, zero: what Sally was left with). Grandma was chagrined. Rudy was nonplused. Amad was disappointed. Chi-Chi was inexplicably triumphant ("Told you!"). Stephanie, who was launching a career on this new thing called the Internet, lambasted Sally for "doing it for free." Chevon, the Glock-wielding fury, summed it up: "Catch a feeling, catch fire," meaning you only got hurt when you allowed yourself to believe in love and to be vulnerable. In other words, Sally should have known better.

She felt weak and lightheaded. Never would have thought she'd be the one left to sing the sad, sad song. The notebook couldn't soothe it all. On two occasions when Rene and Chevon were splitting a joint at Sweet Thang's she almost gave in to temptation. Something, anything to take the pain and pangs away. Something to get her off the stress, the questions, the uncertainty, the floating. No Mo. One week left on the cast. No money. Stomach pains. Delinquent payments on all of 168's bills. Eli feverish night after night. A begrudging and vengeful Rodney in her dreams.... Sally started to envy the goofy/relaxed look on her friends' faces. To go on a short trip.

Get that bud! Backyard chanted on the tape player.

Smoke that skunk

To leave worries behind. To fire up and fly

away. Friendly skies, they called it. Friendly fucking skies .

It sounded good until Sally thought of Rudy. Party-girl Rudy. The one Mike had known. She was an aspiring model back then. Did a photo shoot or two after dropping out of high school and still had a portfolio at Grandma's to prove it. Nice shape, pretty face, nose a little too big, but those eyes, those eyes.... Everybody knew Rudy loved to play, but nobody denied she had a future. Rudy was on her way until something vicious got a hold of her. Sally was sure it had started innocently enough: Just this once; just to lift my head up; just to stop thinking; just to forget about things.... Was it the unexpected pregnancy? Mike's philandering? The demands or disappointments of a competitive and high-pressure career choice? Sally had never dared ask Rudy how and why and when and what and who. A mother is a mother. There are places you just don't go. But Sally could imagine. She could guess what had turned a blossoming woman into a zombie, the glowing and Afro-toting glamour girl into a bone-thin basement prowler. Sally was sure it had all begun in good faith and good fun. She didn't think she was stronger or smarter than Rudy. She didn't think she was better. She knew that all it took was to start. One weak moment and zap, you were gone.

So Sally got scared and caught herself. "Keep that shit out of my face," she politely asked Rene and Chevon the next time they lit up some green in front of her, on a Sunday made all the more dangerous and tempting because it was gray and gloomy and not really rainy but almost.

Back to 168 one hour later she cut the cast with a pair of scissors, marveled at how pale and shrunken and sickly her arm looked, took a deep breath, and allowed herself to do one last thing before starting her new life, her post-Mo life: She curled up in a corner and cried a good, good cry. It was long overdue, she knew, and only partly because of the breakup. There was much to shed tears about when you thought of it—she'd been a champ and held it in all that time. Sally finally opened the gate and let it all pour out. One for locked-up Daddy. One for strung-out Mommy. One for Sally. One for Amad. One for Eli. One for Rodney & Co. One for all the boys and girls in the ghetto. Sally cried and cried and cried.

When she stopped, she was ready.

Her rebound wasn't so much lucky as it was willed, at least at first. She followed in Rene's footsteps and made it to Upper Cuts. The owner, Delcine, and the two other girls were Jamaican. They were strong-willed, strong-backed, hardworking, and they kept gossip to a minimum. "Throw mi corn," Delcine always said, "me no call no fowl," meaning she stuck to her own business. Though they appreciated Sally's handle on their brand of patois, the women weren't as interested in roots reggae as Sally thought they might be. They had walked the streets of Kingston. They had gone to dancehalls, sound systems, and the Sunsplash. They had grown up on the stuff. To them it was old news.

Sally liked a lot of things about the salon. It was well-equipped, airy, and painted light pink, her new favorite color. Eli and Tyree had a playroom in the back. Camaraderie and good humor always seemed to prevail. The patrons were urban professionals, suburbanites, or neighborhood types. A lot of boys came in to get braids, plaits, twists, and starter dreadlocks. Some of them wanted perms and pimp curls.

Delcine had Sally mostly do prepping or easy stuff during her first three weeks: washing, shampooing, conditioning, relaxing, perming, blow-drying, combing, brushing, curling, grooming, and sometimes coloring. Sally tried to learn how to do it all. Braids weren't all you needed to master. Some of the cut-and-highlight combinations that customers came up with were baffling. And that's not even touching on the weaves, snap-ons, and crochets, which were coming back with a vengeance and constituted a sub-world unto themselves.

Business was aplenty. Tips were good. The long hours guaranteed that Sally didn't have the time to think. She found her new schedule satisfying. Six days a week, open to close. The money was nowhere near what she had expected, but it promised to get better. Though it would take another month to completely catch up with the bills, she managed to keep 168 afloat. It was still very empty, but nothing got cut off. Gas, check. Lights, check. Water, check. Phone, check. Sally opened her very first bank account, smiling all the way and paying rapt attention to every detail because she was anxious to try and understand how this thing called money works.

She thought she was dreaming when Rudy came in her room on a Sunday afternoon to tell her that Pepsi was outside in a limousine. Pepsi who? What limo? "Just look out your window," Rudy said. "It's really him."

Sally looked and here indeed it was, a black and conspicuous thing that took three parking spaces. She checked her face in the mirror and walked down the stairs. The driver got out and held the door for a grinning, suit-and-tie wearing Pepsi. He put his eyes into his smile, for once. "Told you I'd find you," he said, handing Sally a bouquet.

She considered the crimson roses. They reminded her of Mo, a flower shop near Kramerbooks, and happier times.

Pepsi was looking at her expectantly. "What are you doing here?" Sally asked.

The grin widened. "Taking you out."

"Are you, now?"

Pepsi opened his palms. "If you want to."

Sally sweetened a little. "Maybe."

"Just for a night on the town."

The flowers were beautiful and smelled nice. "Make that a half-hour. And only if Eli can come."

"Deal."

She didn't change or do anything to herself other than put on a baseball cap. Her hair had started to mysteriously fall out in the middle. Though Rene assured her of the contrary, she thought everybody could notice. She slipped blue overalls on Eli and stuffed his bag. Rudy came outside to see them off.

"Why can't your mother watch your son?" Pepsi asked as they glided through the small streets.

"He's my responsibility," Sally said. "Nobody babysits for me but Rene."

"I don't see Rudy out on 9th any more. She kicked?"

Sally shook her head. "I give her money."

Pepsi looked up. "You sure about that one?"

Sally nodded. "It's called 'enabling,' I know. But I'd rather keep her close."

"I respect that."

Sally refused his offer and watched him mix a drink for himself. Pepsi appeared shorter, more fit, and more mellow than in her memory. They were sitting across from each other. It took her a while to find a comfortable position on the low seat. She kept Eli in her arms. The glass partition was up. They were this bubble of luxury cruising at sunset. "Where's Blackie?"

"Home."

"How's business?"

"Never been better. How's things at the salon?"

So he knew about that, too. "You've been stalking me?"

"Just doing my homework."

They snatched a bucket of fried chicken (white meat only, mild, Family Meal # 4) from a drive-through and headed toward Hains Point. Sally put Eli on her lap and bit into the food. Pepsi loosened his tie. "Only wore this for you," he said. "I feel like I'm hanging myself."

"Why did you come?"

His sigh was deep and heartfelt. "Feeling tired of everything lately," Pepsi answered, not really answering. "Real tired."

Sally tried the fries. They were good, but you had to eat them fast. "You mean the game?"

"Everything."

"Now that you're on top?"

"Funny, isn't it?"

"Can't you just get out?"

"Only if I disappear."

"Are you going to?"

He put his glass away. "Not yet. I got a lot, but nearly not enough to retire. When I do make my move I'll need a house, a business, a clean front." Pepsi looked straight at her. "That's where you come in."

She held his gaze. "As a worker?"

He dismissed the thought. "As a wife."

Sally smiled despite herself. "Seriously?"

He nodded. "That's what I came to tell you. To ask you, I mean."

"Why me?"

"We have a thing. You know it, too."

"I do. But that's not nearly enough."

He took another sip of cognac. "That's for you to decide. I need about one more year. Then we can pick a place and have us a fresh start. No drugs. No guns. No violence. No past."

Sally rubbed Eli's cheek. "What about my son?"

"Shorty's welcome. I'll make him my own. He and you will have the best of everything. We'll be a family. You best believe I'm gonna bust my ass to make it happen. We can start right now if you give me the nod—drive all the way to the Poconos and never look back."

"Cute," Sally said.

They stopped on an esplanade overlooking the Potomac. The sky was almost all dark behind the smoked glass. You could see the moon, pale and a little fuzzy, and Palisades mansions bathed in scintillating lights across the water.

Sally tried to picture life with Pepsi. How long before the Feds came knocking and they'd have to run? They would need good shoes, the kind Mo wore for Coolidge's track. Good shoes, strong hearts, and a whole lot of breath. "Can it really be that simple?"

"It can."

"I need to think about it."

"Take your time."

The driver took her and Eli back. "I guess I'm trying to be happy," Pepsi said as they stood on the curb. Coming from him, his face, his scar, his reputation, the word sounded incongruous and tentative—strange, almost. "And I want you to be the one."

Sally kissed him on the cheek. Pepsi hugged both Eli and her and didn't seem to want to let go. Sally didn't know he had such long arms.

Chi-Chi and her husband, J.J., pulled up behind the limousine in their new secondhand minivan. Sally waited for them to come out. Then they embraced and climbed the porch stairs together.

"Hey, Cuz," Chi-Chi said.
"Wassup, y'all?"
"Just coming to check on you."
"Everything okay. How's the kids?"
"They're good. Rudy in?"
"She should be."
Curiosity was eating away at the couple. "Who was that?"
"Pepsi."
"What did he want?"
"Me."

Rene: Are you gonna do it?
Sally: I don't know.
Rene: Why not?
Sally: Same old same. Remember how worried I was about something happening to Rodney? How I could never eat or sleep until I knew he had made it home that night? How I saw the Tilden thing coming way before it hit? How I was out cold after Rodney got locked up? That's what life with P would be like, times ten. Only this time Eli would suffer and worry right along with me.
Rene: Didn't P say he was getting out?
Sally: They all say that. It's like the most played-out cliché. Who do you ever see get out? Actually get out? Get out for good?
Rene: I don't know nobody that high up.
Sally: Let's say Pepsi does get out. Then what? We leave everything behind. We furnish rooftops and breed pit bulls. What happens with my mother and brother?
Rene: They'll be all right.
Sally: I'd never abandon Amad. I promised

him. And what about Rodney if I just take Eli away? How does he survive jail without news, without the slightest idea how his son is doing, or if he's even alive? And how does my son grow up without knowing his real father?

    Rene: I hadn't thought about all that. Tyrone don't care that much about Tyree. His wife be the one calling and visiting and keeping an eye out. I guess I'm used to fathers not handling their business, not really giving a shit.

    Sally: There's one more thing: I really don't trust dudes with my future any more. Not like that. When they want you, they want you: 'You don't have to work, baby, uh-uh, no-no. Don't you worry, baby. I got you, baby.' So you get used to depending on them 100%. But guess what: The day they're through with you, you're left with nothing. Nothing. That's what's wrong with us womenfolk: We trust too much. It's gotta be us doing for us. Just so we can deal with these fools on an equal footing.

    Sally to Pepsi: "It's no, P. Sorry."

There were to be no heroes left by early winter. Chi-Chi fell from her pedestal first. "Can't believe I used to look up to this hypocrite," Sally told Rene. Rene pretended that, though she had been hip to Chi-Chi's duplicity, she hadn't wanted to come between the cousins since everybody knows how families go—try to wedge yourself in the middle and you get stuck. "But I been knew she was fake," Rene claimed. ("I been knew," the new catchphrase from the girl who took ghetto vernacular to unprecedented heights, maybe not as a pioneer but certainly as an early adopter, with such timeless gems as "I might can do your hair tomorrow," "She got her hair did," "I was cornrolling her hair," and, "Her hair looks more worser than mines.")

    "I guess I shoulda 'been knew,' too," Sally chimed.

    What happened was, Sally was at Chi-Chi's door on a surprise visit with Eli a couple of weeks after the limo ride when she overheard a conversation through the netted living room window, thought she caught her name, held her breath, and waited before she knocked. "The little girl is a ho," Chi-Chi was saying. "She's after money big time. She fucked that African store dude, Mo, right after Rodney, and now she's fucking Pepsi. I don't trust her around J.J. Every time she's down on her luck she goes and finds men to bankroll her. And the first thing she do to hook 'em is give it up. Nasty. Only God knows whose Eli really is. But that's exactly how these young girls carry it nowadays."

"She seems nice enough," her interlocutor intervened in a timid voice that Sally attributed later to Rosie, Uncle John's girlfriend.

"She talks a good game," Chi-Chi conceded. "Knows how to work those angel eyes of hers. But believe me: Sally's no good. I 'xpect her to end up just like her mother. The only difference between the two is that Sally ain't on drugs. Not yet, anyway."

The air knocked out of her chest, Sally backed away from the porch. Chi-Chi's laughter chased Eli and her all the way home, where she wished she could find a hole big enough to bury herself in.

Sweet Thang was next. She had always been Rene's Chi-Chi—the considerate, helpful, nurturing, and dedicated mother figure. No way Rene could have foreseen the betrayal. No way she could have "been knew." It was all about a man, too. "That nigga Dre be brushing up on me every chance he gets," Rene told Sally. "Feeling on my booty and titties. Wants it so bad smoke come out of his drawers. I was careful never to find myself alone with him in the house. The only reason nothing ever happened was because I know how to duck horny niggas, right? But

Sweet Thang was way too blind to peep game. Got herself a young dude and the insecure bitch in her came out quick. Ain't she been around me long enough to know I don't even look at men under 40? What do I want that puppy Dre for? His broke ass can't help with my bills. He wouldn't even get me off right."

"You should have said something," Sally admonished her friend. "From day one. That was your mistake."

"I thought if I just ignored Dre the problem would go away."

"That's not how it works."

"To think he actually said my name when they was bustin'.... That's wild. No wonder she all upset."

It sounded funny enough: Sweet Thang in bed with Dre, a man half her age and half her size. Dre lost in the moment, Dre conjuring up Rene's face. It sounded sad, too. Big as her heart was, Sweet Thang had never been able to keep a man. Maybe the young guys she dated didn't know what to do with her love. Maybe there was something about her that pushed them away. It was her life's great misery.

Sally sighed. "Now what?"

"I'll leave my stuff with you if that's okay."

"Of course."

"I'm gonna take Tyree and check into D.C. Village. File a bogus battery charge against a bogus boyfriend to speed my Housing application up. I'm eighteen. It's time I had my own place."

It tugged at Sally's conscience to hear that. "It be nothing but crazies down at them shelters, Rene. Just stay in Amad's room. He's only here on weekends. He won't mind."

Rene accepted the offer gladly. "I won't be at

the shelter more than two or three nights, total. Just long enough to leave a paper trail. Sure that's okay with Rudy?"

Sally scoffed at the question. "Rudy signed the lease, but I'm the one running this house."

Rene quit her job the same week. No way she was going to work two booths from Sweet Thang after the latter put her out and embarrassed her in front of everybody on Princeton Place. "Wait until you find something else," Sally had recommended. "Then you can jump ship." But Rene was ready to go. Sweet Thang was talking behind her back, poisoning Upper Cut's atmosphere. Shuffling between the shelter, Housing, 168, and U Street with Tyree and a bag quickly proved too much for Rene. Delcine was sorry to see her leave but she didn't say too much, cautious to stick to her principle: Throw mi corn.

Sally wasn't far behind, even though Sweet Thang never directed her barbs and offhanded comments at her. It was a matter of loyalty. "I should have known better than to hire relatives and friends," Delcine mumbled before hanging a "Help Wanted" sign on the window and wishing Sally luck. Sweet Thang held the door for Eli and her. Sally thought the gesture was meant to be funny or something, but Sweet Thang only wanted to make one last comment out of her coworkers' earshot. "Don't trust Rene," she whispered in Sally's ear. "She be talking to your man."

Sally felt like slapping the fat out of Sweet Thang's cheeks. "Whatever," she answered laconically.

The two friends put their heads together. The holiday season had just begun and mall help was in hot demand. Taking turns to watch the kids, they dressed to the nines, scoured Pentagon City Mall, and filled applications until something popped up. Rene got hired in a shoe store. Sally joined the cosmetics department at Macy's. They took care to put in schedule requirements so that they never had to work at the same time. While one was gone, the other babysat and cooked. "I could do that for y'all," Rudy proposed. "I ain't helpless."

Sally tried not to hurt her mother's feelings. "We don't want to impose, Ma. Tyree alone will wear you out in a minute. And you know Eli's kinda restless, too."

"You don't trust me," Rudy said. "Think I was born yesterday?"

Sally hugged her. "Don't say that."

It was true, of course. There was no trusting Rudy with anything. She had nothing to live for except the next high. Sally didn't even think you could call it that any more. At this point it was pretty much a matter of maintaining viable physical and mental states. Smoking or shooting up didn't take Rudy on trips. She didn't lift up, she didn't kiss the sky, she didn't feel warm, she didn't see colors, she didn't talk to God, there was no rush or somersault in a daisy patch. What it did was keep the body aches at bay and get her through another day.

Whatever it was, when time came to chase it Rudy didn't care about the rest. The need took over. She was blowing $30 a day. If Sally had given her $100 she would have done $100. There was no satiating the need. It took everything Rudy gave and it gave nothing back. The need was ruthless. The need was lawless. The need was pitiless. The need sang the tune and Rudy jumped and Rudy danced.

It drove Sally crazy to be giving up cash she could have used for something else. It weighed heavily on her mind. She saw herself doing it forever to no avail. But what choice did she have? At least Rudy was being careful. She bought her stuff across Rhode Island Avenue and used it in the basement. The place was off-limits to anybody but her various friends, men and women in the same predicament whom Rudy met God knows where. One look at them and you knew. No spirit, no joy, no hair, no teeth, no fat, no sleep. Only the shrewd single-mindedness of a fiend. They came and went so much that Sally started to worry about the neighbors talking. Not all of them kept their hands to themselves, either. Rudy would never steal from Sally or Rene, but her company didn't have such qualms. If it had value and it was there for the taking, then it was as good as gone. One more reason for one of the girls to remain in the house at all times. They hid their valuables as best they could and locked themselves in their respective room each night. When they tired of waking up to empty fridges, empty cabinets, and missing microwaves, they bought extra chains and padlocks as well as bins to store foodstuffs under their beds.

The biggest scare of their lives started with Tyree's dead-on impersonation of a doped-out Rudy one 168 evening: the eyes sealed shut, the dumbly relaxed face, the nodding, the bowling pin that leaned and leaned and leaned but never fell—kind of like that Michael Jackson move. "Crack cocaine for niggas!" Tyree muttered for laughs all through that night, spit oozing from the corner of his mouth. "Crack cocaine for niggas!" Rene and Sally knew they had a problem. Tyree refused to tell them where he'd found the inspiration for both the mime and the utterance. Was it Grandma Rudy? Had he been in the basement? He didn't know. He couldn't remember. "I'll take responsibility for one thing," Rudy declared. "It's me he's imitating, no doubt. That's what we get for not having a TV in the house: all eyes on Rudy. But I'll be damned if I ever said anything like that 'crack cocaine' shit in front of the little bastard. Might not always look like it, but I do got respect. Y'all should know me better than that!"

Sally and Rene installed a dog fence across the top of the basement's stairs in order to limit Tyree's excursions. "He must have been sneaking in there while Rudy and them were using," Sally intuited. She felt like apologizing to her friend for what the little boy was being exposed to. But Tyree's next favorite mantra, "Bitches: We fuck 'em, duck 'em, leave them alone!" which he took to repeating ad nauseam with his arms beating an imaginary drum kit and his feet stomping the carpet, seemed to tip the scales, at least partially, in favor of Rudy's innocence. The girls quarantined Tyree in Rene's bedroom, afraid of what might come out of his mouth in front of company. The mystery of Tyree's burgeoning street education was finally solved when Sally caught him listening to go-go tapes on Rene's Walkman in the middle of the night.

"See what I'm sayin'?" Rudy said, as if she were off the hook.

"He couldn't have gotten that nodding stance from a song," Sally retorted. "You *were* high in front of the kid."

Sally thought about all that when Rudy was admitted to Washington Hospital Center the week before Christmas for a bout of pneumonia. Looking at her mother's wooden stick of a body, she wondered how long life could go on that way.
"Here's one who's not afraid of getting stuck," she overheard one of the nurses tell another, not the first needle joke about Rudy Sally had suffered through.

Rudy was conscious, if extremely weak. "Don't look so scared," Sally chided her. "You'll pull through. You always do."

"She's amazingly strong," Rudy's Pakistani doctor agreed with Sally. "But she should stay on the medication we're starting her on. The infections are going to multiply. Next time we might not be able to bring her back."

"I'll talk to her," Sally said. "I'll make sure she does everything she's supposed to."

"I can recommend a couple of drug-treatment programs," the doctor went on.

Sally nodded absentmindedly, knowing Rudy would never agree to rehab. "When can she come home?"

"In a couple of days."

Rudy shrugged when Sally told her. "I'm ready to go," she said, meaning she was ready to die.

"What about us?" Sally asked, the way she always did. "Eli, Amad, me? What about Grandma? Your brothers? Ain't we reason enough to try?"

Rudy's eyes moistened. She was still as a corpse. Swollen, black with blotches, nails bitten all the way down, hands flat on the white cover. Sally sat on the IV-free side of the bed and started to hum as she caressed her mother's hair. It felt like it always had: She was the mother and Rudy the child. Deja vu, or, as Rene would say, "deja knew."

"This stuff is getting old," Sally told Rudy. "You know that, don't you?"

Back home Sally took her courage in her two hands and ventured into the basement. It was her least favorite place in 168. She was convinced evil lurked there. "Come down with me," she asked Amad. They wore double-soled boots and thick gloves and carried an empty trash bag. "Here you go," Sally said, pointing at the exposed tip of a syringe. They found ashtrays, matches, shoes, useless bits of electronics, empty food stamps books, magazines, food wrappers, two glass stems, pieces of Choir Boy, packs of BC powder, rubbing alcohol, rolling paper, empty lighters, and musty clothes. "Open the window," Sally asked her brother. They removed all the cigarette-poked sheets and the pillows covering the rubber flooring, and dumped them in the bag. Amad was grim-faced as they took a final look around. The noises Rene and the children were making in the kitchen seemed to waft in from another world.

They were on their way back upstairs when Sally thought about something. Amad, who was now much taller than her, unscrewed the smoke detector's cover. "No wonder the thing wasn't on," he told Sally. "Somebody removed the battery." Sally's heart fell out. "Bet you this is how that fire got started up Grandma's Eastern Avenue joint," Amad mused. "They never told us because we were kids. But they knew."

"Rudy's fitting to get us all killed," Sally said. "If anything catches here at night we'll most certainly get trapped upstairs."

"She'll probably smoke to that, too," Amad joked.

Sally shook her head. They fished a battery from Tyree's wrestler doll and put it in. The green light that appeared on the ridged plastic cover made Sally feel a little better. "Leave the window open," she directed her brother before they turned the light off.

"We should start thinking about moving," Sally told Rene that night. As soon as Rudy comes back the circus will start over. Ain't no bringing the lady in from the cold."

"You don't want to wait for my Housing application to go through?"

"It might take too long. They won't give you more than a two-bedroom anyway."

"I guess we could try to find something," Rene said.

They decided to put it off until later.

Thanksgiving had been a blast, but Christmas took the cake. They had a tree, a nice dinner, presents for everybody, and that most treasured of gifts: a semblance of peace of mind. Amad, Sally, Rene, and Tyree joined hands and prayed before eating. Rudy was recuperating at Grandma's, where she wouldn't have to worry about Tyree jumping on her stomach from atop the couch. "Merry Christmas," they kept wishing one another. "Merry Christmas." When thoughts of Mo, Rodney, or Chi-Chi threatened to make the day bittersweet, Sally took a look around. She had Eli. She had a job. She had her brother, her friend, Tyree. Toys everywhere. More food than they could eat. What else could a person ask for?

Eli's first birthday was right behind the new year. "What do you want?" they asked him.
"Gooo!" he answered, grabbing a bunch of Rene's braids.
"A chocolate cake," Amad translated.
"Anything else?" Sally asked.
Eli released Rene's braids only to try and scratch her forehead. "Gaaa?"
"He says a TV would be nice," Amad continued. "A small one. And cable."

They invited all the kids they could manage to fit in 168 at once. Not only did Brenda contribute, she gladly gave a hand.

Sally and Rene lost their jobs one week apart, casualties of the post-holidays slump, and immediately hit the cashier circuit. They were broke, having overspent on gifts and food, but they had no regrets. They got hired by the same drugstore chain but ended up in two different branches after training. Sally went to Georgetown. Rene was sent to far Northeast. It didn't take long for them to start hating everything about their new work environment. "They hire us black folk because we're cheap labor," an old-timer told Sally. "Every ounce of energy will be squeezed out of you but you'll never be made full-time, you'll never get the promised benefits, you'll never see more than a 25 cents raise per year on that minimum wage they start you off."

"Why are you here?" Sally asked the disgruntled supervisor.

"I'm 63 years old," the lady confided, "and looking and feeling every bit of it. Nobody else will have me. I'm giving you the heads up so you know what to expect and don't get to blaming me when frustration sets in."

Their morale sagged after the first couple of weeks. It'd be another fortnight before they got their first paychecks and they were bracing for the pinch. "I feel like going back to doing hair," Rene ventured. She placed a few phone calls and tried to reactivate her list of old customers. It was late January and nobody had any money.

"Next month will be better," Sally predicted. "People are gonna start getting their tax refunds."

They were brainstorming with Chevon in the middle of 168's living room on another gloomy and ice-cold Sunday. Javon, Tyree, and Eli were playing in one of the upstairs bedrooms. Amad had just left for Grandma's. "I'm through with alleys," Chevon declared. "No more hitting dope boys for petty cash."

"You're lucky nothing ever happened to you," Sally told her.

"It ain't about luck," Chevon answered. "I got skills."

"I know you're ready for a 9 to 5," Rene said.

Chevon bared her teeth. Her pointy chin and blond wig made her look fifteen. "Never." She was flush and it showed. Good car, good clothes, jewelry, nice digs, an expensive daycare for Javon. She was living even better now than when Wayne was alive.

And it was all her doing.

Sally fished a handful of chips from the bag sitting in front of the three of them. "So what do we do?"

"Keep looking for something better," Rene proposed. "Get that high school diploma. Find us office jobs. Start low and work our way up."

"That's for squares," Chevon interjected.

"What's your plan?" Sally asked, annoyed.

"A mask and a gun," Chevon proclaimed. "That's all I need to make it in this world. And if y'all had any sense y'all would come with me and start getting this money."

"Robbing people?"

"Not people: businesses."

Sally and Rene shook their heads, rolled their eyes, and had a good laugh about it after Chevon and Javon had gone home. "Love her or hate her," Sally remarked, "you can't knock Chevon's hustle. She has bigger balls than most dudes out here."

Rene nodded. "Imagine the damage if she'd been born with a dick."

Later on that night Sally asked herself if Chevon wasn't right to do what she did: refusing to conform, listening only to her needs and wants, setting herself apart, giving free rein to her rage, eating off the land, taking it all and fuck all of y'all. What if it was the only sane response? The one winning move to counter the hell of a hand all of them had been dealt at birth? Here they were Rene and she, sweating it out day after day in cheesy uniforms and contemplating the long, long way up while Chevon got by trusting only her wits.

They found out just how serious Chevon was about her new career plans when they heard about the latest string of robberies on the 14th Street corridor. Chevon confirmed that she was the waif-like, black-clad bandit the police were looking for. "I hit Dottie's at closing time and Kantouri's in the wee hours. It's much more money out there, but I can't do it on my own. I need at least one more person, I'm trying to tell you. Who's up?"

Chevon wasn't addressing herself to Rene, whose fighting technique consisted of waving a canister of Mace in her opponents' faces, and who couldn't look or act hard if you paid her to try. No way. Chevon wanted rough-and-ready Sally to be her roll dawg. Sally had guts, nerves, and Rodney's gun. "All I need you to do is watch my back," Chevon explained. "We go in, you stand by the door and keep an eye on customers and employees. Make sure they stay quiet and nobody comes in or gets out. I take care of the registers, the safe, and the escape route. We split it down the middle."

"It's no," Sally answered. "And I'm telling you for the last time. I might have hustled here and there when I was young, but I'm no thief. The only thing I ever stole in my life was a shorts set for Amad. It felt bad enough that I promised myself I'd never do it again."

"Scared money don't make none."

"Make that 'dead money.'"

"This ain't robbin'," Chevon insisted. "This jackin'."

"Same difference."

"You're in the news," Rene said. "Don't you think they're on the lookout right now?"

Mischief brightened Chevon's eyes. "It's ways around everything."

"Who are you planning to hit anyway?" Sally asked.

"The Amoco," Chevon said.

Sally felt the wind rush out of her lungs. "Mo's Amoco?" Chevon nodded.

"Are you crazy?"

"It ain't never been done before," Chevon announced. "But I'm gonna be the one."

"Now you're going too far," Rene protested. "Them some real nice people we're talking about."

Chevon looked at Rene contemptuously. "Don't matter to me how nice they are. Their money green, ain't it? Think about it: All they have is old cameras. No Plexiglas, no security guards, only two people on the graveyard shift. Gas and grocery money rolling in all day all night. It's a wonder nobody thought about it before."

"Everybody loves them," Rene continued. "All the good things they're doing uptown. Them ladies watched all of us grow. That's why they've never been robbed."

"Makes it easier for me," Chevon retorted. "They'll be sleeping when I go in."

Sally looked at Chevon as if she was seeing her for the first time. "You're not touching the Amoco!" she warned heatedly.

"Why not?"

"I mess with them people. And Mo still works there."

"That doesn't have anything to do with me."

"It does."

Chevon sighed with exasperation. "He dumped you," she said. "What do you want to protect him for?"

"Doesn't matter if it's over," Sally told her. "The man was good to me and I'll always have love for him. I can't believe you would ask me to help do him in."

"You're broke; you know the place inside out; you have a grudge—or at least you should have one. Makes perfect sense to bring you along. It's not like they're gonna know it's you."

"You're out of your mind."

"I'm not. And I can't believe you would choose a fucking Ethiopian over me."

"Mo's not Ethiopian."

"He sure looks like one to me."

Sally bared her teeth. "Don't talk about him like that!"

Chevon tried a different approach after they had both calmed down a little. "Nobody will get hurt," she said. "How's that?"

Sally's anger rose again. "You're not doing it and that's it."

"Somebody will. It's only a matter of time. I do it painlessly, they take the hint, get hip and start protecting themselves so it won't happen to them again. Look at it like a favor I'm doing them." Chevon grinned. Only she saw the joke.

Rene was ashen. Sally was red in the face. "Don't do it," she warned for the last time. "Anything happens to that store, I'll know it's you."

"And then what?" Chevon shouted. "You're gonna snitch? I gotta worry about you opening your mouth?"

They stood up, faced each other, and balled their fists. Rene got on her feet, too, wondering if she should get in the middle right then. Sally was taller than Chevon, and that's about the only advantage she had. Timidly, Rene tried to intercede. "Come on, y'all." But it seemed a line had been crossed. All pretense of friendship, or even civility, was being abandoned.

Chevon was the first to look away. "You got soft on me," she said with a trace of regret. "I thought I could always count on you."

"Ain't one soft bone in my entire family," Sally affirmed; "We built tough, just like them cars. But what's wrong is wrong."

Chevon picked up her bag and called Javon. The kids were standing at the top of the stairs, cowed by the commotion. Sally wondered why Rudy hadn't come out of the basement. "You don't have my back," Chevon said as she walked toward the door, her pumps and power suit making her look too sophisticated for 168, or any street shakedown, for that matter. "That's what's wrong."

Sally tried to have the last word, but fell short. Her head was swirling. Chevon was turning into a meaner machine than even she had foreseen.

All Sally could think about for the next couple of days was Mo standing at the end of Chevon's barrel. "Think she's gonna do it?" she asked Rene.

"Any girl crazy enough to stab her own mother over rent money can't be stopped," Rene said.

"I forgot she had done that."

Rene nodded. "Ms. Lucille only got what she deserved, mind you. Mean as shit. Remember the beatings Chevon used to get? The black eyes and busted lips? How sorry we always felt for her?"

Sally remembered. "We were her only family before Wayne and the baby: me, you, Stephanie, Tamika. I guess she learned early on how to fend for herself. But hurting people the way she's fitting to do? I don't know, man."

"She'll set the Amoco on fire just because you asked her not to. Chevon don't care about nobody but her son and herself."

"What should I do?"
Rene was adamant. "You can't snitch."
"I know."

They went to work and kept their ears tuned to the streets. Nothing happened for a good ten days. On the eleventh, they heard that the nail salon one block south of the Amoco had been hit. Though shots was fired into the ceiling, nobody got injured. The holdup was attributed to a trio. "It was her," Sally told Rene. "I'm glad she switched targets."

"Me, too," Rene echoed.

Chevon stopped calling and coming around. No explanation or justification needed. Life had brought the Honeys together and life had brought them apart. You could also call it choices, lifestyles, and fate. It was enough for Sally and Rene to be by themselves. They tried to stick to the pact devised long ago: work hard, stay together, help each other, get ahead. No backstabbers (bye, Chi-Chi), no loonies (bye, Sweet Thang), no psychopaths (bye, Chevon) were about to keep them from going where they needed to go.

Did it come as a shock that Chevon went ahead and did the Amoco anyway? Probably not. Sally realized afterward that a certain unease had been sticking to the back of her mind all the while. Something she had seen in Chevon's eyes when they were facing off. Something that had been absent, rather: emotion. Curious how Sally had never noticed before. But that's how she was with the people she cared about—once they were in, they were in. The scrutiny stopped. She opened up, she aimed to please, she misread clues. "Red flags!" Chi-Chi would have shouted.

Red flags. Chi-Chi. Ugh. She kept calling and showing up unannounced to try and see what was wrong between Sally and her. She might as well have been talking to a wall, because Sally never even bothered to answer. She had buried her disappointment deep, she tried not to think about it at all. Chi-Chi's appeal to their relatives was in vain. Because Sally never shared what she had overheard on Chi-Chi's porch with anyone, Rudy and Grandma were mystified. Everybody assumed that she was in the wrong just for being the youngest. Sally and her attitude. Young girls these days.

One thing about her, once people disappointed her it was for good, cousin or not, family or not. Mo was the only person she felt disposed to giving a second chance to if he ever decided to ask for one. Perhaps because nothing had been said to cause bad blood or true resentment. Perhaps because it was cold and she missed him.

Mo. He had been in her thoughts since Chevon brought him up, and even more so now that weathermen across the board were calling for a snowstorm, the first blizzard to hit the city in years. Record fall and accumulation were expected. People were being advised to stock up and stay in. Sally wondered how Mo and Aster were doing up Tuckerman, and if they were readying themselves for the snow, too.

Sally was like that: she cared. Grandma and Amad had all they needed thanks to Uncle Skunk. 168 was packed with groceries and good to go. Rudy had three days' worth of dope that Sally planned to dole out dose by dose. She had made her mother put the baggies in her hand as soon as Rudy came back into the house from the Rhode Island Avenue spot. "I'm not a child," Rudy had complained. "I can pace myself if need be." Sally had given her one before putting up the rest in her closet. It made her sick to her stomach to touch the stuff. She felt even worse knowing Eli slept and played in the room.

The snow came on Sunday night while they were sleeping. A record it seemed to be. Sally was looking at the backyard when Rene joined her in the kitchen around 8 the next morning, the time they were both accustomed to getting up every day. The snow was like a blanket, thick and long, covering the ground. "Beautiful, isn't it?"

"I wish we had a TV for once," Sally said. "Tried the radio, but the news channels fried my nerves."

"Cabin fever?"

"I've been up since 5."

"5? You look like it, too."

"This dream I was having woke me up: Mo had just gotten shot."

Rene stopped stirring her coffee. "Shot? Did he die?"

"I don't know. It was so real I think I wept in my sleep. Somebody wearing a mask walked up to him and pulled the trigger. Mo went down, and then everything got blurry. I opened my eyes and hugged Eli."

"No wonder," Rene mused. "All that heist talk recently. Chevon and her bullshit."

"That's what I thought, too."

"Where was the dream taking place?"

Sally looked at Rene. "The Amoco."

Rene pushed her cup away. "Did you call?"

Sally tapped her fingers on the table. "I don't want to look stupid. What if he picks up? I don't have anything to say to him, really."

"Haven't you forgiven him?"

"I have. But I'll be damned if I make the first move."

"Call and tell him the truth: you're just checking on him."

Sally couldn't bring herself to do it. "I'm too

scared. Would you? Please?"

Rene went and got the phone. "They're probably closed anyway."
Sally tried to remain calm as Rene dialed the store's number. Her hands and feet were doing a manic dance.

"Nobody's answering," Rene said.
"Let it ring some more."
Somebody picked up as Rene was getting ready to hang up.
"Can I please talk to Mo?" she asked.
Sally got closer. When she saw Rene's mouth and eyes open wide with shock, she snatched the phone. "Hiwot? It's Sally. Something happened?"
"We got robbed," Hiwot said in an unnaturally poised voice. "About an hour ago."
Sally clutched the phone tighter and prayed for strength. "Where's Mo?"
"An ambulance just took him away. They were leaving as you called."
"Is he...?"
"He's hurt bad," Hiwot said. "But he's alive."
"Where are they taking him?"
"Howard, probably. The roads are a mess and it's the nearest."
Sally took a deep breath. "Are you okay?"
"Shaken," Hiwot said. "They roughed us up.... I got away with a few scratches. Mo took the brunt."
"Who were they?"
"I couldn't see their faces."

Hiwot hung up abruptly: a detective needed her attention. Sally ran upstairs to put something on.

"Where are you going?" Rene asked.
"To see Mo."
"In this weather?"
"The snow's not coming down any more. You're watching the kids?"
"Of course."

They called both nearby hospitals before Sally left. "Assuming he got here he must be in triage down at the ER," someone at Washington Hospital Center informed them. "I would give it a few hours."

"Just wait," Rene told Sally.

She knew she'd only go crazy if she tried.

It wasn't as bad outside as she had dreaded. The snow came to her knees. She walked in the middle of the road until she reached Rhode Island, already short of breath. The wind seeped through her layers. The quiet beauty of her street gave way to brown slush and tentative traffic on the avenue. People, too, were treading carefully. Plowers had been running all night without being able to keep up. Sally couldn't believe her eyes when she saw a bus. "Running on chains," the driver told her. "Once you get off, stay on main thoroughfares until you reach your destination. Side streets are a no-go."

She went to Howard first. No Mo.

She waited an hour for the Georgia Avenue bus. It took her to Irving Street, laboring and threatening to slide all the while. From there it was a straight walk. Sally's nose burned and her feet were wet. She thought of Mo and prayed and prayed. She didn't want him to die.

Washington Hospital Center was becoming a second home, she realized that much when she settled into the visitors' lounge with a hot chocolate to wait for news. It's where she had had Eli. Where Rudy came whenever the virus gave her a run for her money. Where Ben had been treated for his wounds. Where Mo was now in surgery. Neurosurgery. "He was conscious when he came in with a skull fracture. We're removing bone fragments and putting a titanium plate in. No evidence so far that the brain suffered any damage."

"How long will it be?"

"No more than three hours. You won't be able to see him today, regardless of the procedure's outcome."

Sally sat and waited anyway. Only three other persons were there. Three middle-aged black women. Mothers, wives, or sisters. They were always the ones doing the worrying. Sally thought about Aster.

She called Rene after finishing her chocolate. "I made it."

"Is he okay?"

"They don't know yet. I'm staying put until I find out."

"Don't worry. The kids want to go play in the snow."

"Out front," Sally said. "No farther."

"I'll be right there with them. Rudy wants her baggies."

"They're in my closet. Give her one. Tell her that's it for today."

She had been warned: Mo's dreadlocks had been partially shaved to allow for the scalpel. Still, it was a shock. Here he was lying diminished and defeated, one arm across his chest, no glasses, eyes lost into the ceiling as if neither the TV nor the world outside the wide window held any interest. Sally tried to imagine the scar under his enormous bandage as she walked toward his bed.

She tried her best to be brave. "Which way to the Valley of the Kings?"

Mo turned his head, suppressing a smile. "Don't joke."

He couldn't move, and so she leaned to kiss his cheek. It was true that he had lost weight—the little he could afford to lose. He looked out of it, too. "How did you hear?"

"I dreamt about it two nights ago, and so I called. Got a hold of Hiwot right after the ambulance took you away. She told me."

"You *dreamt* about it?"

"I did. Only it was worse, in my dream. It looked as though you had died."

"ESP," Mo murmured.

"What?"

"That's what it's called."

Sally wiped the tears from her eyes and pulled the room's lone chair closer to the bed. "He's gonna be all right," Doctor Alesi had told Aster and her. "No speech, memory, or motor functions losses. Plate and screws are in. Stitches will go away on their own. Make sure Mo doesn't bang his head for the next month or so. Soccer is out, definitely."

The sun was making the room almost too bright. Sally brought the blinds down a little. Mo turned the TV off. "How's life treating you and Eli?"

"We can't complain."

"Rudy OK?"

Sally shrugged. "Rudy's being Rudy."

"Don't give up on her."

"I won't. I can't."

She kicked off her shoes and folded her legs under her after handing Mo the gifts she had brought. He dug the set of colorful skull caps (polka dot, all-black, blue, Flash Gordon red with little wings on the sides), but didn't recognize the name on the cover of the one book she gave him. "Who's this Alcaly?"

"New guy, goes by his first name. Underground but bubbling. The only self-published author to make Kramerbooks' window and Staff Picks list."

"I'm glad you're reading again."

"Writing, too."

Mo's eyes opened wide. "Will you show me?"
She promised.

"Who's paying for you?"
"Workers' Comp. This here bill won't be anything to smirk at."

Sally helped him get some exercise at the nurse's insistence. They covered the length of the hallway very slowly, Mo hanging on to the bar running alongside the wall. His legs and hips were heavy. He was surprised at how weak he felt, the amount of effort involved in each step. Sally took his arm in the turns. He had trouble holding his bitterness in. "All this for a little whack on the head."

"It wasn't little," Sally said. "Obviously."

"Makes me feel real fragile. Skull fracture. Neurosurgery."

"It could have been worse."

"I guess."

She thought of Chevon. "What kind of gun was it?"

Mo smiled wearily. "I know Kalashs, grenades, and bombs. Handguns are foreign country. It looked big and black in that kid's palm. That's all I remember."

"What did he look like--the kid?"

Mo let go of the bar and rested his arm on Sally's shoulder. She stopped when she thought she saw him wince.

"All three wore scarves around their faces. My guy looked real short, real tiny inside his parka. Couldn't have been that old."

"Mind telling me how it all happened?"

"It was Nikki's decision to stay open through the storm. We took turns sleeping. She and Mariam went out at 7 to try to find bread, milk, and eggs after all our deliveries got canceled. Shelves were empty and breakfast food seemed to be the one thing people really wanted. The store was packed. Hiwot was running the register. I was everywhere at once: cooler, sandwich box, backroom, coffee machine.... I don't think they walked in together. If they did, I didn't notice. I was on my way to pop a tray of frozen cookies in the oven when somebody stepped in front of me. The gun was wrapped in a piece of cloth inside the kid's coat pocket. He took forever to get it out. Meticulous. Small fingers. Thick gloves. Why I just stood there, waiting, I don't know. I looked at the piece and said to myself, Okay, this is a holdup. The kid never gave me a chance to cooperate. He got on his tiptoes and banged me in the middle of the forehead. I dropped the cookie tray. Hiwot screamed. The store emptied. The two other robbers stepped in. They walked behind the counter very calmly, smacked Hiwot, pushed her toward the back, and had her open the safe. I was made to kneel by the register. Blood was falling in my eyes, on my sweatshirt, on my shoes. I sat there half anticipating a bang, the fatal shot, wondering if that was it—the end. When I stopped feeling the metal against my temple, I looked up. They were gone."

Mo got back into the bed and took Sally's hand. "I miss you," he said.

"I miss you, too," she confessed.

Hiwot showed up with Aster and a laptop computer some window-breaker had peddled at the Amoco for chump change the night before. Mo smiled. "Better late than never," he said, and turned the thing on.

Aster and Sally chatted a little. They weren't becoming fast friends. It's just that their concern for Mo gave them something to talk about. Sally wasn't mad. It didn't even matter that Aster hadn't asked about Eli. Aster was a sister, and sisters always want what's best for their brother. Clearly, Sally hadn't been the best thing for Mo. No hard feelings. It was all business.

Hiwot gave Sally a ride in her all-wheel drive. She was the one running errands and making sure everybody got where they needed to go until all the side streets were cleared. She had a bruise on the right cheek but felt all right otherwise. "People tried to warn us. We never believed something like this would happen. Eight years.... We never felt in danger.

Never even thought that way. We made a living and we tried to help. Some of these children got uniforms, school supplies, scholarships, trips.... They saw the inside of our homes." She sighed. "The ones who robbed us probably come in every day and call us 'Ma,' too."

Needless to say, the inquiry went nowhere. They never did, in certain parts of the capital city. The little that the black and white video showed was unusable. Had Sally still been living uptown, she would have heard something. People talked, they talked a lot, just not to the police. This was big enough that somebody had to have seen or heard something. Sally knew in her heart of hearts that Chevon was responsible. "I just can't prove it," she told Rene. "And I don't want to stir things up without knowing what I'm doing."

"She should pay," Rene agreed. "Mo was off-limits, no doubt. But if you say a single word to her it's gonna be war. You might just have to kill the girl."

It's true, Sally thought: Your best friends can become your worst enemies. "I'm not scared of Chevon."

"I know you ain't. But is it worth it?"

"Mo could have become paralyzed. He could have lost a whole lot. She hit him on purpose. To get back at me. And because Wayne is dead."

"You don't know any of that for certain. I'd let it pass."

"So that Chevon can get away with everything?"

"She'll get hers," Rene affirmed. "People like her always do."

"I let Mo down," Sally said.

It was sending her on a guilt trip, what he had gone through. A gun to his face, pistol-whipped like a chump, marked for life. She thought she should have been able to prevent it. "Too bad he and I weren't talking."

They were now. He reported for work with a clean cut and two new scars one week after getting out of the hospital. People had to do a double take to recognize him. All the pretty locks were gone. Some of the customers thought he lookedoutright funny. "I'm growing my hair back," he told Sally. "It's the first thing I did when I got out of Mog, because Yonis wouldn't have that kind of mess in his house. I'm a rastaman at heart."

"What did you father have to say about the robbery?"

"He doesn't know. Aster and I kept it to ourselves. No need to worry the rest of the family. They have their own problems. They have their own bullets to duck."

The kids mobbed him. A few had written while he was away, trusting Hiwot with precious notes hastily torn from notebook pages. Little Dante sent $5 and a drawing of him shooting the robbers with a sawed-off double-barrel pump-action. Mo felt happy to be back, even though he and the sisters knew things would never be the same. They debated putting up plexiglas. Nikki hired three Third District cops to moonlight at the store, every single one of them lazy and corrupt and dimwitted. But the Amoco did get a semblance of round-the-clock security for a while. When it seemed that a big enough message had been sent, the police shifts got reduced to a few random overnights. "It's gonna happen again," Sally warned Mo, wishing she could share everything she knew.

"Can't live in fear," is what he answered.

"You should try and do something else. No more jobs involving cash."

"That's what Yonis keeps telling me: No son of his was meant to sweat it out in a corner store. But I'm the one calling the shots."

"So what's the plan? Stay here until things get better or you catch another one on the forehead?"

Mo smiled. "The sisters are hooking me up. They're helping me get my own hole-in-the-wall gas station. And a car. As a reward for what happened. I won't need to put anything down. Zero. Not a cent."

"What kind of hole-in-the-wall gas station?"

"Something tiny and protected. A booth, four pumps, free air, a vacuum cleaner. Nothing to do all day but count money and push a few buttons. I get to write all I want."

"Where?"

"We're thinking Florida, between New York Avenue and Benning Road."

"What kind of car?"

Mo was almost giddy with anticipation. "92 Impala SS. Black."

"How American of you," Sally said.

Sally, too, had something for him. They went out to eat one evening and she made Mo get a room in Silver Spring. They got in at 10 and checked out a little after midnight. Two hours was all Sally needed to blow Mo's mind. She took him around the world. Everything she had held back in the Tuckerman basement, everything she knew how to do. Chair striptease, bathtub, bed, mirror, dresser, wall. Hooker boots, a so-'80s Apollonia 6 white lace garter belt, a lascivious smile, the radio, Sally the School of Comforters and No Lights graduate. It went like yet another Backyard song:

Oooh
Aaah
Yeah!
Aaah
Oh my Gawd!
Make the pussy go:
Baby, baby
Drive me crazy
Make the pussy go:

Mo went bonkers for her new body. How she had grown his woman-child, his shorty doo-wop.

The Soul, Sally showed Mo, was alive and well. It was in her bump and grind, her up and down, her 'round and 'round. It was in the heat of her lips when she hovered over him and kissed him, gluing him to her. Mo the maneless lion, a pinkish scab paralleling his hairline from the starry fracture spot to the top of the left ear. "I miss grabbing your hair," Sally whispered in the thick of it. "It used to be one of my favorite things."

"Wow," Mo said when they were finished — what else but "wow" was there to say? It's not like she hadn't warned him. He had been anxious about tonight's date, calling her twice at work to make sure she was going to be able to make it.

"I'm glad we're back together." Mo said as he parked in front of 168.
"We're not," Sally corrected him.
"We're not? Why not?"
"I owed you something," Sally said. "And now we're even. Kind of."
He thought he understood: "You're still angry. But I can explain why I never came to see you after that night. I had enough time to think about it, believe me. In that hospital bed, especially. There are a lot of things I will do differently."
She was interested in what he had to say, despite having made up her mind long ago. "Like what?"
"Making you first, for one. It's not easy to be an African firstborn: A lot is expected of you. The responsibility I felt toward my sister got in the way of what you and I were doing. What we were building. It was too much. When you left, a part of me was relieved to let go of some of the weight. But now..."
"I would have helped," Sally objected. "The

worst was behind us. The hard part, I mean. I was getting on my feet, I was willing to do my share.... I don't see what happened as a money problem, you know. You just weren't sure what you wanted."

"I wasn't," Mo admitted. "But I am now. And you don't know the full story.... Coming to this country, meeting you, living with you and your son ... it all made me become a very different person. A better person. You helped me as much as I helped you."

Mo took Sally's face between his palms. His hands were burning like fire. "I love you," he said.

Sally opened the door and ran toward the house. "I'm sorry!" she shouted. "I'm sorry...."

She hid upstairs, surveying the street. Mo didn't leave immediately. He remained slumped in his seat for a good ten minutes, as if driving had become too much of an effort. Maybe he just didn't want to go home. Maybe going back to the single life, the lonely life, was too much.

Mo wouldn't deorbit, hardheaded as he was, and so Sally had to sit him down and break it down to him. It came out like a speech, wooden and scripted and highroad. "It's not me, Sally, you saw when we met. It's my big belly. It's baby Eli. You didn't go with me despite the pregnancy but because of it. The stuff that happened to you in your childhood —and the trauma it caused—defines you more than anything else. You want to help save all at-risk kids, be they unborn, be it an impossible task. That's who you are. That's what you do. You wanted Eli and me to be safe and have everything we needed. You wanted Eli to have a chance, or at least a good start. The start you never had...." Sally started to cry. "It was noble, Mo. It was laudable. But it wasn't love. Not my kind of love, anyway. It was ... some sort of experiment. Or maybe you just saw need and you reached out without thinking about what you were getting yourself into. And, like you said, it got to be too much. I have a lot of baggage, it's true. And then there's your family. When she came, Aster took priority. She's the reason you're here, after all. You're blazing a path for her. You're giving her a new life, a new country. You're opening a whole new world of opportunities."

Mo thought he had Sally figured out, too. "I could argue that you didn't see me for me, either. I could say that I meant everything you were lacking. I could say that each and every one of your moves was planned."

"You're starting to sound like Chi-Chi," Sally said. "I'm not that calculating. No conspiracy, no intricate plot. I saw something I liked and I went for it. Bottom line. We all have reasons to want who and what we want. You've got yours, I've got mine. It's enough that we gave it a shot. I was actually psyched to get your number that day at the store. I was scared, too. Stephanie's the one who called and booked that first Takoma date. How planned was that?"

"You should believe me when I say I love you."

"You want to redeem me. That's not love. That's something else."

"You can't have one without the rest, can you? Loving, helping, caring ... same package."

Sally's attitude soared so high her ears started to whistle and turn red. "I can care for my own damn self, thank you very much. Sorry for taking that chance away from you. Heroes ain't in such big demand any more. You know why? They let you down just the same. I found out the hard way."

"But..." Mo went on. "But..."

They talked about it a few more times. Mo sure had come a long way since the day the dance began. There was no denying that his affection and his longing were genuine. He wanted to make it work, and so he tried to come up with fresh ideas: live together, help Aster get her own place, send Sally off to school, raise Eli, have another baby, walk into the sunset. And he did put some effort behind his vision, trying to woo Sally with sweet talk and flowers and chocolate boxes and Alcalys and mixtapes and space gear. Sally didn't budge. Mo lost all sense of shame and tried to use her dream—the premonition, the ESP. "It was a sign," he proclaimed. "Allah wants us to be together. You're destined to be my wife."

Sally thought she had misheard. "Allah who?"

"Same one be in heaven."

"What happened to 'No God'?"

Mo grinned with mischief. "That's only half the sentence. It's really 'No God but Allah.'"

"Are you trying to tell me something?"

Mo nodded. "I saw the light when my life was in the skinny kid's hands. The chances of me dying right then and there seemed pretty high. The only thing that came to my mind was, Pray, pray, pray. The Fatiha—the Koran's very first verse—came back to me in a flash. I recited it over and over. And I've been a good little Muslim ever since."

Sally was skeptical. "Good for you, Mo. Existentialists did seem like a dying breed, but Islam is definitely on the up and up. You're on the winning team."

"I'm supposed to abstain from fornication..."

"I have no problem helping you with that."

"But I think about you night and day..."

"Sounds like a personal issue to me."

"Now if we did get married..."

Sally's palms turned into a stop sign. "Don't even go there."

"But the dream..."

"Was no blueprint: just a dream. It means we're connected, me and you. Or that I'm good at that thing..."

"ESP."
"There you go."

Mo's window of opportunity shrank to unsustainable proportions. It became a feat of superhuman ability to be able to sneak in the littlest kiss or tender word or intimate thought—they bounced right back. "Give him some," Rudy interceded, "so he can stop looking like a whipped dog."

Grandma rooted for Mo as well. "The man just got his head split open, for God's sake! Of course he's desperate for a taste. Can't you be nice to him? I hate to see him begging like that."

Rene blamed Sally for Mo's condition. In her eyes Sally had been too heavy-handed in doling out her brown sugar. "You shouldn't have worked him like you did in that motel room. That stuff be powerful. Now he's dazed and confused, lost in the memory, hooked for life."

Sally shrugged. "I was only trying to make it up to him for not stopping Chevon. Guess it backfired. Oops."

Mo hung in there as long as his diminishing pride and his breath allowed him to. He took his favorite portrait of Sally (a C.T.U. ponytail and white T-shirt summer day snapshot on which she looked enticingly copper in the afternoon light and mysterious and bewitching and good enough to eat and, well, superfine), had it blown up and framed, and made it—take that, Aster--the one object decorating his living room wall. He got "Sally" tattooed in cursive on his right shoulder, newfound religion and common sense be damned. He stood awake many a night trying to find the right words, the perfect move, the winning pitch. But once Sally pronounced that fatal sentence of hers, "That's all she wrote," Mo knew there was no need to insist. "Friends?" he proposed.

"Friends," Sally readily agreed.

Mo braced himself. "So you have somebody new?"

She took it easy on him. "Yes and no."

"Who is he?" he insisted.

"Sure you wanna know?" she asked, mindful of his bleeding heart.

"I can take the pain," Mo affirmed, a man's man at his best.

She told him.

He did take it well, asking if she was sure. She said yes, before commenting, You don't even seem surprised. The man you're choosing sits on impossibly high moral ground, Mo declared: His claim to the prize is righteous and nearly undeniable. I think so, too, Sally concurred. You've got a lot of work to do, Mo added. I'm aware of that, Sally told him.

"You understand what it means?" Mo asked.
Sally nodded. "Time for boot camp."
"I know camps," Mo said. "And I know journeys. Will you accept my expertise?"
"Gladly."

They shook hands, wrote a five-point list, devised a strategy, and set a deadline for midsummer.

It was to be Sally's third or fourth new beginning in as many years. They called the venture GOAL, for Get Out At Last. Not everybody was in the know, but when the lucky few asked, "Out of what?" Sally took the pain to enumerate: "Out of the ghetto; out of poverty; out of ignorance; out of self-defeatism."
"Good luck," the lucky few invariably said, and, "More power to you."

The ground to cover was dreadful in its immensity and arduousness. Sally and Mo took a step back and gazed at the range. "This is serious business," Mo told her, his reincarnation as wizened mountain elder close to perfection. "This is about leaving all the negative forces behind. This is shaking you free of the tentacles of oppression. This is wiping your template clean and writing your own fate. You, my friend, are at a crossroads. THE crossroads. You shall rely on five S through your endeavor: Self-discipline; Self-knowledge; Self-reliance; Sacrifice; and the Soul. Especially the Soul. May it be with you always. May your gaze be steady and your footstep assured. May your heart pump no Kool-Aid. May your mind open up. May your spirit soar."

In other words, Mo resolved to try and teach Sally everything he knew. He became the big brother, the mentor she had never had. The method was simple: They pondered obvious, wide-open, all-encompassing questions such as, What are the skills necessary in order to survive and thrive in today's world, and, What makes a good and decent human being, and, Where do I want to be six months from now, and, How do I get there, and, Who's coming with me? They pondered all those questions and set out to find the best way to answer them.

G.O.A.L. quickly took shape as a three-pronged entity whose components Sally and Mo identified as Character Building, Tools, and People. The first element, Character Building, comprised such subsections as Ethics, Discipline, Blackness, Fitness, Accountability, Responsibility, Values, Religion, Spirituality, Volunteering, Diversity, and Citizenry. Tools was an eclectic mix as well: Scheduling, Planning, Education, Health (physical and mental), Etiquette, Parenting, Attitude, Speech,

Social Skills, Budgeting, Homemaking, Personal Finances, Matrimony, Close Combat, and Appearance. People was all Relationships: family, guilt, brotherhood, motherhood, the ties that bind, friends, loyalty, backstabbing, jealousy, holding back, letting go.

GOAL was an ambitious program. Some people—may the Soul crush all naysayers, nonbelievers, hypocrites, and their acolytes—might have deemed it overambitious and amalgamative.

"It boils down to this," Mo pointed out: "What you're going to be doing every day. What time you wake up. What you have planned. What needs to be accomplished. How you acquit yourself of your different tasks and responsibilities. How your actions and thoughts meet your short- and long-term goals. Which means, basically, that you need to be on a schedule..."

"I can do that."

"...and that incorporated in that schedule must be each component and sub-component of GOAL."

"That's trickier."

"Indeed."

"The 'boot camp' part of boot camp."

They both took a deep, deep breath. "Ready?"

"Ready."

Sally started to get up each day at six, good night or bad night. She cooked breakfast for the household. She studied for her GED while everybody was asleep. She washed and clothed and fed Eli and Tyree and played with them after they woke up, wrote if she could manage, gathered her local and mainstream media news from *The Post* and her alternative news from WPFW. She then prepared lunch. When Rene came home Sally caught the bus to her job, reading all the way in and on the way back as well. Then came dinner, fooling around with the kids some more, and more studying after they had gone to bed. Coolidge's track at the crack of dawn three times a week with Mo. Quizzes on Thursdays and Sundays—her days off—as well as workshops and seminars, visits to museums, libraries, and free computer centers. "Idleness," Mo told her, "is thy enemy." The only shopping they did was for Tools: a good dictionary, finally, the "Chicago Manual of Style," a watch, an alarm clock, a book bag, school supplies, the "New York Public Library Desk Reference." Mo had his eyes on Britannica but Sally wouldn't let him embark on the purchase, reminding him that she was on the go. He did, however, get her subscriptions to *The New Yorker* and *The New York Review of Books*, at the risk of overwhelming her. "Do what you can," he told her. "As long as you get the idea. These are all basic things that are expected of you: build yourself up, inform yourself, acquire skills, know what's out there, understand what the ground you walk on and the air you breathe are made of. The point is to make a decent showing in this race called Life, and not to embarrass yourself while you're at it. GOAL, my dear, is a lifelong pursuit."

Soon Sally felt confident enough to show Mo her manuscript. Laid out page after page were her world and her people. The story was low on bitterness and self-righteousness; neither oversimplified nor dramatic; unadulterated and unsweetened; all true. Mo saw promise. "The only thing," he said, "is to find your own voice and to listen to it. That's the golden rule, corny as it sounds."

"How do I achieve that?"

"Practice. They say it takes about 10,000 hours. And intense, sustained focus."

"So there's hope, you think?"

Mo nodded. "Watch your punctuation—you tend to write the way you speak. There are such things as dots and commas. I'll advise you to keep the "Chicago Manual of Style"—it's the orange, brick-like book we just bought you—closest to your heart. It's a writer's best friend, the guiding light, the ultimate, the Shangri-La. Tough read at times, definitely weighty, but worth every pound, I'd say. Gain knowledge and biceps at the same time. You'll never be wrong or skinny again."

Sally's ears started to burn. Critique is never easy on a novice's spirit and good intentions. Critique is only light on undiscerning, unkind, and unperceptive dispensers. Critique stings and jabs and chokes. "You're killing me."

"Better grow a thick skin, baby. My comments are nothing compared to what agents and editors will take you through. Love everything you commit to paper. Be proud of it. Defend it tooth and nail. But try and manage to look at it with a detached eye. Know how to let it go when necessary."

Sally thought it prudent to switch subjects. "How's your own stuff going?"

Mo made a so-so gesture with his hand. "I kind of lost track during my stay at the hospital. Got myself a computer but now the ideas are gone. I'm taking a sabbatical."

"Don't give up."

"I won't. I can't. For the sake of literature and humanity as a whole, I must acquit myself of my mission."

The irony of things didn't escape Mo. Soon, it seemed, the student might surpass the master. He had always thought Sally smart, but more of a street-smart kind of smart. He saw now that she had what it took to succeed on the academic and professional levels as well. His job might get reduced to keeping her motivated, to throwing riddles her way in order to keep her focused. "Unstoppable," he complimented her. "That's what you're going to be. They won't see you coming." He made himself a mental note to add courses on Empowerment, Sexism, Glass Ceilings, and Harassment to her curriculum.

When they tackled GOAL's human element Amad was near the top of their priorities, second only to Eli. "How are his numbers?" Mo asked.
"Up in attendance and grades," Sally reported. "Up also in behavior."
"What's he clocking at?"
She consulted her notes. "3.4"
"What's the problem?"
"Math. Can't blame him on that: it's in the genes. Going

through the same thing myself. If I flunk the GED it'll be because of it."

"No excuses. I'll tutor the both of you at the same time."

"Thank you."

"Back to Amad: Do you know his friends?"

"His friends, their mothers, their home addresses and phone numbers."

"Teachers?"

"They all have 168's coordinates."

"Girlfriend?"

"No."

"Look better. There's gotta be something. They're sneaky at that age. You must *chercher la femme*. Talk to him about sex yet?"

"I did. When did you learn to speak French?"

"I don't speak French. That's one of those sayings that belong to the world's patrimony—know how to drop them and you instantly look sophisticated as hell. Make sure Amad gets the point, all right? How are we doing on cigarettes and weed?"

"Grandma sniffs his shirts; she searches his pockets. I'll know if and when he starts using. The boy will never be able to fool me."

Mo remembered something just as they were getting ready to move on. "There's a legal issue with Amad, isn't there? The guardianship transfer?"

"Grandma and Rudy are okay with it. I already have steady employment. All I need to complete my paperwork is a lease on a two-bedroom bearing my name."

"We'll work on that."

"There's plenty of time," Sally concurred.

"So we're in good shape?"

"We are."

They took a break.
"Who's next?"

Sally went back to her notes. "Rudy."
"That's a tough one."
"Tell me about it."
"How is she?"
"Problematic as always."
"The basement?"
"Got her a fan. A big one."
"Smoke detector light?"
"Still green."
"Any luck on programs?"
"Plenty of them around. She won't go."
"What's *she* clocking at?"
"$30 a day. I refuse to go any higher."
"That's more than enough. Any possibilities?"
"None that I can think of."
"We have to find a way."
"I'll just turn my back. How's that for a way?"
"You can't. That's Mom we're talking about."
"Just kidding. She's got a special friend."
"She do?"
"Name of Greg. Shoplifts, shoots up, goes to sleep."
"How do you feel about that?"
"I don't like it the least bit."
"Jealous?"
"A little."
"Rudy needs love, too."
"I know."
"Think Greg knows her status?"
"He's got a status of his own."
"Oh, boy. Can Rudy get pregnant?"
"Always a possibility."
"Oh, boy."

"I'll just kick Greg out. Tell him he can't come around. How's that?"

"Oh, boy."

Something dawned on Sally. "How did you find out that Rudy's sick?"

Mo looked her in the eye. "People told me everything about you, Rodney, and your family as soon as they saw the two of us talking. No, I won't name names, so don't insist. Rudy's HIV was one of 1,001 reasons why, according to those well-intentioned souls, I shouldn't mess with you. I kicked all of them out of the store."

Sally lowered her gaze. "Sorry for not telling you myself."

Mo rubbed her cheek with his thumb. "I understand."

Rene was next. Not that there was much to say.

"Housing?"

"Still waiting."

"Tyree?"

"Still bad."

"Old men?"

"She's been taking a break since the C.T.U. security guard."

"Money?"

"She's saving up. Same as me. That's the good thing about Rudy's voucher: free rent. Rene and I split the bills and that's it."

"Sweet Thang?"

"Gone, just like Chi-Chi."

"That means Rene has no support system outside of you."

"Rene's a grown woman. She'll survive. We all

have to be on our own sooner or later."

There was one person left. "How's my Sally?"
"Maintaining."
"Tell me when it gets to be too much."
"So far, so good."
"Still thinking about getting out?"
"Still."
"I'm gonna be busy for the next month or so. Hiwot found a gas station for me near Gallaudet. Financing went through. They start training me in ten days."
"I'm happy for you."
"Can I get a pound?"
She hammered his closed fist. He hammered hers. They bumped knuckles, slapped palms, snapped fingers, and pointed their right index at each other. "Got your back," Sally said.
"Got your back," Mo repeated.

Mo asked Sally to interview him in order to prepare himself for the deluge of public attention threatening to overpower him soon after the publication of "Searcher," even though, by his own account, the book was nowhere near completion. "You have to practice those things," he explained. "Early. The more you do it, the better you get. I want to be ready for the flashes and microphones and nosy questions. Same way I be thinking every day about ways to spend and not to spend my seven-figure advance and subsequent royalties."

They were sitting face to face in a soul food joint near Howard University, a crushed meal between them. Sally was game. "Just tell me what to do."

"It doesn't have to be friendly at all: Push me hard, no holds barred. Never mind that I'm this huge star, this literary phenom breaking all kinds of records. You're a gifted MTV journalist, fresh and cute and popular. Rapid-fire style, ambush tactics, killer smile, plunging neckline. You're fleshing me out for the hordes of screaming fans waiting outside the Times Square studio. We're live, of course."

"Of course. Why MTV?"

"I'm the mouthpiece of my generation. Instant name and face recognition. Instant. I've got all the kids reading. Nerds are hip again thanks to this guy named Mo. My books matter."

Sally closed her eyes. When she opened them back up she was in character. 22-year-old Leila, highly paid onscreen personality, educated enough to have credibility with upper management, street enough to have an edge, adored in the 15-to-35 demographic, Hollywood ambitions of her own. Golden hues gracing her skin, flowing curls, brains behind the painted face and pouting lips, perfect Crest Kid teeth, a slightly nasal but soothing voice, shiny nails to hold the mic, bangles, chic blouse with one shoulder out, designer skinny jeans, designer open-toes. Easy on the lighting inside the studio. Audience on bleachers. A tan-colored couch. View on Broadway and the hordes through a huge glass panel. Rain outside. No, make that drizzle. Drizzle outside and pretty lights.

It went something like this:

__So the pressure is on. You're this writer with crossover appeal. More like a hip-hop star, really. Most Valuable Writer two years in a row plus a bevy of minor awards. Sweeping them clean. How planned was this?

__As planned as MTV branching out into literature and the movies. It's all love. A man's got to follow his dream. Blueprints help.

__Your work is liberally peppered with references to the Soul, and black America's culture in general. Yet you weren't born in this country. How do you know so much? How legit are you?

__I take offense to that. I'm as legit as God made me. There isn't a subject I haven't studied, a place I haven't visited in my mind. I'm free to appropriate any identity, expression, or attribute that I deem fit. Once it's mine I can change it, use it, put it back into the world, pass it on. That's what artists do. If I can get enough mileage out of a Public Enemy line to write a whole book, then it should be, More power to Mo, no?

__Fair enough. What defines Mo the person? Is it Mog, the hometown you fled in the midst of a civil war? Is it Dadaab refugee camp? Is it Washington, D.C., your adopted home?

__I'm the quintessential immigrant. Came from nothing. I clenched my teeth and put in work. Always on the humble. Car washes, burger joints, corner stores, street sweeping ... I did it all. It took me about twelve years, but here I am.

__What kept you going?

__An all-consuming drive to accomplish things. As a man, you want to go and do stuff. Not just survive, but thrive, achieve, build. It's personal gain. It's pride. It's the people depending on you. It's the plight of the needy. It's the larger global issues affecting not just everyday life but the future, our children, civilization as a whole, the planet. You want to say things that matter. You want to do good. You want to help bring about a better world. You want to leave a decent track record.

__Much has been made of your spiritual forays. You've been linked to Social Scientism, Existentialism, Buddhism, and now Islam.

__"Searcher": that's me.

__Your take on racism?

__Something that shouldn't exist, but does. You have to mock it. Once you take it and turn it on its head people realize how stupid the whole thing is. That was my whole reason for doing "Better Will Come."

__Writing rituals?

__None. I carry a pen and a notebook wherever I go. The antenna's always up. I've written in walk-in boxes, meat freezers, warehouses, grocery store aisles and back rooms, gas station booths, speeding cars, concert halls, restaurants, tow trucks, and hospital beds. Wouldn't dream of emulating Proust or the paralyzed French dude who wrote that "Diving Bell" novel using only his eyelids and pinkies, but you get the drift.

__Any advice for unpublished writers?

__Want it. Want it so bad it keeps you up at night. Want it until it almost drives you crazy. Want it until you become a force unto yourself. Study the game. Know the players. Pay your dues. Pray for luck.

__The endorsements controversy?

__Product placement has been around for years and years. Don't blame the commercialization of literature on me. I take notes with Mont Blanc, type on my Mac, sit at an Ikea desk, untie my ultralight Nike track shoes with the neon air bubble, check the time on my Tag Heuer, drink 16oz Deer Park water, snack on Planters. So do my characters.

__You cosigned a Nike-hugging statement with Michael Jordan to give the corporation a much-needed facelift at the darkest hour of the sweatshops scandal.

__Beaverton got caught doing dirty. No denying the problem. Phil Knight personally assured Mike and me that the wrongs would be rectified.

__Excessive branding has also surfaced as an issue.

__I'm not the one with a Swoosh forehead tattoo.

__You've been spotted training with the Washington Wizards.

__I like the relentlessness and determination of pro athletes. Artists at the top of their game can be just as physical. The only reason Marvin Gaye didn't play with the Detroit Lions is that their insurance company backed off.

__Mike Tyson is another good friend. Both he and Jordan happened to publish best-selling autobiographies last year. Your critics, and theirs, call the coincidence improbable. They see your hand, your talent behind those two books.

__*Les chiens aboient. La caravane passe.*

__The beef with Pelecanos?

__Squashed.... I was after the Top D.C. Writer crown. Pelecanos seemed an easier target than that Alcaly guy, who's so underground nobody's ever met him. And Pelecanos, his stories start to sound so much alike after a while—you know, killers and guns and detectives and pushers and addicts and snitches and The Stylistics ... it was becoming embarrassing, embarrassing—the guy used to be my hero, for God's sake. And then Little, Brown, they hook him up with second-rate editors who allow the stuff to come out with typos in it, [bleep] typos, mind you, and all kinds of mistakes. Like, one of Pelecanos's rare white characters, an ex-police officer who ends up getting killed, I think Quinn was the guy's name.... This Quinn, he gets in a Chevelle one day to go bother some project kids down in Southeast D.C., to ask questions around and what have you. The Chevelle, it has a nice chrome grill on it, see what I mean? A "grill," not a "grille," and by the time Quinn arrives to his destination the car has become a Caprice. Unimaginable things like that! So all I did was walk up to Pelecanos at a book expo down at the Convention Center and say to his face what most people were saying behind his back, which is, "George, you're slippin'." He took it the wrong way and said something back to me in Greek. Now I don't understand Greek, but I know when someone is cursing me out, and so I cursed right back, in plain English, and that's when we got to swinging. The *Post* ran a story on it. People started to pay attention. More mistakes were exhumed in my man's workload. And I think the public appreciated the fact that I didn't pull the race card on him even though he was wide open. Wide open. Guess who's on top now....

_Tell us about your scars.

_War wounds. Mog, Kalashs, RPGs.... I saw my share of action. Stuff you wouldn't believe.

__You live a very private life. People voted you Sexiest Bachelor Alive in the under-thirty group category. When you're not wearing glasses, that is.

__Not my fault. The woman I love, she left me, which makes me—I guess you can call me a bachelor. Nothing sexy about that, though I've accepted People's nomination gracefully and I plan to accept it next year as well. Truth is, I'm alone. Alone in the wilderness. Alone until the girl comes back to her senses. Baby, I know you're watching. I miss you and that's for real for real. I should have told you I love you. I should have stuck with you. I'm still available, baby. Let's do this.

__You've conquered the publishing and movie worlds. What's the next frontier?

__Marriage. That's the hardest thing to get right nowadays. Marriage, family, and children. You've seen the numbers? All those broken homes.... Makes you want to give up before you even try.

__Closing words?

__When everything is said and done, this is what I want to be remembered by: He wrote stories that didn't suck; Something great took place in his lifetime and he was part of it.

__This is your host Leila. You've been watching MTV's "Iconz of Our Dayz." Thank you, Mo.

__Thanks for having me.

__ We're out.

The wildest thing Sally and Mo did together after the earthshaking motel romp was to ride the Impala too fast and scrape a row of parked cars on 16th. Mo was teaching Sally how to drive.

"That's what you call a crash course," he muttered as he surveyed the damage. Exhilarated, Sally jumped on his back and covered his neck with I'm-so-sorry kisses before they wrote a bunch of notes and left them on the damaged cars' windshields. It was early May. Sally had obtained her diploma at the third attempt and they were out sort of celebrating. Mo was growing his bush back. His uptown groupies still found him cute, calling him Curly Top. Sally thought otherwise. "You know the difference between a good haircut and a bad one?" she asked.

"Money?" Mo suggested.

"Three months," Sally said.

Had it really been that long? They were all on different grooves. Mo and Aster were taking turns in the booth, whose setup and day-to-day operations were vastly different from the Amoco's. Barely any shelves, no coolers, no foot traffic, no shoplifting, no gas theft. "Half the business, half the headache," is how Mo described it. He refused to stock glass stems, cigars, pipes, rolling paper, and the mini Ziploc bags used to parcel out coke, weed, heroin, and crack—his was a booth with a conscience. When they weren't working, Aster went to school and Mo wrote and volunteered at Martha's Table up 14th, mostly because he wanted to keep in touch with the kids he had gotten to know at the Amoco. When news spread that the city wanted to shut down Clifton Street's Boys and Girls Club, Mo took part in the No More Condos grassroots protest and even got to say a piece on the "Donnie Simpson Show." "Community involvement" became a constant part of his vocabulary. "Mo loves the kids" was also a favorite of his.

    He got better with Eli. Learned how to get down on his knees and scuttle around, funny faces and funny noises all the while. Eli got really attached to him, too. A very good hugger, he would wrap his arms around Mo's neck and stick the top of his head under Mo's chin and just kind of stay there as if this were the place to be, the best spot on earth. "I'm gonna miss this when you're gone," Mo always said.
    "You can come visit," Sally invariably assured him. "Anytime."

    They spoke every day and saw each other several times a week. Sally was getting closer to the July deadline and looking good on her balance sheet, too. Everything was on track. She hadn't stopped at the GED, considering it a mere stepping stone toward her next goal: a real estate license. It took a little arm-twisting, but Mo obtained a lease in Sally's name from his landlords. Sally bought cable service for the Tuckerman basement and had a couple of other bills mailed there. Those documents and her pay stubs, brand-new degree, and proof of enrollment in the real estate program got her custody of Amad after the basement passed inspection. It was no small victory.

Sally become a different person. Her hair grew back in the middle. She lost her baby fat. She started to dress more like a young woman. She worried less.

At Brenda's place for Mother's Day, she got to speak to Rodney for the first time in a long time. He had called to wish his mother a good one and here was Sally, all shy and embarrassed and hesitant. It was very awkward, at least at first. "How's things?" Rodney asked.

"Better," Sally said. "What's good with you?"

"Thinking about becoming a Muslim."

"I hear it's the new thing."

"Thanks for taking good care of our son," he went on, not getting the joke. "Brenda's been telling me."

"I'm tryin'," Sally answered modestly.

Rodney took a deep breath. "I never apologized," he said. "Guess this is as good a time as any."

"For what?"

"Everything. Not listening to you. Wrecking your life. Leaving you out there to fend for yourself."

Sally wondered if those were tears in his voice. Memories of the two of them filled her mind. The movies. C.T.U. Her first red roses—how funny she had felt holding the bouquet. No more than little kids. What did they know? She had been so alone. So lost. So scared. "I forgave you a long time ago. Do you forgive me for not sticking by you?"

"That was selfish of me to ask. Nobody should have to put up with that. You're young. I want you to be happy. As for Eli ... I trust your judgment. Do what you think is best until I come home to do my share. I'll try and be in his life as much as I can from the inside. We'll find ways."

Sally felt herself crying. "I might come see you."

Rodney laughed despite himself. "Yeah, right."

"I'm for serious."

"Don't tease."

"Just watch," Sally said.

"Love you," Rodney told her.

"Love you, too," she answered.

She gave Ben the phone and hurried home to try and keep the promise she had made Amad to do something with Rudy for the holiday.

They didn't venture farther than the McDonald's on Rhode Island. Sally thought it was because Rudy disliked being in public (the telltale signs and symptoms of her addiction were readily visible, now more than ever, and people stared and sneered and whispered). Could have been mere paranoia: Her sister, Ella, had been arrested for possession with intent a few days ago. "We could have gone shopping," Sally told her mother as they sat across from each other. "I wanted to buy you clothes."

"Just give me the money," Rudy suggested in her hoarse voice.

Sally gave her the $100 she'd set aside without second thoughts, for once. "Happy Mother's Day, Ma."

"Thank you, baby."

Amad pulled a card from his jacket and gave it to her. Tears fell from Rudy's eyes when she read aloud the poem he'd written, something straight out of 2Pac. It made Sally sad to see her mother struggle to make sense of the words. Eli was surprisingly quiet. He didn't try to wrest himself from his uncle's embrace to go explore the floor.

Nobody was hungry. They ordered light, nibbled, and took their time walking home. Sally was glad they hadn't gone to the mall after all. The crowds, the lights, the forced enthusiasm.

She, Mo, Rene, and the boys were at the Laundromat when the cops raided 168 and plucked Rudy from the basement three weeks later. It's good that nobody was there to see it. "It would have broken your heart," Mr. Arnold, the retired teacher who lived next door, told Sally.

Sally didn't cry, contrarily to all the other times Rudy had been hauled away. Nobody said a thing, come to think of it. They all remained quiet as they lugged the trash bags full of fresh clothes to the second floor. Tyree went to lie down. Eli picked up a toy truck and pushed it around the same corner over and over. Mo excused himself after Sally assured him that she and Rene could take care of the mess the cops had left behind. The first thing she did was check on Rodney's gun. She found it where she had stashed it. "Let's start with the basement," she told Rene after handing her a pair of gloves. "Watch out for syringes."

She gave Rudy three weeks before going to

see her down at D.C. Jail, enough time for her to kick heroin and pick herself up a little. It was a drag that they couldn't touch or sit next to each other. "You look good," Sally told her mother. "Gaining weight and looking healthier already. Your cheeks are full."

Rudy didn't waste time on niceties. "It was you who snitched," she accused Sally. "You turned me in to the police, didn't you?"

Sally didn't flinch. "Don't say things like that. You're my mother. I would never turn my back on you."

Rudy's eyes burned a hole into the partition. "I know it, Sally. I feel it in my gut. You can lie all you want.... I made you, remember?"

"Whatever."

"Dirty bitch."

Sally took the high road. "Do you want me to leave? I'm missing work to come see you and this is how you treat me, this is the thank you I get?.... Fucking accusations?"

"You did it!" Rudy shouted. "To park me somewhere before you roll. It's all a part of your plan!"

"If anybody did it, you're the one. What, you thought Five-O would never catch up with you? How dumb do they gotta be?"

Rudy wasn't done. "It's all your fault anyway. I knew I should have never signed for that house."

Sally shrugged. "What's done is done, Ma. Try and make the best of it."

Rudy shook her head. "My own daughter.... Ain't that some shit." She slammed the phone on the receiver and left.

"She'll get over it," Sally assured everybody.

They went to check on Rene's new apartment the next day. It was on the eighth floor of Temple Courts, the Sursum Corda projects' only high-rise. Teenagers crowding the sidewalks at noon. Women in slippers and do-rags and bonnets and shower caps. Cars honking and double-parking. Predatory eyes scanning each new face, each passerby. The vibe of an open-air, anything-goes market. "Deja vu," Sally said.

"Deja knew," Rene corrected.

The inside of the building wasn't as bad as they had feared. "The elevators work? Are these people for real?"

Rene took an instant liking to the place, mainly because it was hers and hers alone. "Finally," she said. They sat in the middle of the living room floor and switched furniture around in their minds. The voices of Tyree and Eli covered the hallway noises. "The kids like it, too."

Sally went back to see Rudy ten days before her departure. She found her in a much better disposition. Maybe the money order deposited into her commissary account had helped improve her spirits. Maybe it was the methadone they were giving her. "I still think you did it," she told Sally. "But I ain't mad no more."

"Good," Sally said. "'Cause it's my last time seeing you for a long while."

"Never thought you would actually leave," Rudy said. "I know you've been talking about it for months, but..."

"It's not you I'm leaving," Sally assured her. "It's this town."

Rudy nodded. "You're doing the right thing. This motherfucker sucks your soul right out of you."

"You can come join us when you're ready," Sally proposed. "I meant to tell you."

"Down there with them racist sons of bitches?"

Sally laughed. "It's not that bad."

"Write and tell me how you like it. Then we'll see."

Sally looked at her mother intensely. "Take care of yourself, hear? I want you to be around for Eli. And Amad. And me."

Rudy held her gaze. "I'll try," she said. "Don't know if I can beat this shit or no, but I'll try."

They got up. The partition stood in the way of their kiss but they gave it their best shot anyway. Rudy had one last thing to say. "You might think it's just old fucked-up Rudy running her mouth, but I want you to know I'm proud of you. Sorry for being such a sorry-ass mom."

Sally felt something open up inside of her. She didn't know how to describe it. Only that it felt good, it felt light, it felt peaceful. "It only made me a stronger person," she said.

Her last two days were devoted to goodbyes. Sally disposed of Rodney's gun in the Anacostia river. She emptied 168 and gave away everything she possessed (such was the nomad's way) except for her books, which were left for Mo to ship after she got settled. The notebook was traveling with her, of course. She dared not leave it behind.

"Got a name for your novel yet?" Mo asked.

"'Skillet,'" she announced. "The title of my favorite band's latest CD."

"Backyard?"

Sally nodded. "I hope Big G and them won't mind."

"I was thinking 'Guanguanco,'" Mo said.

"What's that?"

"A Latin rhythm. Gil Scott-Heron swears it symbolizes rebirth and regeneration. Thought it might be appropriate, with you going from one phase of your life to the next and all."

Sally laughed. "I'm gonna stick to my guns."

She hugged her grandmother. She told Rene she loved her. She scratched Tyree's head. She packed two bags. Three if you counted Amad's backpack.

Their bus left early on a Saturday morning. Mo drove them to the terminal behind Union Station. They were fifth in line. It was exciting just to be there and smell the air. "Keep an eye on your sister," Mo told Amad. "You know her attitude be gettin' her in trouble."

"I will," Amad promised dutifully.

Mo and Sally left him with the bags and went to sit for a while. "You should have flown," Mo said.

"Takes the romance out of it," Sally answered. "And it sounds like something Aster might say."

Brenda and Ben came to see them off. "How gutsy of you to go," Brenda commented.

"It's now or never," Sally acknowledged.

Ben's depression seemed to have improved. He still limped badly, but he declared himself happy with his warehouse job. "I run the forklift with my good foot." Mo and he didn't speak or make eye contact even as they stood at the snack counter together. Macho, macho men.

"I'm holding his paychecks for him," Brenda said of her younger son. "He wants a car. As soon as the money amounts to something I'm putting a deposit on a one-bedroom in Maryland. Ben's moving away. Ready or not, like it or not."

"Ain't you going with him?"

She shook her head. "I like my place fine. If I

ever leave it'll be for a house. Ben's gonna have to learn to be on his own."

Brenda kissed Eli and played with him for five good minutes. "Time to go," she finally decided.

Nobody had thought about bringing a camera. "Stay in touch," they all told one another.

Mo, Sally, and Eli got closer to the line. Sally started to get butterflies. New state. New town. New life. She had no idea what she was in for, what she was going to find. All she had was Eli, Amad, a few bundles of clothes, food for the trip, and enough cash to last her three months. "When are you coming to see us?" she asked Mo.
"October," he told her for the tenth time.

The bus pulled up. Fifteen minutes later passengers got the OK and started to embark. Mo held and kissed Eli before handing him to Amad, who took him to their seats.

Sally and Mo stepped out of the line. She had one last question for him: "Do you think I'm like my mother?"
"You're nothing like your mother," he replied. "Nothing at all." She wrapped her arms around his neck. He started to give her his cheek but she kissed him full on the lips. Mo from Mog. Glasses, skinny as ever, beard, curly top. Lover, mentor, ally, guide.
"Thank you for everything," Sally whispered.
He looked at her. Sally the redbone (she hated when people called her that). Hair pulled back, slanted eyes, full lips, full nose, full cheeks, white T-shirt, jeans, running shoes. "Thank you, too," Mo said in turn.

She turned to look at him from the top of the steps. I'm glad to know you, she told him in her head. Friends like you are what we all wish for.

Seeker

Amad came looking for me one day in September. I should say "us," for Eli was still with me. Kind of there but not really. It's hard to look back and see him in the picture fully. Walking like a big boy now. A few words, "daddy" not one of them. Growing up in the fringes. Dirty, snotty, whiny, always hungry. Chips and juice and Happy Meal toys. Only half dressed if we stayed in. Left to mind his own. Locked in a room if we had to roll and nobody could babysit. I took care of him when I remembered. Other people did, too. Juliet. Rene. Willie. Neighbors. Tyree never came back. Rene didn't seem to care. We were having too much fun, busy doing nothing. Snorting. Smoking. Chasing. Drinking. Clubbing. High after high after high.

It was almost funny, the way I looked square into my brother's face without recognizing him. He was growing his hair. His eyes had turned from green to brown. Pimples dotted his forehead. More bass in his voice. "You never called," he said plaintively, accusingly. "I waited and waited. What, you just forgot about me?" He was worried to death. Didn't know what I was up to. Didn't know where Rene lived. Just that name: Temple Courts. He came anyway. Waited around. Talked to people. Found me.

I had trouble meeting his eye. Could he tell I was using? What did he see when he looked at my face, the room, the apartment? I perfunctorily asked about Grandma and Rudy. Amad barely answered, his mind somewhere else. Eli was a welcome distraction. He walked in from an errand with Rene, recognized his uncle, and threw himself at him. I hadn't noticed how close they had become. Uncle and nephew. Amad and Eli. They held each other and played and played. Eli got to do and feel more than he had gotten a chance to in a while. When Amad left, not surprisingly, he remained by the door and cried. "Go to bed," I told him, shaken by the visit. I paged Juliet, who rescued me from the blues with a loaded pipe.

Amad started coming around regularly. Though I'm sure he became hip to what I was doing on the very first visit, I never heard a word of reproach come out of his mouth. His way of helping me save face, I guess. His turn to protect me. I knew nothing of his routine, his life with Grandma, his high school, his teachers, his friends. "Okay" was his favorite word. He was okay. Grandma was okay. School was okay. Everything okay.

He took it upon himself to rid me of Eli as much as he could, just like in Beaumont. Holidays, afternoons, weekends. He would pop in and take him to Southeast. I was always glad to see my son go. Relieved. More freedom, more latitude, more time. Less guilt.

The day came when I had to stop piggybacking: I needed my own drugs. Work held no appeal—not the regular kind, anyway. I knew I could have put together a decent enough bullshit package to help me get an admin or clerking job. Eight hours in a confined environment sounded like more torture than I could handle, however. So I went down 9th to try and convince my uncle Skunk to give me a job. Hustling came easy to me, and at least I'd be close to the stuff.

Dapper in knee-length chinchilla and gold-rimmed glasses, the Night Vision Man trembled with righteous anger and dismissed me with a brief sidewalk scolding. "Don't you ever show your face here again, Sally. We've washed our hands off you. Rudy might have forgiven you, but you're dead to the rest of us. Anybody in the family who so much as says hello to you will have to answer to me personally. Ratting on your own mother! Are you crazy? You're lucky we didn't pull a Fredo on you. Get! Get! Snitch-ass bitch you!"

I got! got! and happened to meet Stephanie on U a little moment later. It had been almost a year. "You look good," she lied.

"So do you," I told her just as truthfully.
"How's Eli?"
"Good. How's Stephan?"
"Wonderful. What are you up to?"
"Trying to find me a job."

Stephanie looked me up and down. A sly smile progressively relaxed her face. She took a drag from her cigarette. "Nothing green about you any more. I'm glad."

"Never was green," I said. "It was a matter of places I didn't want to go."

Stephanie nodded, still seizing me up. "And now?"

I shrugged and lowered my gaze. "It's whatever."

She took me to a studio at the corner of 11th. "This is where I hang," she said, pulling the heavy black door marked Youngin' Records and Urban Entertainment after pressing a buzzer. "All day, every day."

It was dark and smoky inside. A reception area equipped with a desk and a sofa gave way to a wide control room and a recording booth. The walls were covered with egg trays, keeping the seediness in. Lonnie was sitting in front of the soundboard, mixing an instrumental. Up close he didn't look like the sex fiend Stephanie had always made him out to be. Regular guy if you checked past the big head and flat face. Regular guy if you asked me. Didn't even seem to be from the streets. Next to him was his boss,

Wouncie. No more than twenty-five, muscular, clean-cut, knowing eyes, Iverson jersey, diamond in each ear, rope chain, restless.

They wasted no time getting down to business. "We're looking for a red girl for the part IV of our 'Uptown Freaks' series," Wouncie told me after shaking my hand, sounding very important. "The model we counted on just quit without notice. Very unprofessional. Let's see what you got."
I looked around. "Here?"
He nodded impatiently.
Stephanie smiled encouragingly.
"Hell no," the old me said.

Stephanie caught up with me outside. "Wouncie's a dick," she readily agreed, Devil's advocate, heels and makeup and no bra on, whirlwind all around us, people and honking cars and construction work, a new sort of energy for this once-forsaken neighborhood, we got put out of C.T.U. for all the luxury apartments and condominiums going up, a minor inconvenience, we were just part of the area cleanup. "And I get where you're coming from, hon. But don't you need money?"
"Who don't?"
"I get you," she said again. "Half of the time I don't feel like doing this shit. But one lousy shoot pays for a whole month."
I shook my head in disbelief. "We used to be good girls," I said. "What the fuck happened to us?"

Stephanie shrugged. Shreds of our childhood friendship came back just then: laughter, complicity, talks, trust, dares, days without a burden, moments without a care. "Life...." she said. "Ever tried Molly?"

I took my clothes off and laid them on the couch. The carpet felt nasty under my feet. Breadcrumbs and pointy things and God knows what. I was too disgusted to look. Too disgusted to try and find out. Disgusted. With the place and the people. With myself. With impossible choices. With compromission. With all the things I had been doing recently that were totally unlike me. Things that boxed me in, clipped my wings, chained my ankles, put a lock on my future. Things I couldn't take back. Things I would judge myself and be judged by for the rest of my life. It was door after door after door, farther and farther into what? Into the unknown. Into the dark.

"There's power in it, too," Stephanie said of what I was getting ready to throw myself into. She sounded as if she was merely reflecting on her own leaning curve. Could be that she, too, was grooming me. "Unexpected, but true. Like casting a spell. Like being wanted by the whole world. Like becoming the center of things. Like having all the roads lead to you. Like holding lives in the palm of your hand. Puppet master."

Right then, standing naked in front of strangers, in a strange and grimy room, that wasn't how I felt. The girl sure knew how to spin a tale, sell a dream. Maybe there was something in it for her. Power? Does an object have power?

The men's eyes burned holes in my body. "Turn around," Wouncie asked.
"Butt's a little small," Lonnie commented. "Titties, too. Good skin, though. Nice feet. No stretch marks. No scars, except for that C-cut. Face isn't bland-looking."

Wouncie took out a cigar, took his time with the clipping and the lighting and the puffing. "Ever did it for the camera?"
I shook my head.
"Not even with your boyfriend?"
I shook my head again.
Wouncie sighed. "This ain't amateur hour, baby girl. But I guess we all have to start somewhere."

I couldn't put my clothes back on fast enough. "How much?"
"$2,500 for a two-hour session. That includes role-play, foreplay, three positions, and a decent finish. We can discuss extras if the vibe is right and you feel like making more. No preservatives. Shave your pussy and underarms. Put on something nice and easy to slip out off. Stephanie can help with the makeup. Bring your own baby oil and lube if you don't like our brand. Show us a clean bill of health. Sign off on all the rights before we shoot. That one-time payment is it. No royalties. No residuals."

"$2,500 upfront it is. Who's doin' it?"

"Me," Lonnie announced.

I turned to face him. "You'll need to take a blood test as well. And I want to bring a bodyguard. No offense, but I don't know you guys."

"Not a problem."

I went to the clinic and then the head shop. The electric-blue wig I settled on came to my shoulders. Blue nails and contact lenses as well as fake tattoos glued to my back, arms, and C-section scar achieved the transformation, or so I hoped.

Wouncie didn't like the package, but I told him to take it or leave it. Not much there to argue about, especially after Lonnie himself covered his face with a bandanna. Online pay-per-view didn't seem all that kosher to me all of a sudden. I made sure to count the money before putting it in my purse. Juliet, Rene, and a rent-a-tough from our building remained parked out front with a pistol.

The room was behind the recording booth. Windowless, painted red, huge bed, fake plant, crusty sheets. All four of us popped X and snorted coke before we started. I froze on Lonnie for the first couple of minutes. Chances were he'd had unprotected intercourse several times during the last month, which essentially voided his blood test. The piece of paper he'd shown me meant nothing. If he had AIDS I would catch it, too. But the X kicked in and I felt aroused almost despite myself, stage fright out the window. Wouncie reminded me to smile, look at Lonnie, make noises, stare into the camera, and generally act like I was having a ball—"pun intended."

"You're a star now," he said after Lonnie and I were done and the lights had gone off. I was sweating. I was sore. I was glad it was over. "Let's do it again."

By the way the three of them laughed, I understood it was an old inside joke. I shrugged and walked off, almost surprised I could still look people in the eye, keep my head up high.

"Ain't you forgetting somethin'?" Stephanie asked once outside.

"Wouncie got your commission," I told her. "I worked too hard for this money to give you a cut."

I knew from the look she gave me that news of my performance would be all over our old haunts before sunset. They had me on tape. Clifton, Fairmont, Euclid, Columbia, Girard, Harvard, Park, Kenyon…. They would all know soon enough, and go watch, and talk. But Stephanie was Uptown Freak One, wasn't she? But who in their lifetime has never ever had reason to do something a little ugly, something a little uncouth? So the hell with it. So let them.

The ride to Temple Court was very quiet. Solemn, almost. It was like that bluesman on his way back from the crossroads. Shaking hands with the Devil. Bartering your soul. Letting go of the one thing you had to your name.

Eli was in front of the TV. I craved his touch, for once. I needed it. I had thought about it in the car, I had pictured it all the way home. Him running to me with open arms. Squeezing him against me to wash away the filth. Me holding it all in. Me trying my best not to cry. Mommy did the unthinkable, today. Mommy did. Many years from now someone will throw this to your face. To hurt you. To make you feel small. Like when schoolmates were making fun of me, Your dada's in jail and your mama's on crack. I hope you never go looking for facts, Eli. I hope you never get confronted with the truth. I hope you feel enough for me to fight. I hope you have it in you to defend my honor. Because a mother is a mother, even when she's wrong.

But as I walked in Eli raised his head, saw it was me, saw the look in my eyes, and went back to his cartoon. He had gotten tired of being pushed away. Toddlers have feelings, too. They have pride. They know the meaning of dignity. They keep grudges. They learn their lesson. The damage had been done. I'd killed Eli's joy. I'd snuffed his beautiful, beautiful spirit, and loosened our bond, possibly beyond repair. This, too, I had done.

After taking a long shower, I went to sleep. Rudy was in my thoughts for the rest of the week. She might have been what she was but she'd never done anything like this. I had just achieved the dubious distinction of surpassing my mother. Not only was I a dope addict, I was a whore. I felt like calling Chi-Chi to congratulate her. She had seen through me before anybody else. She had seen through me before I did so my own damn self.

Rudy didn't rub it in when she got released and immediately came to visit sometime in November. She didn't lambaste me for sliding so far off track while she was buckling up to finally get herself together. "I would have never thought...," is the first thing she said when she saw me. Amad had informed her that I was down at Sursum Corda using and keeping bad company, of course. Seeing it for herself left my mother speechless. What could she tell me: Just say No? Don't do drugs? Crack kills? She'd long ago renounced any pretense of parental guidance or moral superiority. Preaching by example might have worked, since Rudy was now completely clean. It might just have. But I didn't think Rudy had anything to teach me. I felt on top of things. I thought that I could beat back my demons anytime I chose to. I thought I could outsmart the Devil.

It was good to see Rudy, though. She looked much better. More hair, more weight, nice skin. On the other hand, she appeared not to have much energy left. Moved slow. Talked low. Sat real quiet. Pursed her lips and clasped her now-pretty hands as if holding on for dear life, as if her days were numbered and she felt the need to pace herself. It seemed the light had gone off behind her eyes. She had given a lot and only got so much back. Her body and her spirit were out of step, clean or not. No full recovery from long-term abuse. No shaking off HIV. Fresh start didn't mean a clean slate. She was done. A shell of a woman before she hit forty.

I looked at my mother and saw what awaited me. I saw it clear as day. Payback would come and it would be a bitch. But not today. Today I felt all right, with a full supply of the good stuff in my closet, a meal cooking on the stove, the TV blaring, my friends Juliet and Rene close at hand, Willie walking in and out, people dropping by. Today I was the queen of the crack den.

"Eli's nothing like I remembered," my mother said, finding her voice. "What did you do to him?"
I covered my heart with my right hand. "*Moi*? Nothing. Nothing at all."
"I'm serious, Sally."
"Me, too, Ma. I haven't done to my son anything that you didn't do to me."
It pained her to hear that, but she had no comeback. Good thing, too, because I had insults to go. One wrong word and I would have let her have it.

It was only the first day. Rudy was on an intelligence-gathering mission. Recon Rudy. Seeing with her own eyes, hearing with her own ears. Plotting her next move. I pulled a rock from my pocket and taunted her just for the heck of it—"Want some?"—the way one might offer a guest a drink. Rudy showed class and a lot of heart by refusing to go down that road with me. I stopped short of smoking the rock in front of her. We weren't meant to be a mother-daughter team like so many C.T.U. families. No hunting and copping and scoring together. No help finding a decent vein.

We danced around each other for a few weeks. Not straying too much into each other's business. As polite and mindful as two strangers can be. I looked for signs of a relapse in vain. "Bet she won't make it beyond the three-week mark," I told Amad.

But Rudy hung in there. Got a job sweeping floors and stocking shelves and bagging groceries. Got herself on that Medicaid medicine cocktail and took her pills religiously. Came by every other day for no other purpose than to check on me and her grandson. Kisses and concerned eyes. Fresh fruit and sweets. Tons and tons of guilt. It was new, this looking at my mother as the success and me the failure. Funny, almost. Now there was a philosophical tale for you. There was a gut-wrenching twist. There was a parable.

"Come stay with us," Rudy asked after one month.
"Who's 'us'?"
"Me. Grandma. Amad."
"In Southeast?"
"We'd be glad to have you. Forget what Skunk said. That Fredo shit never made sense to me, even in the movie. I kept fucking up, not listening. You did what you had to do."
"No."
"Why not?"
"I'm into lighters too much. Wouldn't want to start another fire."

"Stop joking."

"It's no, Ma. I'm happy here."

She looked at me. She looked at the living room. She looked at my life. "You call this happy?"

"Yeah."

She took a deep breath. "Then let Eli come."

"Why?"

"It's what's best. At least for now."

I raised my voice. "Are you trying to say I'm doing him wrong?"

"No. I'm just asking you to give me a chance to prove myself. I fucked up with Amad and you, but..."

"But you're finally ready for the job," I completed. "Congratulations!"

"I mean it," she said.

"What makes you think you can just take Eli?"

"I'm his grandmother. And I'm not 'taking.' Just trying to relieve you."

"We'll see."

I thought she was talking just to be talking, but Rudy kept asking. Amad, too. I might have already been beyond help, but Eli could definitely be saved, and they wanted him. Watch out: The Flying Harrises coming to the rescue! Get the kid out of there before Sally kills him! Dirty house! Roaches and mice! Anything can happen! Drugs everywhere! That old pervert Willie! Dumbass Rene! Juliet the ho! Sally stoned out of her mind 24/7! Lord knows what Eli sees every day! Poor little baby! Locked inside a room when they go out! Fed any damn thing! Never clean! Rashes! Scabs! Coughs all the time! Teeth growing all wrong! Never sees a doctor! How serious he looks! Listless! Ghetto child! Let's go get him! Our blood! Our little Eli!

Who was I fooling? I was glad to see my son go. I had been ready for him to leave ever since Beaumont. Amad and Rudy took him and stopped coming around. Good riddance.

One more door. One more step toward the deep, complete, unforgiving dark.

I was left to my own devices. Everybody had given up on me just that fast. The years I had spent standing by Rudy and helping Amad meant nothing, it seemed. Now that it was my turn they found themselves unable or unwilling to stick around. Family....

You're looking at it the wrong way, something told me. Rudy and Amad know better than anyone what you're up against. Rudy, especially. Been there, done that. She knows you're doomed. She knows this path you're on leads nowhere. Can't blame her, and your brother, for not traveling with you. You're gonna crash. Something's bound to happen. Something bad. You're a lost cause. Lost cause. Lost cause.

Who cared? Not me. I was now free to self-destruct all the way. So were Juliet and Rene. It was like Eli's presence was the only thing that had kept the household from plunging into total chaos. Though not much of one, the last barrier. With him gone there was no reason to show restraint. It was sex-sex-sex, sleep-sleep-sleep, crack-crack-crack. The stuff stayed out on the table, in steady supply thanks to Willie, who knew that in order to keep Rene happy he had to keep her and her friends flush. So we smoked. We smoked in the living room. We smoked in the car. We smoked day and night. We smoked like there was no tomorrow.

We would have smoked to death if the marshals hadn't put us out a week before Christmas, showing up at Rene's door with guns drawn and tightlipped Ms. Perez, the building manager. "You're being evicted for drug use within the premises," she told Rene, sticking a stamped piece of paper under her nose. "A clear violation of your lease."
"This whole building is a drug use," Rene countered. "Why make an example of me?"
"You have one hour to pack," one of the marshals said. "After that we're coming in."
"Y'all can't throw us out in the cold," Juliet protested. "That's against the law."
"One hour," the marshal repeated.
"Aren't we supposed to get a notice?" I asked.

Ms. Perez turned to confront me. She was on a roll, scratching lines off the legal pad clutched against her flat chest. We were just one of several units she planned on emptying today. Virtuous, self-righteous, disdainful, and prematurely aged by the demands of a stressful job, she had no patience for my kind. "You're not on the paperwork," she snapped. "Stay out of this."

"Careful how you talk to people," Willie intervened. "Your friends will be gone in a little while, and then it'll be just your ass and us disgruntled tenants."

Ms. Perez looked at him, and then at the marshals. "Do I discern a threat here?"

Willie, who had two vials of Deader in his pocket, took refuge in silence, asking himself, no doubt, where to transplant his love nest and what would happen to his little chocolate girl.

Rene seemed just as thunderstruck. Shame, shock, confusion, and wonderment made of her eyes a lively and entertaining display. Nothing like your first eviction: being escorted out of the building, having your furniture thrown out on the sidewalk, salvaging your possessions from bums, enduring the chuckles and "concerned" inquiries of neighbors, wondering where you were going to lay your head tonight and how to go about pursuing the one interest of your life now that drugs wouldn't be so readily available as in Temple Courts, where quality stuff came to you thanks to your lover and you didn't have to deal with Mr. Pusherman—your mama, your daddy, that nigga in the alley.

"One hour," the marshals chanted together. Big boys with small pants, heavy belts, and dusty shoes, they had eyes only for the clock and the flesh poking through our skimpy outfits. Joking back and forth, they stood by the door while we grudgingly started to pack.

I felt like laughing with them. Nobody gets put out of the projects, nobody, what was Ms. Perez talking about, "drug use," what exactly was that, and laugh in Rene's room I did while stuffing a trash bag with papers—she wanted us to save her papers—until I picked up a bunch of envelopes from the bottom of a drawer and recognized Rodney's handwriting. The stamps and mailing address were old but it was Rodney all right, pre-Miranda Rodney, sharing and describing and hoping and confiding. Something Sweet Thang had told me the day I left the salon came back to my mind. It didn't matter at this point, of course, because Rodney was history and I didn't see how anything more than a platonic correspondence could have taken place, but in my drug-induced paranoia an outburst felt not only like the right thing to do but the only thing to do, and so berserk Sally went, dumping the trash bag full of documents at Rene's feet before spitting at her, hawking a thick glob that caught her in the right eye before my mouth tore her to pieces, the backstabbing and scheming bitch. Rene being Rene, she just stood there and took it all, ears burning, lips quivering, saliva dripping from her face, useless and hopeless till the end. I walked out, grabbing my purse and a lighter and a small thing of nail polish on the way.

Out on the street at 9 in the morning, coming off a high. No money, no plan, no ideas. The cold got to me after the first half-hour. What a day. I sat in a park. I sat at bus stops. I went inside coffee shops. I went in and out of the library and convenience stores. I went downtown and I went uptown, just like the girl in my favorite reggae song—Shine Eye Girl, she trouble to herself.

Chevon. Maybe I'd bump into Chevon. Long time no see, dawg. You have $10 I can use? Cool. You don't suppose I could stay with you, do you? Let's go rob a bank after breakfast. Any bank. Heck, a couple of them. Me and you. Let's start a gang and run this town. Bonnie & Bonnie.

I rang Wouncie's buzzer. Hello there, I'm here for the sequel. Let's go in the backroom, pop something, turn on the lights, let the camera roll. I'll do the whole package today, extras included. Nothing to lose. I rang and rang, but there was no answer. Wouncie had gotten what he needed from me, hadn't he? Another bear. Another rabbit caught daydreaming in the woods.

9th Street. Skunk in front of his house conferring with Never Scared, both of them looking through me as if I've become a ghost. Even the bodyguard is too good for me now. The damn bodyguard. Get, Sally, get! Skunk, I used to be your favorite niece. What happened to those days?

Eye contact. Make eye contact. Smile at every passerby you see. Find New York Joe and ride him in the wheelchair. Flag Murphy down and let him fondle you all he wants in the back of that cruiser. You want me, Murphy? You want me, Mr. Cop? Here I am. Let's pretend I'm still 15 and you're not a molester, a corrupt piece of shit. I won't tell if you don't tell. As long as I get paid.

Need a girl to take home today, sir? No? It won't cost you much. I'm friendly. I can be your wife for a moment. Yours for the length of a dream. Harem fantasies. $50 early bird sleaze special. We can do things. No?

Try harder, Sally. Switch that ass, the little that your mama gave ya. You know these dudes want some. Take them into the alley, stick them for their cash. Stick them with what? The lighter. Use the lighter. Give up your dough or I'll burn you to death. Flick that Bic so fast they won't see it coming. Unlike me to be out here without a blade. What I get for rushing.

I thought of Atlantic Avenue. Grandma ... Grandma would fix it. Grandma wouldn't turn her back on me. Lizzie's hands. Nothing like Lizzie's hands. Bomb-ass apple pies. Rudy, Amad, Eli. Merry Christmas, y'all! Just thought I'd check on you. Sure, I'll take a plate. A gift? For me? You shouldn't have! So kind. So, so kind. I love you, too. Hi, Sonny. Look what Mama got you. It's a Tonka truck. It's a Schwinn. It's a Game Boy. It's a set of Matchbox cars. It's a Gap jumpsuit. It's Air Jordans. Now what do you say? You're welcome, baby. Let's go sit by the fire. Let's roast marshmallows. Let's take a shower. Let's wrap ourselves in warmth. Let's walk all the way to Youngstown, Ohio, to see Grandpa Mike. Bet that'll make him happy. Hi, Dad, it's me, Sally. I was in the neighborhood. Miss me? I miss you, too.

Cold, man. What a day. What a motherfucking day. How did this come to be? Out here with nothing. Panic like a drill in my head. Dreading the dusk. Dreading nightfall. No one to call. How?

Not as strong as before, Sally. Remember two winters ago when you didn't have a coat? Rocked your thin sweater without a problem until Mo bought you one. Yet here you are crying after five minutes in the wind. Bet you Mo would scoop you another one if he happened to see you like this. Nice guy, this Mo. Super-nice. SuperMo. Mo from Mog. Coming-to-America Mo. You should have stayed with him, Sally baby. You should have looked the other way when he dropped the ball on that Aster thing. You should have stayed. Shared his kingdom, talked to the elephants, ruled over vast swaths of land, Sally the Queen of Zamunda. Mo. Oh, why didn't you stay, you dummy? What was your problem? Why wouldn't you sit still? What was so hard to put up with? You could have had it all. The diamonds, the white gowns, the dancers, the elephants, Zamunda. It was Rodney. You had Rodney in your crosshairs. Thought you'd go and make history, didn't cha? First woman on earth to wait for a man. Guinness Book Sally. She stood by him, you know. All that time. She married him in jail, yes she did. She raised his son. Worked four jobs. Bought a house and a car. Never missed visitation Wednesday. Thought she had it figured out. He had a Miranda, you see. At least that's what he said. Ran a good game, this Rodney. Three plays ahead. His stroke of genius was to act like he was letting her go. Put himself in an impregnable, irrefutably ethical position. Mmmm hmmm. Sat on his pile of make-believe and watched it appreciate. Regained ascendency. Let guilt blacken Sally's heart. Pronounced himself a Muslim to pack even more rectitude and moral weight. New religion, new image, new man, new era. Then came the news of the sentence reduction, icing the cake of possibilities. The seed of hope was planted, and blossom it did. Not only did Sally go back to him, she ran all the way to the penitentiary. When it all came crashing down she was left with nothing. It only took a second to destroy everything she had been trying to build, her sense of self included. Downhill she went. Let it all go. Threw it all to the wind.

Some days I think that I had a good reason to break, a perfectly good reason. Some days I think I had a bomb ticking inside of me anyway. It was just a matter of time and circumstance. The built-in Great Weakness. Lurking. Waiting. Biding its time. You can run but you can't hide. It's in our blood, Sally. It's in our genes. That's who we are. That's who we be. That's what we do. We do drugs. We get high. We give up. We ruuuuns. I should become an existentialist, man. Take responsibility for everything. Say, You know what, it's up to me, man: I can do this. I'm in charge here, okay? Everything that happens inside and outside of me is my fault. I fuck up? My fault. I fail? My fault. I give up? My fault. Poverty? My fault. Messed-up schools? Me again. Crime rate? Guilty as charged. War? You guessed it. Ozone layer? It's your girl. Income gap? I'm sorry, man. Oil prices? Couldn't help myself. So now Sally's got the blues. All kinds of hues. Blues and purples, too. Only okay when she smokes that shit. Screws her head right into place. Different light. Warmer sun. Heart beating fast and strong. Courage to face another day. Crack. Crack cocaine for niggas. Backyard said it right: Get that bud.

Mo has to do a double take before he recognizes me. I look nothing like the girl he used to know, the girl I used to be. Almost pulls a gun on me. On me, though! He's just closed the booth. He's alert. His head is on a swivel. He's watching his back. Thinks I'm out to jump him, sitting as I am by the Impala. Awash in mystery, away from the canopy's floodlights, a woebegone thing holding scrawny knees by the iconic grille. Rocking back and forth, talking to myself, shivering, singing, *I've been walking / All night long / My footsteps make me crazy / Oh baby / It's been so long / I'm wondering*…. Where in the world did I ever hear that song? Looking, smelling, feeling a mess. Damn near delirious after wandering for hours in the cold, my head pounding, my mind going zoom-zoom-zoom, withdrawal making me shake and twitch, around D.C. in a day. What if he wants nothing to do with me?

The lot is small and tidy. He sweeps the grounds and wipes the pumps and empties the trash regularly. No loiterers, no panhandlers with squeegees, no whacked-out zombies out for a buck or opportunity. No project kids hanging out just to be seen. Not commuters looking to score. Nothing but cheap gas and window transactions. Uptown Amoco this ain't. Good for you, Mo. Good for you.

"Long time no see," he murmurs, rather matter-of-factly. Perhaps he's been expecting me. "Which way to the Valley of the Kings?"

I manage a chuckle from where I'm sitting. "Long time no see," I mumble through chattering teeth. Anticipating an earful, at the very least a heartfelt soliloquy. But he spares me the Oh-my-God-what-happened-to-you skit. And I'm grateful for the restraint. I truly am.

He helps me to my feet. He holds the door for me. I hurry in. He looks like a better version of himself, unlike me. He looks like comfort, hard work, confidence, health, purpose, sanity, bearings, solidity, peace of mind aplenty. All the things that, when you're out binging and partying and stupefying yourself day and night, can seem pretty boring. "I was hoping," he muses as we drive up North Capitol, heat blasting full force, a beneficial wave radiating. He turns toward me. "I probably shouldn't, but I've been waiting."

From deep inside my seat, legs folded under me, trying to keep it together, I can't help but sneer. Get angry. Snap. Show some teeth. "For what? Me to fall back into your lap?"

"Not at all. Nothing like that. Took me a while, but I accepted everything. Losing you, I mean.... I did. If anything, I fault myself for hurting you.... For starting something that I couldn't finish. For … not going all the way. You clearly deserved better. If only I…. Truth is, you should have never been on that bus, Sally. I let you down. I think we all did."

So he knows what I've been up to. Of course he does. Amad told him. Rudy told him. Grandma told him. He's all caught up. He's in the loop. He's all filled in. He knows everything about the fall, the ride on the wild side, the guanguanco, the doors. Not the type of epiphany he had in mind for me, I'm sure, but hey.

We're on Blair Road. Where is he taking me?
"This one is not on you. Or Rodney. Or Rudy. Or the rest of the world. It's not on anybody but me. I take full responsibility."
He finds that hard to accept. He finds that hard to believe

We veer off Blair, into even less traffic. Residential, from the look of it. The words we have just spoken last us a while. They are earnest and honest on both ends, I can tell. They come from the heart. They come from lots of thinking and water under the bridge. They are tinged with regrets. He still cares, it seems. Hard to be sure, because my radar is off. Has been for a while. It'll be a minute before I trust my instincts again. Either way, I'm not jumping out there. That's not what I'm here for.

Mo still cares. Do I? Should I?

The street, dark and empty and leafy and quiet, looks eerily familiar. "Where are we?"
"Takoma. About four blocks from the old digs."

The house is small and fenced in. We skirt the front and go into the basement through a glass door. There are a slide and a swing in the backyard, colorful under the moon. I'm thinking aww, how sweet, kids at play, a family lives upstairs, but Mo says no, renting got old, I live by myself, this is all mine, I have a mortgage now, aren't you proud of me?

Not much light inside the basement. Sparse, basic. Bare walls. A sofa. A table. A pile of books. A desk. A chair. A ream of paper. A box of pencils. Another cabin in Montana. Another Walden. Another mystic's cave. Is this where he writes?
"No, Sally. Not me. Hopefully, this is where *you* do."
"Longhand?"
"That was more for effect," he laughs. "The

laptop's upstairs."

I don't know if I should get upset, relieved, or happy. I am starting to feel awfully unsteady on my feet. "Who says I'm staying?"

Mo raises his palms. "Just trying to be a good friend."

We sit. The shaking subsides, but not the nausea and twitching and pulsating and restlessness. I'm mad that he's seeing this. I'm mad that he's seeing me like this. But we're past the niceties, aren't we? Something is calling from each and every cell in my body. Something urgent and insisting. I'm ready for a hit. Ready for a shower. Ready to lie down and sleep for days. Ready for Mo to tell me what he plans to do with me. "I don't suppose you keep a stash of rocks and aluminum foil handy? I could use a smoke right about now."

He smiles without smiling; a little tense; a little shocked.

"A bit of methadone, at least… No? Didn't think so.…"

"That would be…"

We say it at the same time: "'enabling.'"

Why does it all feel so much like old times? The jokes. The instant connection. The vibe. I thought I'd been doing enough changing for a few lifetimes, yet here I am, here we are. Even the silences are familiar. We were never ones for small talk. Being in each other's company was enough.

Mo looks around. "I tried to prepare the best way I could," he says. "You'll have to tell me what you need. I'll get you anything you ask for. Anything but drugs and alcohol. That stuff scares the shit out of me. No matter how much I love you, that's a road I will never travel with you. I'll need you to respect that. If you must do it, do it … outside. Sorry for sounding judgmental."

"I get it. Everybody has their limits. I used to have limits, too."

"Does that mean you're staying?"

I look at him. "Truth?"

"Truth."

"I don't know."

He takes a deep breath. "Why did you come, Sally? Why tonight, I mean?"

Telling him everything is beyond me. So is lying. "I had nowhere else to go. It's been a pretty shitty day, starting from early this morning. Night was about to fall. The poison in my system started kicking in. I felt sick. I needed to make a decision. Sleep in an office building porch or bank lobby? Try a shelter? I wasn't feeling any of those options. You just popped in my mind out of the blue."

"For money?"

"For money," I admit readily. "For a hug. For old times. For a place to crash. For all those things…."

"Doesn't matter," Mo says. "I'm glad. Just stay. We'll figure this out."

"How long?" I ask.

"Forever," he answers.

"I'm not ready," I stammer. "I'm not ready for anything."

"I know. I'm not asking."

"Maybe just tonight."

"Just tonight," he agrees.

And my head falls back. And I struggle to keep my eyes open. And I start slurring my words. And I start to feel cold all over again. And my heart pounds-pounds-pounds. And I fold into myself. And I wrap my hands around my shoulders. And I hold myself as if to console myself. You're all right, Sally. You're all right.

I'm on a cliff, merciless winds pushing me nearer and nearer the edge. Not resisting. Not wanting to die, either. Not yet. Not really. Just a little clueless about how to proceed. A little uninspired. A little confused.

Bile rushes through my lips. I run to the bathroom and do my business over the bowl, not daring for one second to look at my face in the mirror. Then, out of breath and lightheaded, I slump to the floor. Sally the wretched heap. Sick from the retch, sick from the crack beating me up, sick from the smell, sick from the taste, sick from the words, sick from the world.

Mo drapes an arm around me. He pulls me on my feet. Helps me undress. Helps me get in the shower. Unable to stand up, I sit at the bottom of the tub. He scrubs me, rinses me, rubs me dry, wraps me in a white bathrobe. I've never felt so helpless. I've never felt so cared for. Is it love or is it pity? It fills me up and depletes me in the same sweep. I cling to him like a lost child. His jaws are clenched, his eyes full of tears that, unlike mine, just won't fall. This must be the hardest part for him, too: my withering anatomy. Poking ribs, empty chest, spidery arms, pencil-thin thighs, baby-chick legs, cheap tattoos. Blink and I turn into an elf. Blink twice and I vanish.

 A shadow darkens his face. Through it all, his hands remain firm.

 Back in the living room he pushes the table before unfolding the sofa. Then pulls sheets, a blanket, and a pillow from a closet.

 Mo flicks the light off. Moonlight floods the interior, unlike in the Tuckerman Street hideout. It will be nice in the morning once the sun is out, if the sun is out, looking at the garden through the huge sliding door. Nice and homey. I think that Mo is about to leave, but he sits on the carpet and wipes the sweat from my forehead. "Truth?" he whispers.

 "Truth," I manage to say.

 "Some nights I would drive around Sursum Corda after getting off in the hope of seeing you. It was killing me. I couldn't stop thinking about you. How to reach out? How to reconnect? I didn't know what to do. I just wasn't sure. It was clear that you had changed. A lot. Who was I to assume anything? Maybe you didn't want any help; maybe I was no longer welcome in your life."

 Cold, nauseous, and sad, I pull the cover over my head. Tears start to free-flow as again. It's hard being loved. It's impossible to believe. To trust. To soften. To open up. To accept. I don't know that I ever want to go there again. Love always hurts. Love damn near killed me.

I think of the slide and swing out on the grass. It's easy to imagine Eli playing in this yard. Easy to see all of us living here. Throwing our corn, calling no fowl, minding our own. Fulfilling better and sunnier prophecies. "What street are we on?"

"Butternut," Mo says.

I raise myself on an elbow. "The house ... is it pink?"

Mo nods. "Unfortunately. How do you know?"

I let myself fall back on the mattress. "ESP."

He blows me a kiss and disappears. I realize I've forgotten to ask about Aster, "Searcher," Yonis, Mog, the war.

I close my eyes. I let the silence engulf me. I wait for the pain. One night. A couple at the most. Then I'll go.

I couldn't have slept more than an hour. Couldn't have. All night, I tossed and I turned. I ran to the bathroom. I sat on the floor. I splashed water on my face to cool the burn. I pressed on my ears to quiet the noise. All night, I fought a good fight.

But I open my eyes and the sun is already high. Mo's long gone. There's fruit on the table. There're keys atop a scribbled note. There's money. I still feel like a train wreck, but I have control. It's still winter, but I no longer am cold. But maybe I'm getting ahead of myself here. Maybe I'm getting a bit too cocky. Can't expect it to happen all at once. Recovery is a long and winding road.

It's like taking stock of a hurricane. Ruins and devastation. Nothing left standing. Nothing in one piece. Utter dismay at the damage's scope. It's easy to feel overwhelmed. To turn around, to give up before you even try. Where to start? Where to begin?

The mini playground is calling me outside. I slip on the robe and open the sliding door. Steadier on my feet than the day before. The grass is crunchy under my toes. The yard is planted with beautiful and ancient trees. The spring will be pretty. The summer even more so. When was the last time I heard birds sing? When was the last time I felt the sun on my skin?

Both swing and slide are old and worn. Just like my body feels. Just like my soul. But they are secure in the ground. They aren't peeling, they aren't torn. I climb the small yellow ladder. I go down the short slide and let out a laugh, sounding to my own ears like a different person. I sit on the swing. I push and I kick until I am happy with the speed, until I'm out of breath, until I feel the wind, until I am no longer afraid.

I search my heart. It is filled with gratitude, I find. For Mo. For my folks. For life. And there's something else. Something bubbly and elating and hard to pinpoint. Joy. This must be joy. It's been so long. And I know, just then, that I have what it takes. I have it in me. Pick through the debris. Clean up. Rebuild. Bring myself back from the brink. Make amends. Live.

Where to begin? I am a mother. Of all the things I've let go, everything I've renounced, it is the one that counts the most. So it is where I start. It is where I begin. Eli. Eli. Eli. Will you ever forgive me? I missed Christmas, I was all the way sick, I didn't dare show my face. But today, on your birthday, I am here, and you are here, and I can't get enough of you, and I swear I will make it up to you. And as you wonder who is this stranger clinging to you I hold you closer still, I smother you with kisses, I close my eyes and I reclaim you, my son, my love, my heart.

ACKNOWLEDGMENTS

Special thanks to Marthe, Issa, Nathalie, Ngone, and Paul Lo; Ieasha, Isaiah, and Anthony Morris; Susan, John, Johnny, and Katie Palmont; Keith Johnson.